DEATH OF A PSYCHIC

DETECTIVE NISHITA SERIES BOOK ONE

B. WELLS

CAVEL PRESS

KENMORE, WA

A Camel Press book published by Epicenter Press

Epicenter Press
6524 NE 181st St.
Suite 2
Kenmore, WA 98028

For more information go to:
www.Camelpress.com
www.Coffeetownpress.com
www.Epicenterpress.com
www.BWellsAuthor.com

This is a work of fiction. Names, characters, places, brands, media, and incidents are either the product of the author's imagination or are used fictitiously.

Cover design by Scott Book
Design by Melissa Vail Coffman

Death of a Psychic

Library of Congress Control Number: 2024940331

ISBN: 978-1-68492-250-5 (Trade Paper)
ISBN: 978-1-68492-252-9 (eBook)

*To my husband without whom
I would have never kept writing.*

ACKNOWLEDGMENTS

With deepest thanks to the kind and generous writers I met in critique groups, Malcolm, Julie, Jo, Elissa, Cali, and the Ninja Writing Salon. You inspired me and when needed gave me a friendly shove to keep going, I will always appreciate your spirit and humor.

But mostly to Jennifer McCord at Epicenter-Coffetown-Camel Press who said yes.

The first time I died, I was fifteen. When the doctors and nurses revived me, it felt like I'd been gone for a long time. You see, while I was "dead," I was given a gift: seeing many futures before me. One with fortune and glory, one with political activity, and one with secret ambitions. I only had to choose. But at fifteen, do any of us consider the consequences of our actions?

—Lena Rezenchov
at the Conference on Spiritual Awakening

ONE

THE BASE OF TOPANGA CANYON ROAD begins at Malibu Beach. From sandy shores, the eleven-mile road climbs up the Santa Monica Mountains to a scenic overlook with a panoramic view of tree-filled hills and the Pacific Ocean. As the roadway twists and turns, signs caution travelers to remain on the path by depicting silhouetted pictures of rattlesnakes and falling rocks. The warnings deter most except for those who arrive in the darkness to secretly dump old water heaters, stolen cars, or sometimes a body.

On this Monday of a holiday weekend, a husband-and-wife stunt team and their crew chose to cycle up the hill for fun. To keep a positive attitude during the grueling eleven-mile, two-thousand-foot climb, each switchback was christened in honor of a dramatic car chase from a movie: *Mad Max*, *Deathproof*, *Fast 5*, *Bourne Identity*, and the Steve McQueen, which was the only curve named after a movie star because of *Bullitt*—a movie featuring the actor in a classic car chase that was filmed on the streets of San Francisco; there was no argument, Steve McQueen was the king of cool.

The team gathered at the Las Tunas parking lot at 6:10 a.m. They unhitched their bikes, powered through a warmup, hooked onto clipless pedals, and saddled up to conquer the mountain and return home before brunch.

As they pushed off, they agreed it was a perfect day for a ride and placed bets on the winner. Once they reached the first hill, the *Mad Max*, all chatter stopped, and they powered on.

As they began the *Deathproof* switchback, a call came from the last rider. "Hold up!"

The call traveled up the line each rider calling forward. "Hold up." "Hold up." All riders pulled over to the gravel shoulder. The leader turned back and called down, "What?!"

"Car!" the wife shouted. "Might be an accident," she added her voice breathy.

The car was on the opposite side of the road from the riders. Along this section, there were no guardrails or streetlights. Driving downhill, cars occasionally accelerated too fast, misjudged the turn, and skidded off the side. The woman had glanced up and spotted the edge of a dove-gray roof embedded in a thick hedge of coyote bushes.

The crew rode down to join her and set their bikes against prickly bushes. The husband noted the car's engine wasn't running and there weren't skid marks off the gravel shoulder. They wondered when it happened. No one could determine how long the car had been in the ditch.

They murmured back and forth about the type of car. One man said it was an expensive car and most likely stolen. The wife said, "This doesn't look good. Do you think anyone is stuck inside?"

Her husband in a big booming voice called, "Hey! Anybody there?" No answer. The bushes were pressed hard against the side of the car. "How can we get down? There's no room on either side."

Checking out the terrain she said, "If I can get to the back of the car, I'll climb over the top to the windshield." She took off her warm-up jacket and handed one arm to him. "Lower me."

The others tied their jackets together lengthening the makeshift rope, linked arms, and braced as they lowered her down the scree and brush-filled path. When she got to the car, she said, "Someone's inside." She knocked on the windshield, "Hello, are you okay?" She was quiet. The crew exchanged glances. Her husband was about to call out to her when, in a guttural voice, she said, "Call 911. Now."

Without pause the husband lifted his phone out of his zipped chest pocket and dialed. He put it on speaker and held it out. "911 emergency. Do you need police, fire, or paramedics?"

"Yeah, we found a car off the cliff on Topanga Canyon Road," he said, noticing how dry his mouth had become.

The operator asked, "Do you need emergency services?"

"EMTs." His insides shook and he wondered why. He'd seen accidents before, some deadly. But this felt off. Maybe because it was an expensive sports car, and that always spelled trouble.

Calling from the car's roof, the wife said, "Don't touch anything. Move away from this side of the road." She gasped several times once she reached the crest, "We need police." When she reached the final step out of the bramble and onto the road, she looked frightened. "She's dead."

My near-death experience terrified me. I wasn't afraid of dying but living. Returning to my body, the world had shifted in ways I had no language for. People and places I'd known since birth were unrecognizable to me. I ran as far and as fast as I could. I landed in Santa Fe.

—Lena Rezenchov
at the Conference on Spiritual Awakening

TWO

DETECTIVE TED NISHITA GRUNTED, FINISHING THE last lunge. With shaky legs, he stumbled over to the metal weight rack and set down the twenty-five-pound dumbbells. The familiar clank of metal hitting metal coupled with a sigh of satisfaction filled his apartment. Grabbing the towel draped over the set of weights, he wiped his head, neck, and hands. He noted red and raw callouses from the workout. Good, he thought while flexing his fingers from tight fists to open hands. He liked roughed up hands; it signaled he was no desk jockey. There was nothing better than to meet a suspect in an interrogation room and shake hands. The startled look on the suspect's face delighted him. People dismissed him, being only five-foot-ten, but he could hold his own. He was no superhero, but he'd thrown down big guys. They forget that ankles and feet are weak spots.

Three steps to his kitchen, and he poured a glass of water. Leaning against the counter, he stared at the framed map of the Los Angeles area that filled the wall next to the refrigerator. It was a gift from his parents when he graduated from the academy. Cities nestled inside the LA basin were circled with pastel colors. Light blues, reds, greens, yellows, and orange bubbles were labeled: Santa Monica, Venice, Brentwood, Westwood, and on and on. It reminded him of a basket of jellybeans scattered on green plastic grass.

One red section caught his eye, the district next to the Los Angeles airport, a small area surrounded by grassland and a long stretch of road. Nineteen years, seven months, and ten days ago, his brother's car was found there, shoved off the roadway and into the watery ditch. Police told his family it was a hit-and-run accident and they'd do their best to solve it. With no security cameras along the Balboa Wetlands, finding the driver of the other vehicle wasn't promising. He was ten and the loss of his brother left a wound much like knives that score bread dough. Unknittable.

He'd decided to become the youngest detective on the force and solve the case himself. His mission chosen he enrolled in karate and taekwondo classes mastering each level. Once in high school, weightlifting and cross-country running became his passions. Last year, he achieved his goal and became a detective, but he was no closer to solving his brother's mysterious death.

His cell on the kitchen counter buzzed and when he read Santa Monica Police Department, he answered, "Detective Ted Nishita."

"Detective," Captain Cooper spoke with authority. "I have a case for you."

It was early, half past six in the morning and from the strength in his voice, Nishita wondered if the man ever slept. "Yes, sir," he answered.

"I've put you as lead detective on a case out of Topanga working with an officer from that branch." He stopped and shuffled papers. "Officer Scott Fisher." Nishita was about to say something, but the captain plowed forward. "This is a velvet glove case. Be on your toes. I can give you one uniformed officer. Who do you want?"

Without pause, Nishita said, "Officer Camilla Leila." The silence on the other end sliced through the line. Too late to rethink that request, he recalled the friction between Officer Camilla Leila and Captain Cooper. His mouth readied to list her abilities: she culti-vated trust and unearthed answers in unexpected corners, and he and Camilla entered the academy together - he'd trust her with his life. Faced with the cold silence at the other end, he held his tongue.

A long sigh came from across the phone, "Keep me informed of developments." He hung up.

"Thank you, s-" Nishita stared at the phone, momentarily speechless. A case, and as the captain said, a velvet glove one. The Santa Monica Police Department isn't as high profile as other stations throughout the Los Angeles area, but it has what is called old money; wealthy families that can trace lineage back to the silent movie era. He'd heard the captain's velvet glove speech before. It was a cautionary tale of mistakes made while investigating a public figure, a politician, a movie star, or a celebrity. Fans lingered around every corner and were known to record police behavior. The captain always said that while emotions are fleeting, videos last a lifetime.

This would be his first velvet glove case. He felt good, confident, on top of his game. Then he remembered what today was: the day his parents hosted a neighborhood picnic and barbecue. It was one of the events they did to ease the pain of losing his brother Allen.

For the first six months after Allen died, his mother and father passed through the days as if their feet couldn't touch the ground. From the emptiness in their eyes and the hollow sound of their voices, grief had replaced his loving parents with empty replicas. As time passed, his parents took different paths to solve Allen's case. His father had hired a private investigator who tracked a lead to Las Vegas that then went cold. His mother stepped in and engaged psychics, mediums, and a shaman living in New Mexico. They'd spent a lot of money but nothing significant was revealed.

His sister had finally had enough and said she was still alive. She needed her parents back. It was a remarkable moment and got them to honor Allen and return to the living. Each year after that, they hosted a spring barbecue for the community. It grew to become the favorite event in the neighborhood.

He wouldn't make it this year. His heart sank.

His call buzzed. Officer Camilla Leila's name spread across the screen in bright green letters. "Hey," he answered.

"We got a case," she said in a bright voice. Officer Camilla Leila was a single mother of a twelve-year-old son. A few months ago, she failed the detective test. The failure crushed her and her normally playful wit turned acerbic. After an unfortunate spar with Captain Cooper, she was placed on probation. The month leading up to the test, her life fell apart. Her rent went up, her car needed new brakes and tires, and her son, Nestor didn't like his babysitter. After failing, she almost quit the force. But her older brother stepped in and built an apartment for her in the basement of his house and convinced her and Nestor to move in. It was a good move because things stabilized for her. But hearing Captain Cooper's voice, it was clear she hadn't set things right with him. If she'd only apologize.

Who was he to judge with a string of former girlfriends and unspoken apologies? Nishita said, "Are you at the station?"

"Yep."

"Give me thirty." He was ready to hang up but then said, "Oh, I got the velvet glove talk from the captain. Do you know who it is?"

"The victim is Lena Rezenchov," Officer Camilla Leila said, her voice hushed.

"The psychic?" Nishita pictured his mom and chewed his lip.

"Ted, you still there?" she asked.

"Sorry, I was thinking of my mother. She's a fan."

"I'm sorry. Lena Rezenchov had a large following. The books she wrote, the retreats, and those contemplation cards . . ."

Nishita wondered if he should call his mom and tell her privately, make her promise to keep it to herself. No. That wouldn't do, not before her big event. She'd have to find out when everyone else did, from the news. Eventually, he'd tell her he was working the case, but not now. Nishita said, "We've got a long day ahead. Pick up coffee." He heard his abrupt tone and then added, "Please."

"One more thing, it might be a hit-and-run," Officer Camilla said.

Nishita drew in a breath. "Okay," he whispered and hung up.

Statistics report twenty thousand hit-and-run accidents a year in the Los Angeles area. Eight thousand have casualties, and out of that number, approximately three hundred are fatal. Nineteen years, seven months, and ten days ago, Allen was one of those fatalities. Soon Allen's case would turn over to the cold case files, and if Nishita was lucky, a group of podcasters might take it up and dig into areas for which officers didn't have the time or resources.

Nishita set his cell on the counter and glanced back at the map of Los Angeles. The jellybean colors had paled now that the sun had passed the window.

With no time to dwell, he stripped, showered, and shaved within a matter of minutes. He had to be at the front door before Camilla lost patience and honked. The neighbors wouldn't appreciate that, not on a holiday morning.

His cell pinged with a text message as he was tying his shoes. He knew it was Camilla outside waiting.

Camilla texted: 60 seconds then I honk.

He answered: Did U get coffee?

Camilla texted: Drinking mine now. Tasty.

Camilla could rub people the wrong way, but he just laughed. She'd tell the truth no matter how brutal. A few noses got put out of joint, and yes his did too. He picked up his cell, filled his pockets with keys, smelling salts and two linen handkerchiefs.

Once on the passenger's side, his seat belt buckled, he faced her. She had a cup in her right hand, red lipstick marks along the top and pointed to his cup in the center holder. He mouthed "thank you" and sipped. It was just as he liked, two creams and no sugar. It's funny how little things such as knowing the way someone takes their coffee means something. Tiny moments of being known weave together and make a friendship. Watching her he thought, she should have had made detective. Yes, she was annoying in the way a loud-mouthed kid sister can be, but when the situation called for it, Camilla delivered.

"Tell me what you know," he said.

"The accident happened on Topanga Canyon Road," Camilla began.

"Are we calling it an accident?" Nishita asked. "I thought it was a hit and run."

"It's undetermined," she said. "Let me catch you up on this morning's event. There was an eighteen-wheeler that jackknifed across the 405 near the Getty Museum exit ramp blocking four of the five lanes. As you can imagine, a massive pile-up of over fifty cars has stopped traffic cold. The 405 has been down to one lane since early this morning."

Traffic was bad on good days; this would be epic. He whistled.

Camilla continued, "Consequently, along with the highway patrol, Topanga and Tarzana police are sorting that out. There are two fatalities and many casualties. It's crazy. The only good thing is it's a holiday, so the usual morning traffic isn't riding up their backs. Anyway, when a body was found along Topanga Canyon Road, the Topanga Sheriff's Office asked Santa Monica for assistance. Hence you and I."

"Busy holiday." He sipped.

They drove in silence along the quiet streets. It was early February, and the sun crested above the buildings. Turning onto Pacific Coast Highway, the ocean came into view. At this point, the road was sandwiched between the shoreline and the cliffs. He'd lived in Santa Monica his entire life and could count on his fingers the times he went to the beach to swim, but he couldn't imagine living anywhere else. Knowing the ocean was within walking distance reassured him.

The sky and ocean mirrored one other in slate gray against a backdrop of fog. The gray-green color stirred his memory, but he had to verify. Opening Lena's file on the laptop, it was as he thought. Lena Rezenchov had that same color of eyes. Last summer, he'd been working on a robbery case when she was booked on a DUI. Police followed a strict protocol when a celebrity is arrested.

They are fingerprinted and photographed as normal, but a high-powered attorney arrives long before the celebrity is placed in a holding cell with prostitutes, shoplifters, fraudsters, and the like. The attorney, to hide their identity, gets them out the side door, placed in a dark SUV, and escapes the media.

None of that happened for Lena Rezenchov.

Held for hours before someone came for her, Lena made as many friends as possible, uniformed officers, detectives, suspects, and cell mates alike. She wasn't judgmental at all, and if asked, gave palm readings, spoke about past trauma, and what it takes to create a new future. The female cellmates embraced her, told her which rehabilitation center had the best food and the softest beds. When her husband came to pick her up, the ladies sang a farewell song.

But he couldn't shake the question as to why she was left in that cell for hours. No one posted bail. No attorney or husband or friend came to rescue her. It was curious. "Lena Rezenchov, the Psychic to the Stars," he muttered.

They reached the intersection of Pacific Coast Highway and Topanga Canyon Road and stopped at the light.

Camilla turned and asked, "So, changing subjects, have you seen the posts on social media?"

He knew she referred to his former girlfriend Emma and her star-studded wedding attended by the rich and famous. "Yeah I saw them. Emma looked good." He pretended it didn't matter.

"Ted, it's me. Cam." When he didn't answer she said, "I didn't know Emma knew that guy long enough to get married. I mean the wedding pictures were gorgeous, and those sunsets in Majorca. Wow. It was all over social media and on the front page of the gossip papers at the coffee stand."

Clearing his throat, he said. "Very impressive."

"He's a movie director. Did that one where teenagers save the world from zombie destruction." Cam giggled, then continued speaking with an air of complete authority on the subject. "His father is a producer of those car movies, like all seven or whatever number they're on. That's whatcha call Hollywood royalty."

"Yeah, I guess," he said.

"Oh, come on. Emma is an entertainment attorney; she was bound to connect with someone like that. Besides women like that always marry up. It's an unwritten law." Camilla saw the traffic light had changed and pulled into the right lane to turn up the canyon. She checked in on him. "Well, as they say, 'marry in haste, repent at leisure.'"

He gave her a sharp look hoping she'd back off on the brutal honesty. She gave him an "I told you so" look. He swallowed, his throat very dry, and stared out the side window.

After a twenty-minute drive from his house and they were in a different world of rolling hills filled with rocks and scrubby trees. It wasn't green like in farm country. It was wild with a touch of danger. Coyote bushes had thorns that could pierce soft-soled tennis shoes. If one wasn't careful, a rattlesnake curled up sleeping under a bush might strike passersby. Daytime sun, magnified by the hard rocks, burned tender skin through clothing. If a person wandered off the road and into these hills, it wasn't good.

Red and blue lights flashed as they reached the blockade. Camilla showed identification and an officer let her pass.

"I suspect they're trying to keep the press out," she said.

"Give us a breather," Nishita answered. He wondered who was going to make the formal presentation to the public. A celebrity like Lena Rezenchov generates curiosity over how she died. The press would drag up old clippings, her Oscar party shenanigans, the DUI charges, and her stint in rehab. If it was a slow news day, she'd be front-page fodder, but perhaps with the trouble on the 405, this might pass under the radar for a day at least, give him time to wrap his head around what happened and why.

They reached the emergency vehicles parked across the road. A young deputy waited by the shoulder, obviously from the Topanga Sheriff's Office.

Camilla chuckled. Nishita turned to her and said, "Be nice. He looks still wet behind the ears." Her response was a sly smile. Nishita noted the dark gray forensics van parked to one side. He thought he caught a glimpse of the big guy Luis, head forensics technician.

"Was that Luis? We lucked out; he's the best," Camilla said. She got out and addressed the deputy while on her way to the gray van. Nishita took the time to send a text to his sister, Hyacinth. He'd let her know about his case, as his mother didn't live with a cell phone tied to her hip, much as he wished she did.

He texted: Got a case. Won't make it today. Tell Mom pls.

Hy texted: Keep me posted. Saw pix of Emma's wedding. Fancy-Smancy.

Nishita smirked and put the phone in his breast pocket and got out of the car. He noticed the air first. It didn't smell of the ocean like in his neighborhood. It was dry and had a musty smell, like old dirt. He checked the surroundings and noted the curves to the road and lack of guardrails. It was a lonely stretch of road.

Another thing he noted was that the road was relatively straight in this section. There wasn't a curve to justify swerving—unless, of course, the driver lost control higher up and finally succumbed over the edge. This stretch had the deepest drop. Nishita approached the shoulder and examined the bushes and surrounding gravel. The bushes had fresh breaks where they were broken behind the sports car. Had some of the bushes been placed to hide the car? Nothing else was disturbed. He wondered if the car was guided off the cliff.

Det. Nishita walked up to the ambulance and greeted the lead EMT. The man said his name was Steve. "Do we know when the car went over?" he asked.

Steve shook his head. "A group of cyclists spotted the car this morning." He pointed to the muscular men and one thin woman standing off to the side near a collection of expensive bicycles. "They saw the car at 6:35 a.m. Called 911 immediately."

"Were they heading uphill or down?" Det. Nishita asked as he examined the sightlines from both directions.

"Up. They do the tough part first, then turn around and . . ." Steve made a zooming sound to illustrate rocketing downhill.

"Sounds fast." Det. Nishita chuckled at the thought of racing downhill on a bike. In that second, his mind flashed to a memory, and all present senses dissolved. He felt the air whip across his face as his short stubby legs pedaled his stingray, doing his best to keep up with his older brother riding a sporty two-wheeler. They rode along the boardwalk laughing and smelling the salt air. He was desperate to keep pace with his older brother, who taunted and teased him to keep up.

Nishita gripped his hands into fists to stop the memory and return to the present. He caught Steve watching him. He cleared his throat and said, "Yeah, going downhill might be too fast to focus on the road and spot a car." He asked, "Why were you called?"

"The bikers, well, the main guy, thought the woman was still alive. But once it became obvious she wasn't," Steve shrugged, "by that time, we'd already been dispatched."

"What had him change his mind about her condition?" Det. Nishita asked.

"His wife went over the top of the car to see if anyone needed help. She saw the body and told them of her condition." He lowered his head. "But there's something else." Steve pulled Nishita to one side and said, "I'm no detective, but this feels staged."

Once Steve said it, Det. Nishita realized he agreed; something was off. It had started with the moment he arrived and noted the lack of any tracks near the cliff.

Steve continued, "Her injuries, the ones I saw through the window, were head trauma. Her face was hit by something, and not the steering wheel of that car. Also, she doesn't smell right."

Det. Nishita thought that odd. "What do you mean?"

"I don't know. I can't put my finger on it," Steve said and pinched the bridge between his eyebrows. "I can't place it."

"Well, maybe the coroner can figure it out," Det. Nishita said. "Okay, thanks."

Det. Nishita walked over to view the car. Luis nodded to him as he spoke with Officer Camilla. They had a brief exchange and Officer Camilla turned to Det. Nishita.

"They can't get the body out until the car is pulled back from the road," she said.

"Do we have a truck coming?" he asked.

Officer Camilla held up her cell and answered, "I've called. They'll have to send one of the secondary tow businesses. It's still busy up at the 101."

Nishita lowered himself to view the back of the car at bush level. Why here, he wondered. This area was picked for a reason. Was it the lack of guardrails, no streetlights, or because it was the steepest drop?

He walked over to the cyclists and thanked them for their call, took their names and phone numbers in case he might need them to answer questions. They got back on their bikes and continued up the hill. Then Nishita pulled out his cell and began to take pictures of the gravel, the broken branches, the surrounding area, and the road facing uphill for his records.

When satisfied, he walked to the patrol car and checked the file on Ms. Rezenchov. Her mug shot appeared. His impression from that day was that she'd looked happy, almost relieved. He'd seen that look on people before, as if their lies were finally over. Reading further, the report stated she was married and had a daughter. Curious, it listed her daughter as the emergency contact, not her husband. The address was in Santa Monica, but it also showed Lena owned a bookstore in Topanga.

Getting to the family was of primary importance. The last thing he wanted was for them to hear about this on the news. He worried about her body reaching the morgue because someone on staff leaked information about sensational or celebrity deaths to podcasters. Then the media circus would begin. Money and fame had that effect.

Officer Camilla guided Officer Scott Fisher over for an

introduction. Nishita looked Officer Fisher up and down, noting his baggy uniform. Nishita wondered how recently he'd passed his exam.

Fisher held his mouth tightly. He seemed to struggle with words. "Thank you for coming in. As you know, our team is at the 405."

Nishita watched the young officer struggle. "How well do you know the family?" he asked.

"I went to school with Anya." Officer Fisher looked back and forth between Camilla and Nishita. "The daughter," he said.

"Right," Nishita said. "Are you able to check the bookstore and inform anyone there of Ms. Rezenchov's death, alone?" he asked watching Fisher to check for hesitation or awkwardness. "Can you do that?"

"No one will be there," Officer Fisher answered quickly. "I mean it's a holiday. They're closed."

Det. Nishita noted his attitude. "That's not what I asked. Will you check the bookstore and if any family are there, inform them of her death?"

Officer Fisher stiffened his stance. "Yes, sir."

"Call Officer Camilla with details," said Det. Nishita quietly yet firmly.

"Yes, sir," Officer Fisher said.

"Officer Camilla and I will go to the Santa Monica residence and see if we can connect with Anya." He felt the pull of a long investigation and welcomed it. It would be something to focus on—not his former girlfriend's spontaneous marriage or missing the barbecue celebration for his brother.

At sixteen I changed my name from Linda Rodgers to Lena Rezenchov. People have accused me of pretension. My answer is this: I was legally dead for twenty minutes. I emerged reborn and knew that the life I'd had vanished. Does a caterpillar keep its same name when it has emerged from a cocoon?

—Lena Rezenchov
on the jacket of, *Beyond Death and Dying*

THREE

A FLATBED CAME INTO VIEW AS IT rounded the curve. There was a sign on the side door: Gus Post Towing 24/7. The truck arrived quite fast and Nishita wondered if it came from the service station at the base of the hill. If that service station had security cameras, it might have captured other cars. Maybe he'd get a time when the accident happened, but he'd have to ask the tow truck driver about cameras when the moment presented itself.

An older Black man stuck his meaty hand out the driver's side window and waved. He checked the location of the accident and deftly jockeyed into position to pull the car from the ditch. When he got out of the truck, Nishita was surprised. For a big man he moved with ease.

He appeared to be someone comfortable in any situation. "Can't say I was surprised to get a call," he said with a deep, resonant voice. "Lots of kids love to speed along these hills late at night. More car than they can handle, but there is no stopping a boy with his toy." The elderly man had an arch in his voice when he said "boy" as if he didn't mean a young man but an older man hanging on to lost youth in fast cars.

"Detective Nishita," he said holding out his hand. "Are you Mr. Post?"

"Call me Gus," he said and accepted Nishita's hand. His hand wrapped around Nishita's with room to spare.

"We have a dead body in the car and can't remove it until the car is out of the ditch," Det. Nishita said.

Gus shook his head and said, "Sorry to hear that."

Nishita checked Camilla and saw her with Luis taking pictures at the upper curve of the road. That was good, but he needed her and signaled for her to come down.

Turning back to Gus he asked, "Will it distress you to work with a dead body inside?"

"I've done it before," he said with a weary sigh. "They really should put some guardrails along here. Can't tell you how many times I've written to the honorable mayors of Topanga and Malibu about the dangers of these curves, but nothing." He wiped his face with a large red cloth. It was one of those cloths that men who work on cars always carry. "Let's see what we have," he said. Gus studied the bank and noted the loose gravel along the shoulder. His mouth tightened to a hard edge when he saw the back end of the dove gray car.

Seeing the man's reaction Det. Nishita asked, "You know the owner?"

"It belongs to the bookstore people at the top of the hill," said Gus. "Do you know who?"

"Lena Rezenchov," Det. Nishita answered.

The words startled Gus and he fell silent for a moment. Nishita wondered if he was praying. Gus turned back to the truck and pulled on large chains with metal hooks. The rack of the metal chains echoed in the canyon. Gus said, "Three folks from the store drive it."

"You knew her?" Det. Nishita asked.

"Lena came in to fill up. It's an older car, so it has to use leaded gas. We carry that in the back," Gus said. "Sometimes the other one, Marta, would drive it—but not often—and the husband, Dudley barely fits."

He moved to hook up the car, but Nishita stopped him. "Wait. I need you to wear these," he said and handed him a pair of blue nitrile gloves.

Gus smiled a half smile and held up his large palm. Nishita knew officers on the force who complained that even the extra-large gloves barely made it to their wrists.

"I've got a pair." Gus pulled worn leather gloves from his back pocket. They fit like a second skin and although aged were cared for with oils to retain suppleness and shine. "I've got some per-snickety customers. Rich folk don't like prints on their cars. I keep several of these in the truck."

Nishita saw his opening and asked, "Do you have security cameras at the gas station?"

"Sure do," Gus answered while he continued to work. Pointing to the car he said, "I imagine you'll want me to take this to the Santa Monica station?" He checked for an affirmative response, then continued, "After I drop it off, an officer can come to the station, and we'll sort out the footage."

Nishita watched with a bit of fascination. Something about Gus reminded him of his grandfather. He hadn't thought of his grandfather in a long time. He pushed the memory away telling himself to focus.

Gus said, "I'm going to need to clear some of these bushes to reach the chassis. That okay?"

Officer Camilla stepped up and said, "Luis has photographed the entire area, but I'd like to record removing the car. We can't miss any details."

Camilla moved into place and positioned her camera. Gus made his way down to the car. When he looked in the driver's side window, his face changed. Shaking his head, he bit his lower lip and then crawled under the side of the car to hook it to the chassis. Once he succeeded, he climbed his way back to the road.

Nishita noted his overalls and thought Gus was either smart or lucky they were thick, but a few thorns had attached to the pants.

The winch motor started. Gus wiped his face with the red cloth. "These cars are better-cared-for than people. They are held in an air-conditioned garage, hand-washed and polished like a diamond."

The car lurched and Nishita heard the crunch of car parts. Dragged out of a ditch, no car survived scratch-free, but this one was meant to be driven on slick streets arriving at star-studded events. Gus took it slowly to reduce the wear on the car. The rear end of the car made its appearance and Nishita stared at the rear side fender. His heart stopped. It had damage consistent with a car when it is clipped. Cars get this in high-speed chases when police must get the driver off the road. Using a push bar, they clip the driver's side fender causing it to spin. The speeding suspect is then surrounded before they harm someone. Lena's car had this type of damage.

A final thrash of the bushes and the car was pulled over the last hump and rolled onto the road. Luis went to work photographing all angles. Nishita checked the rear fender.

Gus spoke to him in a hushed tone. "When I got up to the window, I didn't know if it was the car or," he took a breath as if to control his emotions rising, "or the lady, but I swear it smelled like those disinfectant wipes. You know the ones I mean?"

Nishita wondered if that was what Steve had smelled. Steve and crew wheeled a gurney towards the car. Nishita held out his hand to stop.

Approaching the car alone, Nishita looked in the driver's side window. The body had slumped to the right, toward the center of the car exposing a head wound on the left side. Long dark hair covered her shoulders and blue shirt. On the passenger's side floor was an expensive handbag. She wasn't wearing a seat belt. The wound on the left side of her face showed a deep gash. There should have been blood down her neck and on the steering wheel, but he saw no trace of it.

He opened the crumpled car door put his head close to Lena's body and inhaled. An odor was present of some kind of cleaner. He touched Lena's shoulder. It was cold, but if the car went over the cliff last night, she would be cold. When he reached down to her thigh it felt hard, too hard for someone who died within the last six hours. "Steve," he called. "Gus said he smelled a disinfectant. See if that matches what you smelled," Nishita asked.

Steve leaned into the car and got down as close he could to her feet. "She's clean. Makes me think she was kept somewhere."

Looking at Steve he asked, "If she were stored somewhere cold that would mask the time of death. Correct?"

Steve answered, "Yes."

Nishita whispered, "Somebody's smart."

A teacher warned me of clinging to judgmental thinking . . . If carried to the extreme it divides us into I'm right and you're wrong. If you find yourself stuck, allow the marvels of our universe to touch your heart.

—Lena Rezenchov, *Let Your Light Shine*

FOUR

THE SUN, HAVING BURNED THROUGH THE clouds, warmed his skin. By its position, it had to be close to eleven. Nishita never doubted his determination, drive, and desire to solve cases. However, keeping his emotions under control while viewing victims of homicide had been an unforeseen challenge. He'd helped dig bodies out of shallow graves, untied them from piers, and retrieved them out of dumpsters, each victim affected him. He wasn't the first detective to shed tears at a crime scene and he wouldn't be the last. If he ever became the bitter, hard-drinking detective he saw portrayed in old movies, he'd quit.

While waiting for Lena to be removed from her car, Nishita didn't know how he'd react. When she'd been at the station, she was accessible and radiated kindness. In an unexplainable way, she made him feel important standing next to her.

A gurney wheeled close to the car. Luis held up his hand to stop them. He wanted more photos of the car, particularly the scratches along the fenders and Lena's position inside. He paid attention to the position of her purse and the vodka bottle.

Luis finished and nodded to Nishita. No one moved. An eerie silence fell upon the hillside; no birds sang, no insects buzzed, and no planes flew overhead. It was so quiet Nishita heard his lungs take in air.

Steve and crew set about lifting Lena from the car. The driver's side was cramped and her body stiff in the seated position. Finding the best way to remove her proved awkward.

After a struggle, they succeeded. Nishita fought the lump growing in his throat. His mind flashed to the moment when she was brought into the station for booking. Lena was stunning, in that old-time, ageless Hollywood movie star way, with black hair, caramel-toned skin, and large gray eyes. Male and female officers alike stood in awe. In the brief moment he had made eye contact with her, Lena made him feel perfect as he was, that he didn't need to justify his existence.

He was filled with an urgency to contact Lena's family members. As soon as her body arrived at the coroner's office, word would get out and spread like wildfire across the web. Before approaching the gurney, Nishita changed his gloves. There could be no cross-contamination. He saw the gash on her left forehead, but when he moved her hair to the side, he didn't expect to see a bruise on her right jaw. Faint bruises appeared along both sides of her throat. He checked her hands and noted several fingernails were cut to the quick and her hands were clean. A faint odor filled his senses. Leaning close, he checked the cuffs of her shirt and saw a stain along the edges.

"Bag her hands to her elbow," he said and stepped back from the gurney. Camilla tied off Lena's hands. After she was done, she glanced at Nishita. Their contact spoke silent words. It was clear Lena had fought her attacker.

The crew gently placed Lena inside a body bag and zipped it closed. In one swift motion, the gurney was wheeled to the back of the van and pushed inside. The doors slammed shut and the hollow sound reverberated in the canyon.

Staring at the ambulance, Nishita wondered what had happened. She was a successful author with thirty books in the New Age genre, but it was her contemplation cards that catapulted her to star status, a simple deck of one hundred and fifty tarot-type cards.

Written across the top was a quote from a philosopher or poet, and under the quote were Lena's reflections. His mother was given a set as a gift from a kind neighbor to help her through grief-filled sleepless nights. Her favorite was a quote from Aristotle: "It is during our darkest moments that we must focus to see the light." His mother kept the deck at her bedside and the grief encasing her eased.

Camilla touched him to get his attention. "Ted?"

"Yeah?" he blinked as he turned to Camilla.

Gus stepped in view. "I'm set to drop the car off. Do you want to follow me to the station?"

Nishita shook his head. "They'll be ready for you. Thanks for coming." He held his hand out and they shook.

"Your grandfather was Ted Bednar?"

He wasn't expecting to hear his grandfather mentioned. However, most older men in the auto repair industry knew him because of his service station, a successful presence in Santa Monica for years. Nishita nodded.

"I'm sorry he passed."

"Me too," answered Nishita. Gus looked as if he wanted to say more, but Nishita broke eye contact.

Gus got into the cab of his truck, turned around the curve and drove downhill.

Camilla got a radio call from her shoulder walkie-talkie. She turned to Nishita. "Are you ready for the barrier to be taken down? The officer wants to know."

Nishita nodded. After Camilla relayed the message, she signaled Fisher to join her. Nishita faced his team: sharp-tongued Officer Camilla Leila and green-as-new-grass Officer Scott Fisher. He hoped they were up for the challenge because this case had a bad feel.

"Camilla, you and I are to contact Anya Hardwick. Fisher, what can you tell me about the store?"

Fisher took a deep breath, "The bookstore has been around since I was a kid. Before Sophia Stannis and Lena bought it, it was a run-down farmhouse. During the real estate downturn of 1990, these old ranch spreads were cheap. Lena and Sophia bought it and began fixing it up."

"Sophia Stannis?" Nishita caught the new name.

"Oh, yeah. Sophia must be almost eighty. She had a bad stroke months ago; she's confined to a wheelchair." Fisher pulled on his ear as if thinking. "Anyway, they remodeled that old farmhouse into a mansion. The third floor is a complete apartment with a kitchen, four bedrooms, and two bathrooms. The whole family used to live there: Dudley, Lena, and Anya . . . and of course, Sophia and Marta."

"Dudley is her husband, Anya is her daughter, how are Sophia and Marta connected?" Nishita asked.

"Sophia and Marta are mother and daughter and arrived with Lena. They worked together to build Lena's business. They weren't related but like family," Fisher said.

"What was it like there?" Nishita asked. "At the bookstore?"

Fisher widened his eyes. "Very busy. It helped the community to have a centerpiece like the bookstore. Businesses set up across the street. Lena taught nightly seminars. Sometimes they held weekend retreats that brought in a crowd. With the influx of people, everybody's business grew. Happy days. I mean, it could be chaotic, particularly for Anya. One time Lena vanished for six days. No one knew where she was. Dudley wondered if she had run off with one of her celebrity clients. That's rich because Dudley had his parties if you know what I mean,"

Fisher said with an arch to his voice. "But Lena returned, and I thought she was fine, but then her arrest happened, and she was off to rehab for months." Fisher stopped and thought a moment then said, "Sophia had a stroke while Lena was in rehab. But Lena wasn't allowed to leave until she completed her full term. Dudley did that. Not letting Lena out to see Sophia, I mean."

Nishita was impressed that Fisher knew the inner details of the Hardwick household. "Would you say you're close to the Hardwick family?" Nishita pressed.

Fisher blushed. "Well, as a kid, I hung around while the bookstore was remodeled into a mansion. I went nuts over all the construction equipment. The cement trucks, cranes, bobcats, and electrical gear. I considered going into construction—"

Nishita held his hand up to interrupt, "Let me ask this: can you remain neutral during the investigation?" Nishita gave his best hard stare. Fisher squirmed but eventually nodded. Nishita continued, "I will hold you to that." Fisher nodded again. "Do family members still live at the bookstore?"

"Marta and Sophia live on the third floor. Dudley moved to Malibu. The bookstore is closed for the weekend. Marta and Dudley went to Las Vegas for a convention."

Nishita marveled at the torrent of information. "When you get to the bookstore and inform whoever is there of Lena's death, do not go into detail."

Fisher nodded, turned on his heels lifted his e-bike out from the nearby bushes, and started up the hill. Seeing the e-bike surprised Nishita, but on second thought it was probably more efficient than a car in these hills.

Camilla said, "He's a good guy, just a kid. I think he thought this would be his case and got his nose out of joint when we were called."

"Keep an eye on him. Make sure he doesn't talk with reporters," Nishita said. Glancing at his watch, he saw it was almost noon. They had to get moving before fans or podcasters sniffed out Lena's death. Wanting to respect the family, he felt it necessary to deliver this news in person.

Once in the car, he asked Camilla for her impressions of the crime scene. Camilla didn't answer right away and appeared to be collecting her thoughts.

She didn't answer right away. Before beginning, she collected her thoughts. "Aside from the road showing no skid marks or disturbed gravel, the car had little damage. There were scratches along the side from the bushes and a dent on the rear fender but not deep enough to suggest an accident. I can only assume, that car was not in a high-speed crash. As to the body, Lena wore no rings, or a watch. She had pierced diamond stud earrings. Sometimes robbers demand the person take the earrings off or they will cut them off. But with what we know so far, I don't think this was a robbery. Her credit cards were still in her purse as was her cell phone and a bottle of vodka."

Nishita considered her remarks and thought of the bruising around Lena's neck and the damage to her hands. Checking the records of Lena's arrest on the laptop he ran an in-depth search. "Dudley Hardwick's address on file is the Topanga bookstore."

"What is Lena's main address?" Camilla asked.

"Same as Anya's," said Nishita. "Lena renewed her driver's license and put Santa Monica as her address."

Camilla asked, "When did she renew it?"

"Last month on her birthday," Nishita said.

They retraced their drive back to Santa Monica. It was heading towards the warm part of the day, and the activity level had increased. Along the coast, the beaches were filled with picnickers, sunbathers, and surfers. Camilla turned the unmarked car onto the boulevard and wove through traffic to meet Lena's daughter.

Invisible guides are sometimes called angles. You plan to interview at one company, but a different one calls first. You fly to one city, but a storm forces the plane to change its destination, and that alters the trajectory of your life. This is the magic of invisible hands. Be open to these gentle nudges.

—Lena Rezenchov, *Magical Listening*

FIVE

ANYA HARDWICK LIVED IN THE MIDDLE of an eclectic neighborhood; new upscale stores encroached upon older shops that had been a presence since the 1960's. The tell-tale signs of old logos and paint gave it away. There was a plant shop called Rhoda's Den, a Mexican take-out that served "The Best Tacos in Town", and a café patio with chess players circled around small wooden tables. The new stores included designer tennis shoes, a tapas and wine bar, and a jewelry boutique. Nishita hoped the older stores wouldn't get squeezed out by aggressive enterprises. He suspected it was his way of holding on to the past, not unlike people who collect classic cars.

They pulled up to a bright blue house with white trimmed windows and front porch. Nishita noted it was a store called Royal Herbs. When he studied the address on the building it read 757 and when he read Anya's address it said 757 1/2.

"On the side," Nishita said and pointed to the porch that wrapped around to the back of the building. Nishita took a deep breath and opened the car door. Pressing his lips together, he readied for the hardest part of the job, telling family of the death of a loved one. He stepped out of the car, smoothed his hair, and straightened his suit jacket.

As he was about to step onto the sidewalk, the car radio signaled, and Camilla answered. While talking, she waved Nishita back. Irritated, he opened his hands out and mouthed, "What?"

Cam asked the person at the other end to wait. "It's Fisher. Marta Stannis was at the bookstore. She said Lena was staying in town at a hotel this weekend."

Nishita could hear the woman crying over the radio and his heart sank. He held out his hand to Camilla to ask for the mic.

"Fisher, will you express my condolences and ask Marta if I can stop by later this afternoon?" Nishita said over the car radio.

When Fisher returned to the call he said, "Ms. Stannis will be here whenever you arrive. And, Sir? She pointed out some broken potted plants at the bookstore. She says it must have happened during the weekend. She and Mr. Hardwick were away," said Fisher. "It looks like vandalism."

Interesting, the store being vandalized during the weekend. "Take photos of the damage. Check to see if there was an attempt at a break in. Place some caution tape around the pots. Are there security cameras?" No response. "Fisher?"

"Yes, sir. I was checking. Yes, there are cameras. Should I help Marta? She's crying," he asked sounding a bit overwhelmed by the emotion of the moment.

"Give her a moment," Nishita said. "Tell her to take three slow breaths while you count to ten."

Nishita focused his attention on Marta as Fisher counted. People have been known to fake being upset when they hear of a loved one's death. But not being in her presence, he couldn't tell. Once Fisher reached ten, Marta stopped crying. Nishita said, "How I can get in touch with Mr. Hardwick? Will you ask Marta for his number?"

Fisher relayed the question, but this time he held the radio button down and Nishita could hear Marta. Her voice was measured, and cautious as she reported Dudley was still in Las Vegas for the International Gemstone Show held at Caesar's Palace. Then she gave Dudley's cell number.

Handing the mic to Camilla he said, "Dudley's in Vegas. Some Gemstone Conference." He wondered about the broken pots. Was it a coincidence? Experience told him there were no coincidences, not in a murder case. Setting that thought aside, Nishita dialed Dudley's number and it went directly to voice mail.

The male voice was cheery and had a slight British accent. "Hello there, this is Dudley. Thanks for calling. Yeah, I'm in Vegas from the 11th to the 16th. I'll be at Caesar's Palace. Leave a message and I'll get back to you. Ta!"

Det. Nishita relayed a simple message requesting Mr. Hardwick call him and left his cell number. Twice.

Nishita caught Camilla watching him. She pushed her lips into a small twist and said, "It's not always the husband."

"Yeah, but often enough, it is." He stepped to the side of the house. "What does one do at a Gem Conference?" Camilla shrugged.

They turned the corner and came face to face with a wooden door carved with fairies in a forest of flowers. The sight was so spectacular, it took a moment to locate the security buzzer. A bright voice answered the bell, "Yes?" He introduced himself as Detective Nishita and asked if he might speak with Anya Hardwick. The young woman paused, then said, "I'll come down."

Hearing footfalls on the steps, they moved back from the stoop. The door opened and Anya Hardwick moved into the light. She was a taller version of her mother. Her dark hair pulled in a ponytail, wearing a gray sweatshirt, and turquoise framed glasses. She looked from Nishita to Camilla and back, her mouth twisted in a slight scowl.

Nishita paused, readied his thoughts, and took a breath. Not missing a beat, Camilla spoke up. "I'm Officer Camilla Leila, and this is Detective Ted Nishita. Are you Anya Hardwick?" she asked. The young woman's face darkened.

He reached for his identification and the wallet got caught in the folds of his suit pocket. Finally, he freed it and held out his identification. Anya tipped up her glasses, held the badge close to her face, studied it, and handed it back.

"May we come in?" Camilla asked.

She moved aside and gestured for them to enter.

The stairs lead upwards and followed along the outer wall. They rose to a large open area with dark wood floors and colorful rugs placed with precision under the dining room table and in front of the fireplace. The rugs, he guessed, were Persian due to their intricate patterns and vivid colors. Large ferns inhabited corners at the far left by the bay window, and the fireplace mantle was covered with crystal rocks, candles, and marble statues of gods and goddesses.

Anya gestured to the two couches facing one another in front of the fireplace. Nishita sat while Camilla stood behind him. Anya hovered near the opposite couch and didn't sit.

Det. Nishita cleared his throat, keeping his gaze on Anya. "I'm afraid we have some bad news." She sat and her face lost color. He could tell she had no idea what he was going to say yet prepared for the worst.

"Your mother was found in her car on Topanga Canyon Road deceased," he said. He never took his eyes off her, watching her reactions to detect any false expression.

She tipped her head towards him and whispered, "What?"

"Your mother, Lena Rezenchov, has died." Watching Anya carefully, he remembered the smelling salts in his topcoat pocket in case she might faint.

She put her hand over her mouth and began to shake. Her eyes widened and her face turned red as if on fire. She folded in on herself and rocked and rocked. Her sobs got louder. Nishita signaled to Officer Camilla to move in. It was best that a female officer offer support. He said a silent prayer of thanks that Camilla was here. Anya turned to face her and fell back against the couch.

A high-pitched wail pierced the room, and his blood ran cold. Walking over to her he said, "I'm sorry for your loss." He handed Anya the linen handkerchief from in his coat pocket.

Asking through gulps of air she said, "How? When?"

"Her body was discovered inside her Maserati; it had gone over a cliff on Topanga Canyon Road. We think it happened sometime early this morning or late last night," he stated.

"In her car? At night? Oh, no, no, no." She covered her face. "Had she been drinking?"

Det. Nishita thought it a fair question, as a year ago her mother was in rehab. She could have started drinking again. It has happened, even to people with good intentions. They want to remain sober, even promise sobriety, but faced with setbacks in a job or relationship, emotions kick in, and to turn away from the pattern of seeking comfort takes more than willpower. Det. Nishita spoke carefully, "We won't find out the cause of death until the autopsy."

"What aren't you telling me?" Her eyes were suddenly cold.

A cell phone rang in her kitchen. Anya stood, moved to the counter, and saw who was calling. "Daddy? Oh, Daddy, Mum!"

Nishita heard the deep tones of a male voice. The man spoke for a few minutes. Was he advising her on what to say?

Anya stopped listening to the man and handed the phone over. "He wants to speak with you," she said.

Nishita gave a quick glance to Camilla, then walked over and accepted the phone. "This is Detective Nishita," he said.

"This is Dudley Hardwick, Lena's husband. I got a call from Marta Stannis. She said Lena was in a car accident?" Dudley said his voice steady but pinched.

Nishita sketched out the details for Mr. Hardwick. He'd given death notices to family over the phone before and didn't like it. Subtilities in facial expressions lost, he had to rely on his ears to pick up any hint of guilt, regret, or despair. Dudley's voice was steady and controlled. Nishita heard voices in the background and wondered if he was in a public place and trying his best to hold it together.

"Are you in a hotel lobby, sir?" Det. Nishita asked.

"I am. I was at our booth when Marta called me with the horrible, just horrible," Dudley stopped. Nishita heard small sobs.

"Sir, can you go to your hotel room? We need privacy to talk," Det. Nishita suggested.

Dudley made guttural noises then said, "I've got to get home, I have to contact the press. Lena's fans will be devastated."

"Did you drive to Las Vegas or fly?"

"Drove. Left LA on Thursday. I was to return tonight or tomorrow. But when Marta called . . . I have a van full of items for the bookstore," he said with a touch of a complaint.

Nishita thought it interesting that he provided the day in which he left without being asked.

"I don't know what to do next." His voice cracked.

Det. Nishita could hear the pain in his voice and said, "Can you take a moment before driving? You've had a shock."

Dudley took a deep breath. "I will leave within the hour." Dudley hung up.

People see me when grief has overwhelmed them. They're in pain and want a bridge back to normal. They ask, "What is my future? Will I make it?" I slow my mind and focus. At that moment, flashes of light and images ripple before me. Then the person and I talk about what I saw and how to move toward a new life.

—Lena Rezenchov, 2005 Interview on KTLA Channel 5

SIX

RETURNING THE PHONE TO ANYA, NISHITA kept his reactions contained. It was critical to maintaining an impartial demeanor, at least outwardly. With the death of a family member, the fine web that held a family together can break. By observing he'd learn who was dominant, who was the quiet one, and who was the peacemaker. Some family bonds strengthened; some ties were so weak they never rebuilt.

When Dudley abruptly ended the call, Nishita wondered why he didn't ask to speak with Anya again. With a blank stare, she set the phone down the handkerchief still clutched in her hand.

Like a marionette pulled by hidden strings, she opened a cupboard. "May I get you some water?"

Officer Camilla removed the glass from her hand. "Let me." She filled the glass and guided Anya back to the couch. Nishita followed and glanced at the dining room table as he walked back to the living area. The table was filled with neatly stacked folders stuffed with paper. Each pile had a different colored label. He could only read a few but they were cities in the Southern California region: Apple Valley, Hemet, Pomona. It looked like some kind of research.

Officer Camilla sat alongside Anya on the couch and Nishita

took his spot across from them. Anya stared directly at Nishita and asked, "What happened?"

He raised his eyebrows at the change in her demeanor. There wasn't much he could tell her at this stage. "We are at the beginning of the investigation, but the circumstances surrounding her accident look questionable," said Det. Nishita.

"I don't understand," said Anya. She wove the handkerchief through her fingers. "Explain."

Nishita watched her. Her face was calm unreadable, but a hard edge had entered her voice. He imagined she'd inherited her father's fighting nature; however, on her it felt less deflecting and more like digging for truth.

"If you will answer some questions, we'll have a better chance of finding out what happened," Det. Nishita said. "We were told she was at a hotel this weekend. Do you know why?"

Anya leaned back and rested against the soft couch. Pausing while her eyes scanned the room, she began, her voice a whisper at first, "You'll find out soon enough. My mother and father were getting a divorce. My mother didn't want to run retreats and workshops anymore. She was tired and wanted to move in a different direction. She went away to clear her mind." She sipped water.

Nishita pulled out his notebook and jotted down a few things, partially to record events as they unfolded, but it also gave him a chance to watch. If her parents were getting a divorce, was that the reason for the change of address on Lena's driver's license?

Anya continued, "She was starting a new chapter in her life to explore what direction to take." Shrugging helplessly, she wiped the tears from her cheek. "She was writing a new book, a personal account of her life." Anaya glanced around the room.

He followed her eyes. She looked over to the mantle, filled with crystals and statues. There were several boxes stacked in the corner next to the fireplace. "How long ago did she move in?" he asked.

"A little over a month. As you can see, we haven't sorted out the space yet." As she spoke her face changed and she tried to stifle her cries, but small whimpers escaped, a sound lost puppies make.

Det. Nishita gave her a moment to recover. "Where were you this weekend?"

"Here. Except for the occasional trip to get groceries and coffee at the shop across the street. My partner and I are working together on human trafficking in Southern California. We've been able to interview a few of the women through a translator. They were promised work in America and are smuggled into the country. The prettier ones are singled out. They never see those girls again."

Nishita considered the words "her partner". He wanted to know who that was and how to contact them to verify her statement. He quickly returned his attention to her and asked, "What do you do?"

"I'm an investigative reporter," she answered. "Freelance."

"Is that the report on the table?"

Anya nodded. "It's a start. We've got a lot more research ahead." Her face flushed and she used the crumpled handkerchief to dry her cheeks and jawline.

He thought he'd change the subject and give her a moment to breathe. "Can you tell me, what a Gemstone Conference is?" Det. Nishita asked. "Your father is in Las Vegas attending one, I've never heard of them." Truthfully, he knew about the Sacred Stone store four blocks from his parents' house. But an entire conference? That was interesting.

Anya appeared to put on a brave face and smiled. "It's an event where buyers and sellers of all types of gemstones, jewelry, statues, and silks gather and sell, buy, and bargain the weekend away. People from all over the world attend."

Her eyes sparkled and lost a shade of sorrow as she talked. "Conferences are opulent. I've seen rose quart rocks as big as chairs, crystals the size of bowling balls, and amethyst geodes large enough to fill the doorway. And then there are rare stones like white jade and citrine." Anya smiled with a faraway look on her face then let out a long sigh and began to cry.

He wanted to say words of comfort, but he'd hated it when people said them to him at his brother's funeral. Looking down at his notebook he cleared his throat. "Why did your father go?"

"My father and Marta attend each year to get things to sell at the bookstore," Anya answered.

Det. Nishita noted that he had just spoken with Marta, and she was at the bookstore . . . odd. "Does Marta go to every conference?" he asked. He didn't want to tip his hand if there were differing stories of what happened this weekend.

"Yes, when the conference is held in the States. My father travels a lot for business."

"And what is his business?" Det. Nishita asked.

Her answer was clean and clear. "Hardwick Import Export. Before the explosion of the internet, he was the guy to get things. He started with herbs. You know, roots, tree bark, and seeds used in natural tonics, salves, and ointments made downstairs at Royal Herbs. The apothecary? In a few years, he expanded the business to include Persian rugs, silks, brass and copper pots, and kettles. Then he added jewelry." She counted on her long fingers. "Earrings, bracelets, necklaces, and pins. Anything to sell at our bookstore. He traveled to Turkey, Egypt and lately he added Cambodia."

"I appreciate your help. What does he export?" Det. Nishita tried his best to ask the question as if he were merely curious. Anya loosened her ponytail and let her hair fall to her shoulders. She looked tired but he had to press on.

She said, "American leather, cotton, rayon, blue jeans, overalls, silk-screened T-shirts. Anything we take for granted but people want in other countries."

Det. Nishita made a note to check and see if Dudley had ever been flagged for illegal items, cigarettes, liquor, prescription drugs, or cold medicine. "When did your mother leave for the hotel?"

"She left Thursday morning." Anya buried her face in her hands.

Nishita and Camilla made eye contact. Nishita recalled something she had said earlier. He approached this part delicately. "You seemed surprised she was driving at night."

"She doesn't drive at night." Anya lifted her head to address him. "My mother is—was short, and that car had blind spots. It was low to the ground and the sideview mirrors weren't functional. Nighttime became particularly challenging for her."

"You asked if she had been drinking," Det. Nishita said.

Anya pulled on her lower lip with her thumb and forefinger. She nodded. "I just thought, and I have no proof, that maybe, alone, I don't know," she stammered and again stood up.

"She escaped to drink?" Det. Nishita suggested. He shot a glance at Camilla.

Anya stood. "She usually called me, not every day but every few days," she said. "I knew this weekend was a retreat for her, so I figured she wanted . . ." She didn't finish her thought and wandered to the mantle.

It wasn't what she said, it was what she didn't say that piqued his interest. If her mother had escaped to drink that weekend, she must have been under a great deal of stress—a divorce, a change in her business, and moving in with her daughter. These things are emotional challenges. "Has your mother relapsed before?"

She fidgeted with a statue of the Greek god Mercury recognizable because of the wings on his helmet and shoes. He made a note to research the gods and goddesses of ancient mythology as a refresher. There was a reason Mercury was on this mantle.

She said, "When Sophia had her stroke, my mother was in rehab. She tried to leave but wasn't allowed per my father's instructions. She didn't take kindly to that and escaped but only got as far as the winery just down the road."

"Sobriety can be a lonely road." As he spoke a painful memory of his brother flashed in his mind. Allen said life was just better high.

"Marta found her," Anya said. "My mother had a lot of secrets.

A crazy amount. Oh, she was open about her troubled youth and changing her name from Linda Rodgers to Lena Rezenchov-"

"She changed her name?" Det. Nishita asked and made a note to follow up.

Anya nodded. "Lena Rezenchov sounded more exotic than Linda Rodgers. It sold more books. But I'd always suspected that there was something hidden, something she feared." She gripped the mantle as if bracing herself during an earthquake.

Nishita knew that quake; he'd felt it before. His desire to provide comfort fought with his training, which told him to keep his distance and offer support. Her face went through different expressions. Murder floods a family with suspicion. She looked as if she might shatter.

Was there any way he could prepare her for the media frenzy, the internet trolls with their outrageous theories, and the tension between family members? "Anya, we will need to search the bookstore and your apartment," Nishita said a little more coldly than he intended. He had to remind himself, Anya was in shock and to keep an even manner. "We have to look for why this happened."

Officer Camilla shot him a look, then she asked, "Anya, do you have someone that can stay with you for the next few days? A close friend?"

With that question, Nishita knew Camilla was signaling to him that Anya needed a break. He could ask more personal questions at the station, in a formal situation, and record it. "Your mother was famous," he began, ". . . once this reaches the news."

"Yes, I'm aware." There was a heaviness in her voice. "I wanted nothing to do with that part of her life. The fortune and glory as she called it." She gave a cynical laugh. "Fortune and glory. That was her mantra. The parties, the attention, and the fame."

She sounded bitter. Nishita made a note to check all past news articles on Lena, but it brought up a question, and mulling it over he finally asked, "Why did you go into investigative reporting?"

"I wanted the truth. I saw the news was no longer reporting

facts but turning into a regurgitation of gossip and rumors," she said. "My first article was about the growth of rogue broadcasters and how that corrupted news organizations. I had traced a few fringe podcasters and found links to bribery, threats to whistleblowers, and buying stories only to subvert them. My article wasn't published. Must have touched a nerve." She gave a self-satisfied smile like a cat who had hidden something important. "Well, it's all there and one day, one day . . ." She drifted off.

She's a fighter and will need that strength, Nishita thought. "How can I get in touch with your partner?"

"My writing partner lives in Apple Valley," Anya said.

"Ah, I saw one of the files with that label," Nishita said. With that, he stood, asked her for her partner's name and phone number, and echoed Camilla's suggestion to have someone stay with her. Her eyes glassed over as she considered who.

As Anya escorted them to the door, her voice weak she finally said, "My friend Rain Sahota will stay with me. I've known her since I was seven."

Camilla said, "She sounds perfect."

Have you ever known something was going to happen before it did? Have you felt the presence of someone before they contacted you? Everyone has intuitive powers, but we don't know how to develop them. In this book, I give you my step-by-step guide to awaken your power.

—Lena Rezenchov, *The Miraculous Power Within YOU*

SEVEN

WHEN NISHITA REACHED FOR THE CAR door handle, he glanced back at Anya. She'd moved to the porch railing and must have been watching the entire time. He waited until she returned to her apartment.

He brought up his cell and noticed he had three missed calls "I'm going to check messages; will you walk the grounds to see if you notice anything amiss?" he asked Camilla.

"I was thinking the same thing," she answered. She put her cap on and headed out along the side of the blue house.

"Check the alley too," Nishita called to her. Camilla didn't turn back but just lifted her hand in a small wave.

Just then, Anya stepped off the porch and called out, "Detective, I forgot to give you this," She held a flat blue notebook, the type that are bought in a packet of three, as she approached. "It's my mother's prayer journal." She reached him and hesitated before handing him the journal. New tears welled in the corners of her eyes. "I hope it helps."

"Anything and everything will help, no matter how small. If there's anything else you think of please call," Det. Nishita said.

She turned and walked with heavy steps back to the porch, and this time didn't turn back when she entered her apartment.

He set the notebook on the driver's seat and opened his voice-mail and listened. There were several messages, but he started with to the one from the Medical Examiner's office. It was from a staff worker saying he'd tried to keep Lena Rezenchov's death quiet, but there were reporters at the morgue due to the traffic accident this morning. Once they discovered Lena's death, off they went to post video reports.

"Damn!" he said. "The guy was probably slipped a few bucks to alert reporters." He hadn't wanted this to get out so fast. He'd hoped for at least eight hours of unencumbered police work.

Camilla, having returned, asked, "Who are you talking to?"

Nishita made a guttural sound of disgust. "Media trolls They're like insects."

"Did word get out about Lena?" He nodded. "Do you think the family will need security?"

Nishita pulled on his lower lip with his thumb and forefinger. "Not yet. But we should keep an eye on crowds."

"Media trolls must see people as steppingstones. They're not real people to them, they're a way to make money. That's the world we live in."

Her response lingered in the quiet street.

"Well," Camilla got inside the patrol car, "where to, Little Ted?"

Calling him Little Ted was a jab. He was Little Ted to his grandfather's Big Ted, and he wondered why he'd ever told her that family nickname. "Topanga. I want to talk with Marta Stannis before Dudley returns from Vegas."

Camilla started the car and they retraced their route back to the hills of Topanga. Nishita searched Marta Stannis and Dudley Hardwick for police records. He specifically wanted to know if Hardwick Import Export had ever been flagged by Border Guards. Nothing showed up. He'd research old news articles on the company.

He entered Dudley Hardwick into Google search. An immediate video post appeared from five minutes ago connected to Dudley.

There were sounds of cars whizzing past in the background, then a blurry and jiggly shot of Dudley exiting the Vegas hotel. Someone must have been holding the camera while running. Suddenly Dudley was surrounded by people, and microphones and cell phones were stuck in his face. Dudley held his arms up in defense and appeared shaken, his face flushed as one voice asked, "How did you hear about Lena's death?" Dudley, with a severe look, said, "I will make a public announcement tomorrow." He got inside a van and drove away.

If this video was accurate, Dudley left Las Vegas just after three o'clock. He glanced at his watch. It was a quarter to four. "Let's get to the bookstore before the crowd."

They drove through the streets and made it to Pacific Coast Highway. The last of the sunbathers and volleyball players were finishing up gathering kids, towels, and coolers on the beach. It was still considered winter and the sun was low in the sky, the temperature cooling with each moment. There would be another half hour before sunset.

Approaching the road to head up to the bookstore, the sky became a burnished orange. The traffic light changed red, and Camilla pulled up behind a pick-up truck at a red light and waited. In the left lane of the street that crossed theirs, a gray Prius waited for the turn signal. The car, the only one stopped in the left lane, would pass in front of Nishita and Camilla.

Both heard the young woman sing at the top of her lungs along with the radio. It was one of the newest pop songs, and Nishita had to admit the girl sang quite well. The young woman's arm dangled out the driver's side window and twirled to the beat of the music, her wrist covered with bracelets of every color. The light changed, and as the Prius began its turn, Nishita got a clear view of the woman driver. She had rainbow-dyed hair and a round face.

After she had driven past, Camilla said, "What are the odds that that girl is Anya's friend Rain?"

Announcing the Grand Opening
of the Goddess Garden Bookstore

The long-anticipated center for everything metaphysical has materialized in Topanga Canyon. Driving up Topanga Canyon Road, one cannot miss this Victorian mansion with curved iron gates, a wrap-around porch, and turrets. This reporter called in all favors to secure a preopening tour and wasn't disappointed. Entering the beveled glass doors, one wanders past display cases of red jasper from Arizona, amethyst geodes from Argentina, and fire opals from Australia. The mansion houses a large library which has been converted into a bookstore filled with the latest bestsellers of the new age. Riding the gilded elevator to the second floor, one can receive a psychic reading and discover what the future holds. Or one may sign up for an herbal cleanse to purge toxins that damage health. "We offer a sanctuary in which busy people can refresh, rejuvenate, and revitalize," said Co-owner and author Lena Rezenchov. This reporter sipped elixir tea and strolled through the aromatic garden and did just that.

—B.A. Jenkins, staff reporter,
The Valley Breeze Friday, April 23, 2002.

EIGHT

THEY DROVE UP THE HILL AND past the cliff where Lena had been found. It always surprised Nishita how quickly crime scenes morphed back to innocent driveways, businesses, or streets. It was almost as if the road itself wanted to sweep away the crime.

Pinching the bridge of his nose desperate to relieve the headache pounding behind his eyes, he checked the time on his cell. The itch to check social media filled him, but he buried his cell in his pocket. Not yet, he told himself. He didn't need the irritation. He'd check later.

The car rounded the bend and he blinked, staring at the Goddess Garden Bookstore. It was beautiful and took his breath away. He glanced over to Camilla, and she was also gaped-mouthed.

A three-story Victorian-style mansion with turrets and a wrought iron fence filled the left hillside. A few onlookers lingered by the front gate, talking solemnly with one another. Cellophane-wrapped bouquets set along the stone wall were tokens of grief.

On the opposite side of the street were an assortment of flat-roofed modern businesses. The walkway connecting them was lined with large clay pots overflowing with red geraniums. He noted a fabric store, a ceramic business, a rustic neighborhood restaurant with a wooden sign saying The Wagon Wheel Bar and

Grill, and lastly a bakery. Silently, he counted security cameras along the corners of the buildings. They might have collected footage from the weekend.

Returning his attention to the bookstore, he caught a glimpse of Fisher preventing a delivery truck from driving into a gravel alley that circled to its back entrance. Then he noticed the yellow caution tape draped across the alley and wrapped around tree trunks and bushes deep into the woods behind the house.

"Has he completely covered the yard in tape?" said Nishita.

Camilla pulled the car into the paved driveway in front of the garage doors. Nishita marveled at the feat of engineering it took to dig below the house and build a modern garage underneath. Lena owned a classic sports car. Anyone who owned a car like that would never leave it outside or on the street, but why not build a separate building for the cars unless a connected garage lent itself to other activities?

Ted reached for the door handle, ready to chastise Fisher, but Camilla touched his arm and stopped him. "Let me deal with him. You need to speak with Marta Stannis."

"Find out why he strung tape up the hill. This draws attention, exactly what we don't want," Nishita said and felt his irritation rise. He took a deep breath to calm himself. It was still early in the investigation and there was a long road ahead. Getting out of the car, he adjusted his suit coat and straightened his shoulders. Camilla walked past him towards Fisher and the back door of the mansion. It gave him a moment to take in the building.

There was something too perfect about the mansion, almost as if it belonged on the set of a movie and not in a dusty corner of Topanga Canyon. The stone wall was too clean, the wrought iron fence too glossy. It spoke of deep pockets. Understandably, a business wants to impress its customers, but this communicated something extreme. Was being a psychic this lucrative?

Fisher had told him Marta and her mother Sophia lived on the top floor. He shielded his eyes from the sun and looked up, counting the floors. The top row of turrets and glass windows was the third. The sun sparkled on the beveled glass. *They don't make them like this anymore*, he thought. He walked around to the back door and came face to face with a mature woman.

"Hello, Detective. I'm Marta," she said in a deep voice. She was petite, not more than five feet tall, and slender. She had a strength gained from hard work, not sculpted by exercise classes.

Det. Nishita held out his hand to Marta. "I'm sorry for your loss." She accepted his hand and made a curt nod. "Will it be all right if I ask you some questions?" Det. Nishita studied her face which seemed pale next to the redness surrounding her eyes. She'd been crying.

She gestured away from the chaos of Officer Fisher and towards the front door. "I'd like to understand what happened. Perhaps you can fill me in," said Marta. She opened the wrought iron gate and nodded to the fans nearby. The fans remained silent and didn't move. Marta led up the porch steps and through the glass front doors. She pulled down the shades and the room darkened.

Entering the bookstore, it felt as if he stepped back in time. It had an old-world apothecary look. The main area was filled with display cases. Crystals, jewelry, and colorful clothing reminiscent of a Renaissance Festival overflowed the cases. One section of the front room had shelves of clay pots with names of herbs: Willow Bark, Rose Hips, Feverfew. In quiet corners of the store, suits of armor stood guard. Nishita wondered if the suits held security cameras. It was something he'd ask Marta when the opportunity presented itself.

She walked to the back of the house. As they entered the main hallway, a gilt caged elevator was to his right. It was an old-fash-ioned elevator, the type showing metal workings. Curving upward and almost protecting the elevator was an elegant marble stair-case. Its banisters were wood carved into dragons. He looked up the staircase, a stained-glass window graced the wall to the outside sun. It must look magnificent when sunlight pierced through and left colored patterns on the white marble. Marta kept walking and Nishita had to quicken his steps.

He caught a glimpse of a tall room to his left filled with shelves of books and a rolling ladder braced against a shelf. To his right was a small room with computers and a sleek desk. *There is no escape from the modern world, not even here.*

Marta opened a swinging door and set the door stop to keep it open. He followed and entered an expansive chrome and stainless steel kitchen. It looked more like a cafeteria than a kitchen inside a home. Marta gestured for him to join her. He readied himself to ask questions that encouraged Marta to reveal more than she planned.

Personal coaches say: If you want money, you must raise your vibration. They tell you the world is made up of vibrations. And it is, but they tell you when you match your vibration to money, you will achieve wealth. All sorts of people start running, talking louder, waving their arms about to raise their vibration. It creates is a world in which you are not acceptable as you are. What if, now hear me out, what if, there is nothing more powerful than being yourself.

—Lena Rezenchov, *Path to Inner Power*

NINE

MOVING TOWARDS THE TABLE MARTA POINTED to, Nishita was overwhelmed by odors. It was a mixture of disinfectant cleaners. A pine odor was strong as if it was used within the last hour. However, a faint lemon scent, the type he associated with the wipes his mother used, was also present. His mother bought them by the case and every time he visited, she passed off a tub to him. As if he ever had time to clean his apartment.

Sitting across from Marta, he let her see his admiration of the kitchen. The stainless-steel counters gleamed, the floor-to-ceiling bay windows sparkled, and the floor, a marbled gray and white tile, showed no footprints or smudges.

"You have a clean bookstore," he said.

Marta smiled proudly. "Before we closed for the holiday, I set up a crew to do a deep cleanse," she said and scanned the corners.

"When was the crew here?" Det. Nishita asked as nonchalantly as possible.

"Before we left. I knew the bookstore would be empty. You see, I always travel to Las Vegas for the conference." Marta stared at him directly.

He did his best to keep his face neutral, but this was the first break in the timeline. He'd spoken to Dudley. He was in Vegas as of this afternoon, and she wasn't.

"I spoke with Dudley no more than two hours ago; he was in Las Vegas." Det. Nishita remarked with a polite smile.

"Friday morning, I awoke with a migraine. I stayed in the hotel room with ice packs on my head and the curtains shut." She lightly touched the right side of her forehead. By her reaction, it looked as if the pain was still pressing against her brow. "I was useless to Mr. Hardwick."

"I'm sorry to hear that," he said and did his best to show compassion. Marta looked uncomfortable with his chatter. He decided to shift the line of questions. "How long did you stay?" A blank look came over her face. He persisted, "Well, Mr. Hardwick is on his way here, and you're already here. You just said you always go with him to conference."

"Oh, I understand now. I was sick and wasn't getting any work done. Mr. Hardwick ordered a car to send me ahead. I arrived late last night."

"A car? Why not fly?"

"A limousine can carry more baggage than an airplane. I brought back so many boxes from the conference," she said and glanced to her left to an assortment of oddly shaped boxes piled one on top of the other.

"Ah, that is true. No weight limit in a car," he said. "What did you do all weekend? I mean if you were sick."

"I stayed in the hotel room. I mostly slept. I had the television on but couldn't follow anything. Mr. Hardwick ordered room service for me. They delivered outside my door. But I barely ate. Sunday the pain began to ease. All I wanted was to come home. That was when Dudley, Mr. Hardwick, ordered the limo," she said with a small smile.

Softness spread across Marta's face. She went from cold to warm quickly . . . but that kind of swing in emotions can turn dangerous. By how she talked about Dudley, did she think a romance was possible? A break in his marriage might open emotions she'd kept under wraps.

"A limo, that is pricy," he said hoping she'd take the bait.

"Not for high rollers." She blew air through her teeth in a dismissive sound. "Inconsequential. Mr. Hardwick is a frequent visitor and has many wealthy connections."

Now it's getting interesting, he thought. "And how does he know these people?"

Again, Marta turned cold and scoffed, "Through his import-export business and Ms. Rezenchov's clients."

"Ah, of course." Det. Nishita took a few notes and keeping focused on his notepad, asked, "So, how does that work? A limo driver takes you here, and then he turns around and goes back to Vegas?"

Marta spoke calmly with a hint of irritation as if she was explaining something to a child. "Sometimes the drivers pick up a fare and make the return trip. If not, they are put up in a hotel and the next evening, drive a group to Vegas. People don't realize how many limos make the trip back and forth from Los Angeles to Vegas. All for wealthy clients of course."

"Sounds high effort for the driver," Det. Nishita said. It piqued his interest as to how much Marta knew.

"They are paid well," Marta said, "and a night in a four-star hotel is a nice bonus."

"Mr. Hardwick's business must be successful to justify that expenditure."

"It is." Marta thought for a moment. "He is a dynamic man."

Det. Nishita watched her carefully. "Things must have been changing during the last few months. I mean with the divorce pending. How has it affected you?"

"Lena and I have been friends for over thirty years." Marta pressed her lips tightly in an effort to maintain her composure. "We were like sisters." She dabbed the corners of her eyes.

Nishita saw no tears, or was she reserved?

Marta said, "When Lena and I met, we were teenagers, I saw her from across the room. She was encircled by silver light. I saw her brilliance," she said and lowered her head and sniffed. "I edited her books and helped with the design and marketing of her Contemplation Cards. I managed the bookstore and oversaw the accounts."

Nishita reached for the linen handkerchief, but his pocket was empty. He had given it to Anya and forgot to refill his pocket in the car with Camilla. How could he be so clumsy? He looked around for a box of tissues. Marta pulled out a small lace hankie that had been tucked up the sleeve of her cardigan. It was an old-fashioned way to carry a hankie; he hadn't seen that since his Aunt Helen. Watching Marta behave similarly endeared her to him. But as she fiddled with her sleeve, he spotted a row of small bruises on the inside of her wrist.

"How long have you lived here?" He moved his hand in a circle to suggest the bookstore.

Dabbing her eyes, Marta said, "Lena and my mother bought the farmhouse when we moved to Los Angeles. My mother hired Dudley to do some remodeling. I think Dudley fell in love with Lena the moment he saw her. Soon they married and he made connections with unemployed set designers and actors looking for work. The remodeling went on for years. A year on the first-floor bookstore, then our living quarters on the third floor, then they dug out the old coal furnace in the basement and turned it into a garage. That only encouraged them, so they designed this kitchen, then they did the stone wall and iron fence and the gardens."

"That's amazing. Did you live here while the construction was going on?" Nishita thought of the new bathroom his father had done when he was in grade school. It was a mess.

Marta tipped her head to the right. "We lived on the third floor. It used to be the servants" quarters. There's a full kitchen, a living room, bedrooms, and bathrooms. My mother and I were in one bedroom. Lena and Dudley were in another, and Anya was in the nursery."

There was a wistful note in her voice like someone recollecting past moments of remembered happiness. Nishita suspected the actual living of those times might have been more difficult than her memory.

"I didn't realize this place was that big."

"Would you like a tour?" Marta asked.

"I would, thank you."

Do you ever catch yourself judging others harshly? Our world has been divided into right versus wrong thinking. But who does that serve? When I get like that I ask a simple question: What do I truly want?

—Lena Rezenchov, *Let Your Light Shine*

TEN

MARTA GESTURED FOR NISHITA TO FOLLOW. He couldn't help the feeling that this whole situation reminded him of characters from an old movie, the ones with a tough-as-nails gal pal secretary who worked diligently in the background, the handsome successful boss was married to a socially connected wife. The ever-faithful secretary always saved the day by getting the forgotten anniversary present or staying late to finish an urgent report. Marta emitted that kind of selfless dedication. Her tailored pants, crew neck sweater, and curled hair framing her face, echoed the women in those black and white movies he'd learned to love. Do things ever change?

As they entered the hallway Det. Nishita asked, "Is your mother here? I'd like to speak with her if it's possible."

Marta turned to look at him directly and said, "She was at a care facility this weekend." She took a moment to dab her nose. "She'll return sometime late this evening."

"Is she all right?" Det. Nishita asked.

"She is confined to a wheelchair and can't be left alone." When she spoke, Marta tipped her head slightly and fidgeted with the hankie.

"I'm sorry to hear that. It must be challenging to care for her."

"My mother is strong-willed and knows what she wants. Both a blessing and a curse," Marta said and patted her chest with her right hand. "I wish you could have met Sophia when she was younger. She was a force to be reckoned with."

"You call your mother by her first name? I think my mother would faint if I did that." He gave his best smile.

Marta giggled at his comment. "We've been more like sisters," said Marta. As they walked they passed the room with the computers. She stopped suddenly. "How am I going to tell her about Lena?" She held the lace hankie to her mouth and took several deep breaths.

Nishita couldn't help but feel for her. "Is there someone that can stay with you? It's not good to be alone at this time."

Marta muttered something into the hankie. Lifting her head, she looked directly at Nishita. "Maybe Rebecca Lopez can recommend someone from the care center to stay with us."

"Rebecca?" he asked.

"She's the manager at the Elder Care Center. So reliable," Marta said.

"Do you know when," Nishita kept his words formal, "your mother will return?" Marta shook her head. He got the impression it would be a while and knew she shouldn't be left alone. "Would you be willing to allow Officer Fisher to stay with you?" Nishita almost gagged at suggesting Fisher, but who else could he recommend?

"You're right. I'd just spin in my thoughts." She made twirling motions with her right hand. "Scotty Fisher will do nicely." She took a deep breath and put on a brave face. Her eyes brightened, and she said, "I want to give you something." She turned and went into the small office.

He took the opportunity to examine the hallway unsupervised. The antique elevator looked operational. The elderly mother would certainly need it, and if there were clients who couldn't or wouldn't use the stairs, an elevator was perfect. He let his eyes follow the curved stairs to the ceiling. It was a patterned ceiling, not like the buildings of today in which the ceilings are flat and uninteresting. His eyes drifted down the marble stairs and noted its round edges. It made the marble look soft, pillow-like.

He glanced at his watch and wondered where this day had gone; he had nothing on motive or where the murder took place.

"Detective, you might need these." Marta held out a small gift bag. Her eyes were red again. "The more you learn about Lena the better."

He accepted it and said, "Thank you, but I can't accept gifts. It might be misinterpreted. I'll pay for them."

"I didn't mean to compromise you," she said, face flushing and eyes wide. "I want to understand what happened. The officer said she drove off the cliff along Topanga Road, I assumed she was drinking."

"At this moment, we don't know how she died. We are waiting for the coroner to give us the answer," Det. Nishita said. "I assure you, once I know, I will call."

"I will make up a receipt for the books. I put her three highest sellers. They are the ones in which Lena writes about her difficult childhood, the death of her mother, and her transformation into the psychic she became. It's quite a gripping story," Marta said while she wiped a tear along her cheek.

Nishita handed her his credit card, and she slipped back into the office. His cell vibrated in his pocket. He picked it up and saw it was the Santa Monica PD calling.

"Nishita," he said.

"Sir, are you in charge of the Lena Rezenchov case?"

"Yeah."

"Well, we have a guy here who has turned himself in. He says he was at the Goddess Garden Bookstore on Saturday and vandalized the clay pots."

"Repeat that?" Nishita said.

"Yeah, I don't blame you. This guy, goes by Grant Montgomery, showed up at the station and said we're probably looking for him, if not now, we soon will be. He went to visit Lena Rezenchov on Saturday at the bookstore, but she never showed. He said that she never answered the door. He knew someone was there because he could see the third-floor window curtains move. This person ignored his calls to answer the door, and he got so angry he busted two pots."

"Hold him there until I arrive," Nishita said. He considered how long it would take to drive there; rush hour would add time. "I'll be driving in traffic, should be about an hour," Nishita said and hung up. This was both good and bad—good because it was a lead, but bad because he had wanted to catch Dudley. In his mind, he wanted to be here when Dudley arrived. It was always unsettling for the police to be there when a suspect got out of his car. He wanted Dudley to be unnerved.

Well, nothing to be done about it. Right now, he had to grab Camilla and get to the Santa Monica police station. He noticed Marta staring at him and held up a finger in a silent request for her to give him a moment. Then he dialed Camilla's cell.

She answered on the first ring. "Yeah?"

He spoke quietly almost a whisper. "I need Fisher to..."

At first, she sputtered, then caught why Nishita was whispering. "Are you speaking in front of Marta?"

"Yes," he said and elongated the word, hoping Camilla would get what he was implying.

"Want me to make sure Fisher doesn't get weird?" she asked.

"Bingo."

"I can set him up. Anything else?"

"Meet me at the car."

"Be there in a few," Camilla said.

He turned to Marta and said, "I've got to return to the station. Perhaps I can take a rain check on the tour?"

"Certainly, Detective." Marta smiled. She handed over the bag of books, showed him the receipt, and returned his card.

Nishita admired her quiet charm, something older women eased into. He thanked her and exited out the front double doors.

Outside, the sky was a deep violet. He felt the panic of losing critical time. He hadn't heard from the coroner, and he'd have to search the bookstore, but not yet. He wanted a a solid case. Now he needed to speak to this guy, Grant Montgomery. Who was he, and where did he come from? He'd check the police laptop in the car while Camilla drove. Walking towards the car he noticed more flowers had been placed along the stone wall. Word was out. Internet trolls would have a field day digging up her old DUI and her arrest picture but the kind gestures from fans touched him.

Camilla strode up to the car. "So? What's at the station?"

"I'll tell you while we drive. What did you find out about security cameras?"

Camilla smiled. "Fisher did a lot of groundwork. He located two cameras that face the main road. The Wagon Wheel Bar has coverage of the west-facing road and parking lots. Fisher asked the manager and got the entire weekend." She held up a thumb drive. The look on her face was priceless. She thought she had the golden ticket.

"That will be fun to sort through." He sighed and entered the passenger seat.

"Scotty Fisher will meet me at the station tomorrow, and we'll comb through it," Camilla said, buckling her seatbelt.

"Scotty?" Nishita said with an arch to his tone.

Camilla tisked her tongue. "So, what's in the bag?"

"Books by Lena. Marta pulled them for me," Nishita said, placing the bag in the back seat.

"Are you going to read all of those?" Camilla made a face.

"Anything to better understand my victim. You'd know that if you'd become a detective," Nishita shot at her.

She let out a loud sniff and stuck her tongue out. Then asked, "Why the rush to the station?"

"Grant Montgomery."

"Who?"

"That's what I said. He was to meet Lena at the bookstore. She either didn't show or avoided him and he got upset and broke the clay pots."

Camilla laughed. "A lead at last."

Nishita opened the laptop and entered Grant Montgomery into the Santa Monica Police system. A driver's license with a handsome face appeared. It said he was 5' 11" and 185 lbs., with brown hair, and hazel eyes. He was 32 years old and resided in Atlanta, Georgia.

"Oh, handsome," Nishita said.

"Stop teasing. I can't look at his picture while I'm driving." Camilla said.

"You know, there's a family resemblance, around the forehead. Maybe a nephew trying to cash in on rich Aunt Lena in LA."

"Ouch."

"Goes with the territory," Nishita bantered back. But it did make him think of his own family and the struggle they went through after his grandfather died: the bickering on how to close his auto repair shop and divide the money. The money. What a mess that was. Families and money. Always complicated.

It was clear that in this family, Lena was the main event. Dudley's business, if it was completely legal, could hide behind Lena's shining star. In that way, she was the goose that laid the golden egg. If she wanted out of this business, as Anya suggested, and Dudley wasn't ready to get out from under her protective shield, that could cause a rift. Dudley should be returning from Vegas in the next few hours. There was no way he'd get to interview him tonight. Well, Dudley would be top of the list tomorrow morning.

Next thing he knew, they were pulling into the parking lot of the station.

Camilla parked and said, "I'm going to call home and talk to my son."

"I got this," he said as he closed the car door.

His pace quickened. He reached the front desk and asked about

Grant Montgomery. He was told they had him waiting in interview room 2. "Anything I should know before I go in?" he asked.

The officer said, "He's polite."

"He's polite," Nishita deadpanned. "That's it?"

"Yeah," the officer said.

"Okay." Nishita meandered to room 2 opened the door, and stared at the well-dressed, clean-cut, polite man. Nishita knew he was polite because he stood when Nishita entered the room.

"Mr. Montgomery? I'm Detective Nishita," he said and held out his hand to shake.

Grant accepted his hand. "Please call me Grant. Mr. Montgomery was my father, and he was a harsh SOB." He smiled at his soft joke.

Nishita kept a cool reserve. "So, you are from Atlanta, Georgia? What brought you to Los Angeles, Grant?"

"Let me get to the point. I am Lena Rezenchov's, or I should say Linda Rodgers' son. She gave me up when I was born. I can't blame her. She almost died giving birth to me."

Nietzsche wrote if one stares into the abyss long enough the abyss will stare back. I wondered what the abyss was. Perhaps it was the unanswerable, the unknowable, the deep recesses of our patterned behavior.

—Lena Rezenchov, *Beyond Death and Dying*

ELEVEN

THE INTERVIEW ROOM WAS COLD, IT was one small irritant to put the interviewee off their game. If they were wearing the usual Los Angeles wardrobe of cargo shorts and a T-shirt, they would feel a cool draft against the back of their neck. Admittedly, he'd seen some suspects sweat in the cold windowless room. The ones to watch were the ones at ease. It meant they had a strategy planned.

Grant Montgomery stood next to the long table and metal folding chair. Wearing a tailored navy blazer, aqua blue shirt, and charcoal gray pants, he looked like a businessman on holiday. For a guy who had surrendered, he regarded Nishita directly and openly.

Asking Grant to sit, he went over Mr. Montgomery's legal rights. "Before we get started, I do need to mention that you came here on your own accord, are not under arrest, and may at any time leave." He clicked his tongue and put his forefinger up to his mouth. "Let's see, is there anything else? Oh yes, this interview is being recorded," he said and pointed out the two cameras peering down at him from the corners.

Grant smiled and said, "Fair enough."

"I'd like to get a few details." Det. Nishita opened his hard-edged folder and clicked his pen ready to take notes. He said, "What is your full name?"

"Randal Grant Montgomery. I use Grant; my father was Randal."

"And you are from?"

"I live in a suburb of Atlanta called Buckhead."

The way Grant said it, the name was supposed to impress. "And what brought you to Los Angeles?"

"Two things. One, I was invited to speak at a conference sponsored by Grocery Magazine this weekend," he said and lifted from his side pocket a lavalier with a badge. The badge had his name printed on it and under his name said, Guest Speaker. "And two, I came to meet Lena Rezenchov." Grant swallowed, pursing his lips.

Det. Nishita picked up the badge and read the location of the conference. "One of our best hotels. It has a Michelin-starred restaurant," he commented. "Right on the strand, looking out over the ocean, beautiful people passing by, and of course picture-perfect sunsets." Nishita watched him closely hoping for him to relax or engage.

Grant nodded and made a small sneer as if the hotel didn't meet his expectations.

Having interviewed hundreds of witnesses, victims, and perpetrators there was always a twitch, a nervous blink, or a knee that bounced uncontrollably. These behaviors can separate the guilty from the not guilty. Grant sat still, hands folded in his lap. His one tick was swallowing hard. Something had to break soon.

"When was the conference?" Det. Nishita asked.

"There was a wine and cheese party on Friday night; it's a meet and greet kind of thing. On Saturday, there were sessions on upcoming trends, negotiating with unions, resolving complaints, and working with security teams to name a few. On Sunday the candidates running for the board of the Grocers Association give speeches and greet regional representatives. We vote and that night hold an awards ceremony. Monday was a half day with closing ceremonies and announcing the new leadership team." He held up the badge. "I gave a presentation on community outreach. Something our store has accomplished in the last five years."

He noticed a flare of impatience. It was in his tight smile, the harnessed modulation in his voice as if he held the reins of a quick temper. This was the part Det. Nishita loved. He could sit all day looking in the face of someone before he decided if they were lying or not. But enough messing around, time to get rolling. "So, tell me about Saturday at the Goddess Garden Bookstore."

"Wait, can we back up a bit?" Grant asked holding his hand up. Det. Nishita gestured for him to go ahead. "My father passed away last year," he began. "It was unexpected."

"I'm sorry to hear that." Det. Nishita did his best to appear sympathetic but not personal.

"Don't be, he was a cruel man."

Det. Nishita understood the pain of losing a family member, even an unliked one. "May I ask what happened?"

The corners of his mouth curved downward. "Heart attack." Grant cleared his throat and adjusted in his chair. "My family owns a boutique food market. It's gourmet groceries for the wealthy. You know, the finest meats, farm fresh vegetables, an in-house bakery, deli, and coffee shop."

"This food market is in . . ." He didn't finish his sentence and pretended to look at his notes. The point was to see if Grant would fill in the blank with the same information he gave earlier.

"Buckhead, yes. It's a wealthy suburb with a small-town feel where gossip is king. I'd heard rumors that I was the love child of my father and a wild girl. And this wicked girl seduced my father, blackmailed him, and ran away after I was born. Each time my father had an illicit affair with another woman—girls really—I wondered if the story about my mother was true." He stopped. His face tightened and his jaw muscles twitched. "My father preferred teenagers. What better place to find them than in his workforce? When I was in high school, one of these affairs surfaced. Divorce papers were scattered all over our dining room table. Then one day, the papers were tucked away. My mother got a new car, a diamond necklace, and an extended vacation in Switzerland. She returned refreshed." Grant tipped his head to the side and gave a searing look. "That's Southern for facelift."

Det. Nishita couldn't stop himself from smiling. Such a quaint expression. This whole investigation felt like a jump back in time starting with Lena's classic sports car.

"My mother and I are close," Grant said, and a softness washed over his face. "After Dad's passing, she gave me this." He pulled out from his inside pocket a bulky envelope and slipped it to Nishita. Grant kept one finger at the edge maintaining possession. Grief filled his face and he separated out a smaller envelope. "Open it," he said.

To the touch, the envelope was thin containing only one sheet of paper. Unfolding the paper, he saw the words: Non-Disclosure Agreement. As he read further the names of Randal Montgomery and Linda Rodgers appeared as the Disclosing Party and Receiving Party respectively. Det. Nishita asked, "Your mother gave you this after your father died?"

Grant spoke through gritted teeth. "My mother told me Linda Rodgers worked in the coffee shop at our store. A young teenager with a sweet face, yeah, my father noticed her." Grant handed over a brown file-type envelope.

Det. Nishita tilted it, and out spilled an employee identification badge and he came face to face with a young Lena Rezenchov. There was a full-color newspaper ad for Montgomery's Market. In the advertisement a distinguished-looking gentleman held his arms out in a welcoming gesture. To his left was a man wearing a green apron holding a basketful of red tomatoes and to his right a young Lena wearing a pink and white striped apron and holding a cup of coffee. The banner at the top of the page read: "At Montgomery Farms, we treat you like royalty,."

He went back to the NDA. The language was harsh declaring that Linda Rodgers was not to contact the Montgomery family or face serious charges. He read the signatures and saw someone had to sign as guardian for Linda Rodgers. Pointing to the document, Nishita said, "Zahra Hamdy. Who is that?"

Grant stared down at his hands. "Her grandmother, the only living relative Linda had at the time." A silence filled the room while Grant waited for him to understand.

Det. Nishita tried to put the pieces together, Zahra Hamdy was a Middle Eastern name, but he couldn't place the origin.

Grant broke the silence and said, "The age of consent in Georgia is 16. Linda was 14. I doubt her grandmother knew American law against statutory rape. They were frightened and took the money."

"What about Lena's, I mean Linda's, parents?" Det. Nishita asked.

"Her father, James Rodgers, left when her mother became ill. She passed away when Linda turned eight," Grant answered.

Nishita liked to think parents were more invested in their children, but he had seen, time and time again, one parent or the other can't watch a loved one die, so they leave. A thought occurred to him. "How much was she paid? I mean do you know?" Det. Nishita asked.

"Thirty-five thousand dollars and all hospital bills. I imagine to her it was a fortune. At that age, I would have thought so too. Her grandmother died soon after I was born, and I was told Linda left or ran away. Reports vary."

"When did you contact Lena? I assume you sent out the first notice," Nishita said and reread some of the harsh threats against Linda if she ever tried to contact the Montgomery family.

"My mother always kept an eye on Linda, now the famous psychic Lena Rezenchov. She bought her Contemplation Cards and a couple of her books. Hidden of course, from the old man. After his death, it was my mother who suggested I contact Lena. I sent a letter to her attorney. Didn't hear back until last November. She apologized and said she thought it was a scam. I can't blame her, being a celebrity and all."

"Smart."

"Her private investigator checked me out. I passed," he said with a guttural chuckle. "I received, by special delivery, a box filled with cards she'd made for me each year on my birthday. All with personal messages about how she thinks of me and prays for me." Grant wiped the side of his face and swallowed again. "She was bullied, threatened, and coerced by my father and his team of lawyers to give up her son. At fifteen could I have stood up against that?"

Nishita fingered the employee badge with the photo showing her open face. Could any fifteen-year-old?

"I wanted to meet her, touch her face, hear her voice," Grant said struggling to say each word.

Det. Nishita had to ask, had to get an answer now. No waiting. "Did you kill her? To seek revenge?" he asked softly. "I can understand things getting heated."

"No. God no," Grant interrupted.

"You had a violent reaction to being ignored. Smashing clay pots."

"I pushed one over, and the other was hit by the one I pushed over. I felt so stupid. I left with my tail between my legs and thought about ditching the conference, but I was a speaker that night," he said and ran his hand through his thick dark hair. "This morning, while I was packing my bag to catch the late flight to Atlanta, I saw that Lena was found in her car, deceased. The wind was knocked out of me. I knew I'd be on the security footage, and it would look worse to leave so I came in."

"Any cell phone contact with her?"

"I called her while I was at the front door, but she never answered. Once again, I thought she was dumping me. I left an angry message. I'm sure you'll hear it."

That reminded Nishita that he'd seen her cell phone in her purse. It must be in evidence. "Yep, we will."

"Here is the message she left me on Thursday morning," he said and pressed the play button. "Hi, Grant, I am looking forward to seeing you Saturday. I have arranged for us to meet privately. Give us time to adjust."

She then spoke to him as every mom would speak to a son, guiding him on directions to the Goddess Garden, telling him where to park and approximate driving time from Santa Monica. Nishita thought her voice sounded shy and nervous.

"You told the sergeant that you thought you saw her in the top window?" Det. Nishita asked.

"I saw the curtain pull back and I swear I saw a face. The person jumped back when I called out. I yelled that I saw them and to please answer the door. Nothing. So, I kicked the pot." Grant lowered his head. He brushed a tear from his cheek and let out a long sigh. "All that will be on the footage."

"Can you stay in town for a few days? I mean can your job spare you?" Det. Nishita asked.

Grant nodded. "I was expecting something like that. It's not a problem, although I'll miss the store and my customers. I've always loved the grocery business. It's part networking and part predicting behavior."

Nishita was surprised by his comment. Did Grant realize what he had said? That he had a touch of his mother's power? Was psychic power inherited? That was a question to ponder.

"Do you have anyone that can stay with you? I mean it can be pretty lonely having gone through, what, you--"

"Thanks. I called my husband as soon as I saw the news about Lena. He's arriving tomorrow morning," Grant said.

He looked shy confessing to speaking with his husband. Well, shy or not, he'd thoroughly investigate Grant Montgomery and his movements since arriving.

Grant gave his cell number and hotel room number. When he stood, his professional manner from the beginning of the interview had evaporated. He looked defeated as if the bones in his body had melted. The missed moment of connecting to his birth mother was forever stolen. Watching Grant leave Nishita remembered Anya had said her mother had a lot of secrets. Did Anya know about this meeting with Grant?

Contemplation Card # 148

"Very little is needed to make a happy life. It is all within yourself, in your way of thinking."

—Marcus Aurelius 121 AD-180 AD

When I placed happiness on external things, seductive whispers called, "This will ease pain and lighten dark corners." I'd buy the new dress, the fancy pair of shoes, or drink that third glass of vodka. But despair returned stronger, more urgent, until I realized I had to stop listening.

—My best, Lena

TWELVE

NISHITA HELD THE REMNANTS OF THE young Lena: her identification badge, her picture in the colorful advertisement, and her childish signature on the NDA. He wondered how the affair with Randal Montgomery began. No child at fourteen, male or female, can determine which adults are trustworthy. Teens look for someone older to validate their existence. He glanced back at her youthful face, full of hope. By that age, Nishita usually had a grim determined look on his face.

By how the NDA was worded, it was clear she'd been threatened—either by refusing future employment or spreading rumors, of which they'd already proved capable. These men don't play unless they win. She had to have been frightened and took the money.

In Lena's voice message to her son, there was a quiver in her voice. At first, he thought it was excitement, mixed with anticipation, but what if it was shyness or fear?

When Nishita reached his desk, he set the items in a plastic bag and labeled them as evidence. Placing a call to the desk sergeant, he requested an officer be sent to the hotel to ask about Grant Montgomery's movements during the conference, and what he did during his free time. He hung up the phone and saw Camilla, waving her over.

"I'd like to go to the bookstore. Dudley should have returned from Vegas by now, and I'd like to ask if he knew about Grant, and that Lena planned to meet him this weekend," he said while picking up his keys, badge, and phone.

"Ted, I've got to get home. My son and a few of his buddies were trying to get spiders to bite them. I suppose so they could gain—"

"Spider superpowers? Heck yeah, me and a friend did it when we were twelve. You never knew which spider was radioactive, so we had to do it a lot." He sighed in disappointment. "We never found the right spider."

She threw up her hands. "Are there any other preteen boy behaviors you can warn me of?" Nishita shrugged as if to suggest that was how it was and what was her problem. "Well, one kid had a reaction and was taken to critical care. I need the full story from my son. Find out who was the instigator," Camilla said, concern filling her voice.

"Is Nestor okay?" he asked.

Camilla nodded and said, "My brother said a spider bite or two but nothing serious."

"Those things itch like crazy. Trust me. Anyway, I'm sure Fisher will still be at the mansion." Nishita said with a distinct edge. "Give me the keys."

She smiled and mouthed, "I owe you."

"You do, but before you escape, any report on Dudley's movements in Las Vegas?"

Camilla handed him a written report and said, "The front desk confirmed Mr. Hardwick got two rooms for the weekend, and room service went to one room twice a day. Dudley was seen each morning at the continental breakfast, in the conference rooms, and at the evening events. He asked the front desk for a limo service would arrive on Sunday night to take someone to Los Angeles."

"Just as Marta said," Nishita muttered. "See if they have security footage of Dudley at the conference and around the hotel, at the front desk checking in and later checking out. Oh, and get me the name and number of the limo service."

Handing him the keys to the patrol car Camilla said, "First thing tomorrow. I've got to get home."

Nishita followed her out to the parking lot. He gave her one last wave as she got in her car. He took off his suit jacket tossed it on the passenger's side seat and got in. He entered the address to the Topanga bookstore on the GPS and checked the time. It was almost half past eight. The GPS said it would take thirty-seven minutes to his destination. That meant he'd arrive seven minutes after nine. *Too bad*, he thought. *In a murder investigation, I show up when I need to.*

The traffic was light driving through the city. When he reached the service station at the corner of Topanga Canyon Road and Pacific Coast Highway, he turned up the hill. Once past the service station, darkness enveloped the road. Upcoming curves were only seen by headlights. The challenge forced him to slow down. Why would Lena drive this at night?

As he turned the curve before the accident, his headlights caught a car pulled off to the side. A group of people stood by the trunk of the car, singing and playing guitar. Two women sang a mournful song while a man held a lantern. It was a cold night, and all wore ponchos. Nishita pulled in behind them, got out of his car, and flashed his badge. He said, "Good evening. Everything all right here?"

The singing and music stopped. The guitar player, after glancing at the badge said, "Good evening, officer." His voice and manner were respectful. "We're fine, thank you."

Taken aback by the polite reply Nishita said, "People drive these curves rather fast. I don't want you to get hit."

The man placed his hand upon his heart and said, "That's appreciated, Officer."

Nishita suspected they were here for Lena. He had to pursue the question. "A woman died from an accident this morning right at this curve. Were you aware of that?" Nishita asked.

The man lowered his head, and the group followed his lead lowering their heads. "Yes, we came to honor her spirit. I don't believe we're doing anything illegal."

"No, no you're not. Just be careful." Nishita made eye contact with each person. They didn't avoid his connection. Satisfied they were not doing anything nefarious he said, "Well, good night." He heard muted responses from the others. While he walked back to his car, the music resumed. Driving away, he wondered why they chose to come at this time of night and not wait for daylight. Well, those questions were for another time. The Goddess Garden Bookstore loomed ahead.

The back of the bookstore was lit up and a white van was parked in the driveway. It had a banner on the driver's side door emblazoned with the words *McCormick's Elder Care*. Next to the van was a red Dodge truck. Nishita spotted a tall man next to Marta in an animated conversation. As he pulled into the driveway, they turned to face his car and protected their eyes from his beams. Nishita got a good look at the man. He was distinguished-looking in the way Brits have. He wore an elegant dark blazer and a light shirt framing his face. His beard sculpted his jawline and had salt and pepper hair. Nishita caught a vague resemblance to Randal Montgomery, Grant's father. He wondered if Lena saw that in Dudley Hardwick.

Readying his demeanor, he decided it was best to wear his jacket, so he pulled his suit coat from the passenger's seat. "Mr. Hardwick? I'm Detective Nishita."

Dudley turned, his face shadowed by security lights, the beams directed at Nishita. The brightness forced him to squint to catch Dudley's expression. Nishita held his hand out to shake. Dudley remained stoic, arms folded against his chest.

Dudley was tall. His driver's license said he was 6' 2", but to Nishita he appeared closer to 6' 4". When did any man declare he was shorter? Most men brag they are taller. Nishita had done that in high school to get into the wrestling class. Well, that had failed because the coach got out a measuring tape. Lesson learned, never lie again.

Once it was obvious he wouldn't back down, Dudley accepted, and they shook hands. Dudley's hands were large and soft like a well-oiled catcher's mitt. Nishita lightly rubbed palm against palm making sure Dudley felt his callouses. Nishita held his eyes as they shook.

Dudley said, in a voice as soft as a kitten's purr, "I didn't expect to see you tonight, Detective. Do you have any updates on my wife's case?"

"I do. May I speak with you inside?" Det. Nishita noted the delicate diction in Dudley's speech, making him sound as if he'd been raised at an elite boy's school—very different from his voice mail message.

"We were getting Sophia settled. She spent the weekend at the Elder Care clinic," said Dudley as he pointed to the white van.

"I've never heard of them," Det. Nishita said.

"No, you wouldn't have had. They are an exclusive facility in Malibu." Dudley gestured for Nishita to walk in front of him.

"If you don't mind, I'd like to take one more look at the broken pots. Marta mentioned there was a vandal here this weekend," said Nishita, and he moved out of the glare of the floodlights. He kept his eyes on Dudley, wanting to capture every impression.

Nishita walked to the area surrounded by the yellow tape. He examined the clay to see if it was possible to lift fingerprints. He could feel Dudley and Marta watching his every move so, to unnerve them further, he pretended to examine the area closely. Once satisfied, he returned his focus to the back steps and the group gathered there.

"It is very often nothing but our vanity that deceives us."

—Jane Austin

Vanity, the real seed of destructive power with its attention addiction and need for importance. In our current world of the internet, we hide behind a wall of electronics and create personas. We can be anyone we want, can't we? Ultimately, who do we fool? Only our fragile ego.

—Lena Rezenchov, *Who Are We Really?*

IN THE DARKENED YARD, NISHITA FOLLOWED Dudley as closely as he could to the back door, a move that unnerved the man, which was exactly what he wanted. There was a jockeying of position.

Dudley took control and said, "Allow me, Detective." In a graceful move, he grabbed the handle and opened it.

It was a gesture a host extends to a guest, not one granted to police. In Nishita's experience, it wasn't out of welcoming but shock. Dudley had already displayed signs of duress; he'd driven alone, against advice, and brushed off reporters in Las Vegas, which he must have known would resurface. YouTube videos have everlasting life.

The endless flat desert drive from Las Vegas can make the car feel as if it were floating and not speeding through miles. It can test the best of temperaments. Emotions build while driving, and anger irrupts at the slightest trigger. Dudley had to be running on pure adrenaline. How long before he collapsed?

Nishita stepped inside. Floodlights filled the kitchen with beams that bounced off the stainless steel countertops and the chrome-tiled backwash. It took a moment for his eyes to adjust. In the glare, he got a solid look at Dudley and was surprised by his appearance. In the harsh light, age showed in heavy circles under his eyes and pasty skin. Was it due to insomnia-filled nights?

Dudley kept his head lowered while rubbing the back of his neck. Most husbands, or soon-be ex-husbands as was the case here, realize they are considered prime suspects when a wife dies under suspicious circumstances. There was no denying Lena's death was suspicious.

Dudley and Marta squared off in opposite corners. Marta hovered by the sink and Dudley staked his territory to the right side of a table. The tension in the kitchen was as unavoidable as the harsh light. Nishita turned to Marta and noticed she wasn't as friendly as she had been earlier. The odor of cleaning fluid filled his nostrils as if his visit had been washed away. He let his eyes drop to Marta's hands and saw the edges of a pink rash between her fingers. He softened his stance and leaned into Marta. "Did you check the security footage from the weekend? I'd like to follow up on those clay pots and when they were vandalized."

She opened her mouth to answer but Dudley stopped her by holding up his hand. "Yes, we have, Detective. Marta gave Fisher a copy from our files."

Nishita kept his face neutral but noted who was in control of the conversation, and at this point, it was Dudley. He said, "Did either of you look at the footage?" He glanced from Dudley to Marta and back. Neither responded. He continued, "Was the vandal familiar? Sometimes it's as innocent as a local boy. You know how boys are, they play a game of dare and perhaps tossing clay pots was the latest challenge." Nishita watched Dudley who gave no response.

Dudley turned to Marta and asked, "Did the boy look familiar to you?"

Marta pulled her face into a grimace. "It wasn't a boy. He was a man."

Nishita considered his next question. "Do you think this man had anything to do with Lena's death?" Neither Dudley nor Marta answered. Nishita said, "It is strange that the same weekend Lena is alone, a man broke several of your planters." He checked to see if they were following him. Their silence spoke volumes. He took a different track. "Or could he have been an irate customer, someone upset that the store was closed?"

Marta chimed in, "We've always been closed during holiday weekends. It's been that way for over twenty years." She turned to Dudley; he gave a curt nod.

Nishita asked, "I'm not up on business trends, but isn't a long weekend considered the best time to gain new customers?"

Dudley and Marta both began to answer but Marta backed off and surrendered to Dudley's lead. He said," Up here, it doesn't pan out. Customers like to go to the big box stores for sales. Our customers are attracted by Lena's lectures and retreats—or were." Dudley slumped forward and he looked like he'd lost all color. He became pale making the deep circles under his eyes appear darker. Nishita thought he might collapse but Dudley rolled his neck and took a deep breath.

Fisher could be heard speaking with a woman coming down the marble steps in the main hallway. He stopped talking when he spotted Nishita. "Sir," he said.

In his first impression, the woman standing next to Fisher reminded him of Camilla; strong, and confident. There was a graceless moment while no one spoke. Nishita reached out his hand to the woman. "Detective Nishita."

"Rebecca Lopez," she said in a calm voice. She was taller than Marta and a little older. A leather strap was over her shoulder attached to a case.

"Detective Nishita this is Rebecca Lopez the managing supervisor at the clinic. Rebecca this is Detective Ted Nishita, he's working on Lena's case," Dudley said rubbing his hands together as if to warm them up.

Marta broke into the conversation. "How was mother this weekend?" she asked and pulled Rebecca over to the counter by the sinks. They put their heads together and Rebecca took out paperwork from an outside pocket on her briefcase. Marta checked it, they spoke quietly, and Marta signed the paper.

Fisher made his way to him, showed him a thumb drive, and gave him a small wink. Nishita sighed and directed his attention to Dudley. "How are you holding up, Mr. Hardwick?" He didn't answer.

The shuffling of papers drew Nishita's attention back to Marta and Rebecca. An invoice was handed over as Rebecca slung the strap of her briefcase onto her left shoulder. It appeared that she was finished and ready to leave. She stepped to the back door at Nishita's right. They held each other's gaze. He said, "I'm sorry to meet you under such circumstances. Did you know Lena?"

Rebecca nodded. "She was lovely." Tears built at the corners of her eyes.

At that moment Dudley began breathing rapidly holding his chest. He made a painful sound. Marta called out, "Dudley!" Rebecca, the closest to them, sprang forward and reached him first. Fisher on one side and Nishita on the other, they kept Dudley supported and prevented him from falling against the stainless-steel counter.

Rebecca ordered, "The chair." Marta grabbed a kitchen chair from a table and brought it around. Nishita and Fisher jockeyed him, and he sat with a thump. Rebecca kneeled and checked Dudley's eyes and felt his pulse. She held still for a tiny second then in a gentle voice said, "Take deep breaths, Mr. Hardwick." Turning, she asked, "Will someone hand me my bag? I dropped it."

Fisher picked up the leather case and opened it. Inside the case was a neatly arranged set of medical tools. A blood pressure device and a stethoscope were immediately visible. Rebecca placed the cuff on Dudley's upper arm and began to pump. She quickly and calmly had the stethoscope on and was listening to his pulse. Once more she checked his eyes and smiled. "I suspect you are dehydrated and exhausted." Rebecca looked back at Marta who hadn't moved since Dudley collapsed. Nishita followed Rebecca's attention and noted Marta's stare at Dudley. Dudley pressed his hand atop Rebecca's resting on his arm.

Nishita watched this nonverbal communication from Marta to Dudley, Dudley to Rebecca. He tried to cover his observation and wished Camilla was here; she'd notice these charged meaningful looks and be able to give him feedback on possible scenarios. He glanced over to Fisher and saw him by Rebecca's side, busy repacking her leather satchel. Nishita's insides churned and he inwardly grumbled that Fisher was behaving like a schoolboy helping his teacher, and not noticing behavior.

Rebecca accepted her repacked bag from Fisher and turned to Dudley. "Why don't I take you to the hospital?" she suggested.

"I don't need all that," he said. "As you said, I'm tired and need rest."

"Your blood pressure is on the high side," Rebecca said. "I would prefer you have supervision tonight."

"Let me stay at the clinic. We've paid for Sophia's room. I know that room is open at least for tonight," Dudley spoke quite fast.

Rebecca balked. "I don't know, Mr. Hardwick." He gave her a hard look. Rebecca drew in a short breath and backed down. "Certainly, I can call and set up a room for you."

Dudley visibly relaxed and although he whispered thank you his mouth turned to a hard thin line. Rebecca excused herself from the cluster around her, got out her cell from her jacket pocket, and exited the kitchen through the back door. Nishita could hear the beginnings of a call but couldn't make out the words through the door, so he concentrated on Dudley.

"Do you have high blood pressure, Mr. Hardwick?" Nishita asked. Dudley only mumbled. Something told him this whole episode was a bit dramatic.

Rebecca returned from her call. Walking directly to Dudley, she helped him stand and said, "Mr. Hardwick, we're all set for tonight. Our practitioner has a room ready for you, and we can get you started on rehydration therapy." She pointed her finger at Fisher.

He blinked several times, then made a small "Oh." Fisher placed

Dudley's arm over his shoulder and helped him walk out the back door. Nishita was one step behind, he didn't want to miss any under-the-breath whisperings. He and Rebecca met at the door and this time Nishita offered her the door. She nodded, and as she moved, her case strap caught on the door handle. Embarrassed she said, "My bag." They had to twist positions and once her case was freed, she squeezed past him.

Now outside, Nishita observed Fisher helping Dudley into the passenger's seat of the van.

Nishita said, "Ms. Lopez."

"Rebecca, please call me Rebecca." She moved to the van and stopped at the door.

"Rebecca, I'd like to stop by tomorrow and check on Mr. Hardwick. Are there special visiting hours? I wouldn't want to disrupt the other patients." Nishita kept pace with her step for step.

"That is kind of you. I'm sure the staff will accommodate you whenever you arrive." Rebecca got into the driver's side and Nishita walked around to Dudley's window and made a circular motion with his hand for him to roll it down.

"Yes?" Dudley said.

"I'd like to arrange a time for you to come to the station so we can get your statement," Nishita said remembering Captain Cooper's velvet glove order from this morning. *Handle the suspects carefully but firmly,* he thought.

"I will have my attorney present at that time, Detective. And that goes for Marta as well. We will be happy to make statements with our attorneys present. Now if you will excuse me," Dudley responded and started to roll up the window.

Nishita quickly pushed his arm in before the window made it to the top. "I meant to ask you if knew Grant Montgomery," Nishita said the name clearly. Dudley didn't answer verbally but the window stopped. "Well, he came into the police station earlier today and made some interesting comments about Lena. Well, we can talk about that later, right now you need to take care of yourself. I'll stop by tomorrow." Nishita stepped away from the van as it pulled away. Not exactly his best velvet glove moment.

Fisher made his way to Nishita's side looking like a lost puppy all wide-eyed and tail between his legs. This was a murder investigation, and each moment was crucial. That reminded him that Marta was inside. He looked back over to the back door and saw her standing at the top of the steps, her arms folded in front of her chest, leaning against the railing. He walked back to her.

"Will you be all right here?" he asked. She gave him a quizzical look. "I mean alone with your mother, of course. I can send a patrol if you have safety concerns."

"That won't be necessary, Detective. But thank you for thinking of us," Marta said in her reserved, controlled voice. Whatever vulnerabilities she'd had earlier, she gained control over them. "I will say good night now." She turned and went back inside turning the bright lights of the kitchen off. The darkness circled them.

In the city, there is ambient light everywhere and corners are not completely black, but shades of charcoal. It was a different experience at the edge of the city. Up here, everything was in darkness and only the edges of buildings caught a ghostly glow.

Nishita heard a rustling in the bushes and he recoiled. Fisher said, "It's a raccoon family, Detective. They smell the garbage and are trying to get at the bins."

His nerves were a bit frayed from a long day without food or rest. Nishita checked the street and caught sight of bins lined up along the edge. Something struck him as odd. He asked, "How often is the trash picked up here?"

"Because of the neighboring businesses, it's picked up twice a week, Mondays and Thursdays. But because of the holiday, it will get picked up tomorrow. That's why you see them on the curb," Fisher answered.

Nishita peered over at the trash bins and saw a pair of glowing eyes. If there was no one here all weekend, from Thursday until this morning, there wouldn't be any trash in the bins. He went cautiously to the bins and the raccoons skittered away. He opened the lid and shined a fob light down on the trash. There were white plastic bags filled with rags and a couple of take-out containers. If nobody was here all weekend then where did the take-out containers come from?

"Fisher, go in the trunk of my car. You'll see a roll of garbage bags. Get at least two out. And put on gloves; there's a box in the trunk." This might be fruitless, but he had to take the chance. Nishita pointed the trunk release button at his car and the trunk opened. All he could think was, *What if someone was here, as Grant Montgomery had said*? This could be proof. If there was a receipt for a takeout with a date, then he could ask for DNA.

They worked quickly and carried the bags to Nishita's car placing them in the trunk. "Thanks," he said and shook Fisher's hand. "You need a ride home?"

Fisher waved him off and retrieved his bike from the bushes. "By the way, your phone buzzed earlier. You were speaking to Dudley when he was in the van, and I figured you didn't hear it."

"My phone?" He checked the side pocket of his suit, and his phone wasn't there. Fisher pointed to his car. "In my car? You heard it in my car?" Nishita asked.

Fisher nodded.

"Huh. It must have fallen out." He walked around to search the driver's side seat and considered Fisher had very sharp hearing. Good to know. He checked under the car seat. Nothing. Then he looked at the center console and wedged between the passenger's seat and the console he saw the metallic edge of his phone. It must have slid across the seat. "Stupid phone," he muttered. "It's like they're magically slippery."

"I know what you mean," Fisher said. "My Dad one time—"

Nishita held up his hand to silence him as checked his messages. There was one from Camilla saying she would be at the station by eight tomorrow morning and one from the tow truck driver.

"Gus Post, here. I towed Ms. Rezenchov's car to the police garage. Will you stop by the gas station at the corner of PCH and Topanga Canyon Road at your earliest convivence? I have footage from the weekend that might be of interest to you. We're open until midnight. If you get a chance, give me a call." Gus gave his cell number and clicked off.

Nishita checked the time; it was a few minutes after eleven. He debated if he should return the call. He'd had a long day and he was hungry. On the plus side, it was on the drive home so, if it was a short visit, he'd be home by midnight, and that wasn't too bad. He pushed the return call icon and in one ring it was answered.

"The older you get, the lonelier you become, and the deeper the love you need."

—Leonard Cohen

We all face the darkness of living. It shows up when least expected. A loved one dies, or a marriage fails, or after years of dating, age forty arrives and there are no kids, no house, no prospects, and it's clear the world doesn't want your skills. What can one do? Give up? Give in? Create a new definition of love and success by you and for you.

—Lena Rezenchov, *Spiritual Freedom*

FOURTEEN

"GUS POST," THE DEEP VOICE ANSWERED.

"Mr. Post, this is—" Nishita began and was overrun by a deep rumbling laugh.

"Call me Gus, Detective," he said. "Can you stop by?"

"I'm at the bookstore. I could be there in fifteen?" Nishita listened for hesitation.

Gus simply said, "Great."

Taken aback by the one-word answer he stammered, "O-on, on my way."

Placing the phone in his side pocket Nishita smiled. Instinct told him, Gus Post held a wealth of information on the area; he'd know of neighborhood spats and trouble over parking spots, or inconsiderate drivers speeding around corners . . . and because Gus dealt with Lena's car, he just might be privy to the Hardwick marriage. That was too tempting to pass up.

The night was no longer a bleak trip back to his empty apartment. His infamous second wind surged through his body. Often, Camilla asked where he got all that energy. He never knew how or why, just knew he could call it up when needed. As a kid, his mother tried to calm him by playing soothing music at bedtime. The look on her face when she caught him in the living room after midnight watching television was enough. Eventually, he learned to move about silently, a skill he put to use as an officer.

Fisher's voice came out of the shadows. "Detective, if you don't need anything else."

Nishita turned to see Fisher surrounded by the glow of a distant streetlight. Under that beam, he was the vision of a golden teen-ager—the one every high school has, not the smartest, or most athletic, but the likable one. Nishita had strived to be the likable one, but as Camilla told him, there was a darkness in him that he'd never be able to hide. A pang hit his chest, and a long-forgotten memory surfaced. The night his mother had wailed guttural sounds so loud and long he feared his teeth might crack. Nishita looked away from Fisher and let out a sigh. He cleared his throat before answering, "No, you can go home. It'll be a long day tomorrow."

"Yes, sir," Fisher said and climbed on his bike. He swung his leg over the side and was ready to pedal away.

Nishita called to him, "Hey, why did you become an officer?" Fisher turned back. "It's not an easy career; why the force?"

"My uncle was on the force, my step-uncle, actually. I liked what he provided for the community, his quiet strength." He rattled that off quickly.

Streetlamp and moonlight combined to cast an eerie glow, and Nishita stared. It grew into a game of who would blink first, but he was better and observed Fisher squirm and finally caved lowering his eyes. "That's only part of it," he said and held his bike with one hand the other raked through his hair. "I didn't want to," he stopped and pushed out a slow breath between his teeth, "mess up my life, waste it. I wanted to do something that mattered."

Rustling leaves drew Nishita's attention. The wind had kicked up eucalyptus leaves and they swirled in a circular dance. They both watched the leaves curl, twist upward, tumble then return to the ground.

Nishita broke the silence. "Camilla will call early. Best be ready for her."

"Yes, sir." Fisher turned and rode up the hill.

From the third-floor window, a sliver of light spilling onto the bushes caught his attention. Most large estates invest time and money designing dramatic landscape lighting. The physical location of the mansion called for attention-grabbing lights, and yet there were none. He wondered, was it always this dark at the Goddess Garden Bookstore? Someone could approach it without being seen. The mansion was sandwiched between the edge of the Santa Monica mountains and Topanga Canyon Road. Snakes, raccoons, possums, red tail deer, and the occasional cougar filled the rugged terrain. Only someone familiar with the area would take the risk.

Once, he'd heard of a wealthy man who bought a house in the hills for privacy. The problem was he didn't like raccoons digging in his trash. He asked his gardener to use traps to discourage the raccoons. The gardener warned that if he did that, rattlesnakes would take over the yard because raccoons hunt snakes. The man didn't believe him and demanded that the raccoons be stopped. The gardener did as he was told and set up the traps. In one month, rattlesnakes had taken over his yard and gotten inside the man's garage. Frightened when he saw a snake curled up in a corner, the wealthy man backed down and let the raccoons roam freely on his property. His grandfather told him that men try to dominate and control the environment; it was easier to work *with* it.

He started up the engine and cold white light filled the alleyway as the headlights came on. He considered Dudley's anxiety attack. Was it more than exhaustion? A question for tomorrow. He backed out to the street and headed down the hill.

He passed the area where he had seen the singers earlier, but the spot was empty. There was a collection of flowers. Seeing these wildflowers picked from the hills, emptiness overcame him similar to when the ambulance door closed on Lena's body. The hollow sound echoed across the canyon only to fade.

He arrived at the service station. Gus, standing at the front door, waved. Nishita shook his hand. "Thanks for seeing me."

"I hang around late. You'd be surprised how many folks get gas in the wee hours. Particularly the wealthy," Gus said.

Upon entering the station, Nishita noticed it was clean. There were hanging baskets of ferns along the outer windows and next to the cashier's station, planters with big leafy bushes. There was a mop and bucket in the center of the station. It looked like he'd interrupted cleaning time.

A big-screen television was above the cashier's desk. On the screen was a long-haired brunette in an aqua dress. Bathed in sunlight, she stood in front of the Goddess Garden Bookstore.

"Can you turn that up?" Nishita asked as he eyed the snacks by the cash register. A small rumble came from his stomach.

Gus increased the volume, and the clip changed to a picture of the roadway where Lena's car went over. The shot included a collection of people, huddled together holding tall votive candles heads bowed in prayer. Staring at the group, Nishita thought it appeared perfect, and for lack of a better word: planned. These were not the same people he saw in the dark a few hours ago. When he thought of the group from the evening, they had the look of laborers, gardeners, and homeworkers. The people in the television group were attractive and had the attitude of actors.

The television image returned to the young brunette newscaster as she expressed concern about the lack of guardrails to deter accidents and mentioned an activist group that had taken up the cause to have that corrected. The camera zoomed in for a close-up of the young woman as she expressed her condolences to the family.

A creepy thought edged its way into his mind. What if the television spot was bought by someone with deep pockets willing to orchestrate a narrative? Lena's death wasn't the important part of the spot; the cause of her accident was the point. He asked, "Did they say anything specific about Lena's death?"

"No, nothing like that. They've been showing that clip all evening. It'll recycle around in another forty minutes." Gus quickly slid the bucket and mop to the side. "I'm the cleaning crew tonight."

Once the bucket was secured, Gus led Nishita to the back behind the cashier's area.

He entered a small office space with a desk surrounded by metal file cabinets and bins containing invoices and assorted bills. On a shelf were several trophies from local Little League Ball clubs and pictures of young players in uniform.

Gus sat in the desk chair and pointed to a folding chair next to him. "Let me pull this footage." He grabbed the mouse and twirled it on the mouse pad.

"How long do you keep video files?" Nishita asked.

"A week."

"Most stores loop it every 24 hours," Nishita said.

"A few years ago, a couple of guys stole a car while the patron paid for gas. Can you imagine?" Gus snorted in disgust. "Thing is, I knew I had seen those men hanging around the station." Gus winked with a sly smile that spread across his round face. "I couldn't prove it because we didn't keep footage that long. I asked the owner to add more cameras and to hold the video feed. I told him we have wealthy clients and should provide the highest service. It was a way to do that."

Gus focused on the computer screen and clicked on the video. "I gave a copy of this to the officer this afternoon."

The screen went to a black-and-white video. The camera faced the island of gas pumps at the north side of the service station and had a clear view of the corner of Topanga Canyon Road and Pacific Coast Highway. The service station was closed as all exterior lights were out. The traffic lights blinked but without seeing the color change from green to yellow to red and the intersection empty it was a challenge to get the rhythm of the street.

"Is this time accurate?" Nishita asked as he pulled his folding chair closer to the computer. The time stamp said it was 1:46 a.m. Gus nodded.

Tiny headlights appeared in the upper left corner of the screen, coming toward the intersection. A blurry shape of a car pulled into the left turn lane and waited. Nishita figured the driver was waiting for the light to change. It must have given him the correct light because the car made the turn and passed the gas station and up the hill. Nishita watched the car and said, "Wait, stop, back up the clip." Nishita watched the fuzzy image; it wasn't just a car but a limo. The limousine moved past the camera and up the hill. Marta had said Dudley ordered a limo for her. Unexpectedly, a pickup truck sped through the corner, caught up to the limo, and followed it. Although it was impossible to get a clear view of the make and model of the truck it had a push bar at the front. Nishita felt his hair rise. He reminded himself there were lots of trucks with push bars. This was one of the many trucks he'd seen around Los Angeles and not the truck connected to his brothers hit-and-run. Yet there was something familiar. He'd stared at the only security footage from the night of his brother's hit-and-run so often he could see that truck in his sleep. It was recorded near the airport; Allen's car was being followed by a dark pickup truck with a push bar. Nishita tapped his fist against his chin in frustration. He'd find this truck first, that was his mission.

"Just wait a moment, let me fast-forward," Gus said. He set the time of the footage to 3:02 a.m., and a pick-up truck came down the hill and passed the station.

It was grainy and impossible to see who drove the truck, but he did get a better view of the driver's side. The truck went to the corner and turned back in the direction from which it came. Nishita got a better view of this truck; it was older, at least a 1998 or a 1999 Tacoma. No other cars went up the hill. Get a grip, he told himself. His brother's case was almost twenty years ago. This was not that truck.

"Does the limo return?" Nishita asked his voice raw.

"No, only the truck." Gus fast-forwarded the tape.

No cars went up the hill. The small glow of oncoming daylight appeared. Nishita watched as the cyclist's team made its way up the hill. Finally, after a few moments, the ambulance charged up the hill.

Seeing this footage opened up more questions than he thought possible. "You said you gave this to the officer this afternoon?" Gus nodded. "Sorry, how many days do you have on file?"

"From last Monday," Gus answered.

"I'd like a copy of the full week," Nishita said. The first person he thought of was Grant Montgomery. This would be the only logical route if he drove from his hotel in Santa Monica. If he drove past the station, it would be recorded. When Grant drove up to the bookstore and when he returned. If his rental car didn't appear that would put a glitch in his statement.

"Detective, there is something else," Gus said. He fiddled with the computer and set up a different clip. "This is Thursday night, or Friday morning. You can see the time stamp of 12:45 a.m." He pressed the play button. A grainy shot of the night and headlights appeared in the upper right, drove down the hill to the intersection. It looked like Dudley's shiny SUV passed the service station and turned right toward Malibu.

"Curious," Nishita said. "Late to be driving to Las Vegas, isn't it? Why come down all this way? Isn't it faster to drive north from the bookstore and hop on the freeway?" He spoke more to himself than Gus.

"I'd think so," Gus agreed.

Calling the Vegas hotel in which Dudley stayed moved to first on his list. He needed to check the time Dudley and Marta arrived. With most high-priced hotels, they'd have security footage in the lobby and front desk. He reminded himself not to jump to conclusions.

Gus sat back in his chair and stretched his long arms out. "You hungry? I am. I made a pot of chili. Have a bowl with me?" Gus stood and walked past Nishita to a small closet behind the office.

Glancing in, Nishita saw a makeshift kitchen. There was a sink and a counter with a crock pot, its red light on. Gus moved around the tiny space like a king. He pulled down two mismatched bowls and opened the top of the crock pot. The aroma of spice and salt and a hint of tabasco filled the air, and the sides of Nishita's jaw responded. Yeah, he was hungry. Gus grabbed a box of saltine crackers and tucked it under his arm, then picked up the bowls.

"I've had it simmering all day; it should be perfect now," Gus said and removed a sleeve of crackers from the box. He crushed several on top of his chili. "Come on, it's better with the crackers."

"Thanks," was all he could reply. The first mouthful and his senses couldn't keep up with the bursts of flavor. The sweet tang of the tomato sauce, the salty smoked flavor of the meat, and at the last moment a kick of heat. The crackers seemed to even out the experience. He heard himself giggle.

"Right?" Gus said with a big smile.

They ate. Nishita enjoyed the silence.

Once finished Gus picked up the empty bowls and carried them to the sink, that's when Nishita spotted the photograph. He'd never noticed it amongst the chaos around the desk. An old wooden frame showing its age with dirt, stains, and cracked glass held a photo of his grandfather's service station. It looked like a publicity photo from long ago. His grandfather stood in the center surrounded by a crew of grinning young mechanics all in clean blue uniforms with white name badges on their chest. To the far right was a young skinny Gus.

With a life of its own, his hand pointed to the photograph. "You worked with my grandfather?" Nishita asked doing his best to keep the feeling of betrayal out of his voice.

"I forgot that was there. I was thinner back then," Gus said and patted his full belly.

"When was this?" Nishita asked.

"Oh, 1970-71? I'd just returned from Vietnam. I didn't know what to do with myself, and I'd heard Bednar's Service Station was looking for mechanics. He hired me. I was a terrible mechanic. Oh, I could change oil and work on brakes, but anything else?" Gus puffed air through his teeth, "Way beyond my skill set. Mr. Bednar suggested I get into towing. I mean a guy like me, in those days opportunities were limited."

Nishita stared into his soft brown eyes and rich brown skin and understood. He cleared his throat and said, "That sounds like my grandfather." Never one to give a handout but, a suggestion here a small loan there, and someone could build a business and self-reliance.

"I did pretty good. Then the auto club took over and offered towing services. Cut us little guys out. That's when I came to this station next to Malibu where wealthier clients live and set up for private towing with flatbed requests," Gus said.

"How's that going?"

"Good. I know how to work with the rich. They are different," Gus said emphasizing the word different. He adjusted his head and looked around Nishita to see out the office door and pointed to the television screen. "That news clip is on again if you're interested."

Nishita turned around. The television screen showed a man in a dark suit. Nishita stood and walked towards the cashier's desk to get a better view.

"Good evening, we have sad news tonight. Popular psychic and author, Lena Rezenchov has died. Here's KTLA News correspondent Letitia Curtis with the details. Letitia?"

The picture turned to a woman in an aqua dress with long dark hair. *"Yes, John. Let me fill in anyone who may not have heard the announcement today. Lena Rezenchov was found at six o'clock this morning. Her car had driven off a cliff on South Topanga Canyon Road. I am standing in front of the Goddess Garden Bookstore, the business she and her husband started.*

"You can see the outpouring of support for the loss of the beloved author.

"John, let me say, the accident of Lena has fired up an old controversy . . ."

Gus said, "It just repeats from here." He walked back to the office and ejecting the thumb drive, handed it to Nishita.

"Thanks." Nishita accepted it. "And for the chili." They shook hands and Nishita left.

FIFTEEN

MOONLIGHT PIERCED THROUGH THE TURRET WINDOWS leaving patterns on the bedroom floor. The moon centered in the top window was full last night but tonight a fuzzy edge appeared. Staring at it, she couldn't remember who said the moon was a friend of the lonely.

"Waning," Marta whispered and leaned into the soft cushions of the chair. Her eyelids, too heavy to stay open, fell. But as she drifted off her body shook awake as if frightened. Sleep would not comfort her.

Insomnia was a beast with razor teeth. Marta counted the nights of fitful sleep and the days of no appetite. Spending the entire weekend alone was a mistake. She'd cleaned every corner of the bookstore and balanced all the accounts. Useless tasks. How long before the house of cards Dudley built would crumble, and she'd get ensnared?

Her mother gasped and snorted. Marta sat up and listened checking to assure herself Sophia breathed freely. Sophia moved slightly and settled back down to deep breathing. There were nights she'd heard that sound from her room. Odd how a simple sound like snoring at first irritates but as time plodded forward turned to comfort.

When Marta was nine, her mother discovered bruises up and down her thighs. She had promised her father she'd never tell; it was to be their little secret—and they made a pact, like warriors of olden times by pricking their thumbs—a bond that made her feel wicked and smarter than her mother. She knew she was smarter. She could do math problems in her head and knew when a cashier overcharged them, or when the bank made a mistake in their checking account. Her father had promised when she got older, he'd take her to poker games and teach her how to make some real money. She had liked the sound of that.

But as soon as her mother discovered the bruises, everything changed. She demanded answers as if she knew all along but was too afraid to ask. Marta caved and her father's insatiable appetite was exposed. Her mother, angry and crying, promised he'd never touch her again. They waited until he left for work and made their escape. Traveling across three states, they slept in women's shelters that had a bed for them. If not, they slept in their car. Night after night, as Marta was curled in her mother's arms, she heard that snore. Over time, it became the sound that softened her heart, and she learned to love her mother once more.

Soft chimes rang on the grandfather clock downstairs. Four bells. Four o'clock. Soon, her mother would need to use the toilet. She'd reach for the call button on the nightstand to signal assistance. How many mornings had that buzzer jolted Marta? Mornings she wanted to rip it out of its socket to sleep past four. In a brutal twist, while alone this weekend, she longed to hear that high-pitched buzz. It would mean that whatever had happened was a bad dream and things were normal. But things were far from normal. Sophia would learn soon and then what?

Sophia moaned, her bladder demanding attention. Before she reached the buzzer, Marta placed her hand atop hers and said, "I'm here."

Securing her hand under the back of Sophia's neck, Marta lifted her to sitting, swung her mother's skinny legs to dangle over the side, checked to see if she was stable, and then rolled the wheelchair to the bedside. Standing in front of her, Marta leaned forward and lifted her mother's affected arm to her neck. "Grab your wrist," Marta said, and Sophia mumbled a reply.

Once she felt her mother had a secure grip, Marta took ahold of her waist and got her to her feet. Sophia stood uneasily. They did a small shuffle until Sophia had her toes atop Marta's feet. Marta cracked the usual joke. "Care to dance?" The tango to the bathroom had begun. Marta said, "Right," and must remember her mother's right was her left.

Raising her left foot, Sophia followed, and they inched into the wheelchair. Foot after foot, they repeated until she sat, let out a disgruntled grunt, and tapped Marta's shoulder. Marta felt a wave of anger rise but held her tongue. It was a useless argument to remind her how hard it was to jockey her around, let alone settle her gently into the chair.

Standing behind the chair, Marta pushed it down the hallway and said, "Why you insist on staying in the room furthest from the bathroom, I'll never understand." Sophia mumbled and Marta interrupted, "Yeah, yeah, I know, it's the largest and closest to the elevator and the beveled glass windows make rainbows from the afternoon sun." But her mother never did think of the inconvenience to others, least of all her daughter.

Once in the bathroom, they struggled to get her on the commode, her nightgown lifted and her hand gripping the rail until relief. There had been nights they didn't make it and, humiliated by urinating on the floor, her mother had wept.

Sophia said, "Lena?"

The question Marta feared had been uttered. Panic hit her chest. This could be her moment to tell her everything. She'd understand, forgive her, hold her, and say it wasn't her fault. "Yes, she's gone." Her scalp prickled.

"Dnk?" she asked her mouth unable to formulate the word.

Did Marta hear that correctly? "Drunk? Is that what you said?"

Sophia nodded. This was her chance to make the first move, but how, what to say to sway but not point. "I don't know what happened. The police are investigating everything." Did she accept the answer? The stroke may have damaged her speech and movement but not her mind. It's her eyes to avoid because she will see right through her. Dare she say something? She could hint, let her know something but not everything.

"Were you taken care of while at the clinic?" she asked.

"Mumph." She nodded her head. "Reb-b-b."

"Rebecca? She's excellent. So sad about her son and that whole drug episode." Marta prattled as she got Sophia back into the wheelchair. This was her chance to plant a seed and hope it took root. "I had a crippling migraine and spent the entire weekend in my hotel room. I couldn't eat; all I did was sleep with the curtains closed. It was awful. I never saw Dudley the entire time there. But you know how he is at a conference. Networking, parties, and of course gambling until all hours." She heard Sophia grunt in what sounded like a laugh.

Marta pushed her back to the room, and they performed the reverse dance from before, and she eased her mother back into bed.

She gripped Marta's arm. "Lena."

"We will find out. A young detective has the case." Marta caressed her mother's chest, pulling the soft blanket under her chin. "Rest now." In a few moments, Sophia was asleep. Marta curled up in the soft chair and hoped for sleep but knew it wouldn't come.

I'd heard the Pacific Ocean has no memory. On a painfilled afternoon, I went to the beach, sat for hours, and listened. The surf spoke, and I understood. In this bumpy life, learn to forgive. Just don't forget the lesson.

—Lena Rezenchov, *Spiritual Freedom*

SIXTEEN

SLIDING INTO THE CHAIR OPPOSITE HIS, Camilla said, "You've been busy," and gestured at the scattered Contemplation Cards and books authored by Lena Rezenchov covering his desk. She held a cup of coffee aloft for him to accept.

"You're the best." He accepted the cup and inhaled the strong aroma. His grandmother told him one should have bitter tastes to awaken the body properly. He wasn't sure about that, but caffeine helped. He took his first sip.

"Taking free time to read?" Camilla said.

"Getting to know my victim. If you'd made detective, you'd understand that."

Nishita picked up the top book on the pile. "She was a psychic, right?"

Camilla nodded and gave him a curious look.

"So, didn't she see she was in danger? Didn't she get a hint from her ability?" Nishita said.

"My sister-in-law has an acquaintance that's a psychic. She asked him that very question. He said he can't read for himself. It's like trying to see your nose. No one can," Camilla said.

Nishita looked down to his nose. It made his eyes cross to test out the theory and barely seeing it gave up. Touching the pile of books he said, "She was prolific. This pile are her best sellers." Joking, he said, "Last night I read this one." He held up a red-covered book titled *Persistence*. "It's something about science and metaphysics … so intense I fell asleep reading it."

Camilla chuckled. "Anyway, you were lucky last night."

By Camilla's teasing, he knew they must have found something in the trash bags he brought in. A wicked smile spread across his face, and he asked, "Which bit of evidence came through?"

Camilla raised her eyebrows. "Am I going to have to live with your smug face all day?"

"You know, I can call—" He reached for the phone on his desk.

"Oh, all right," Camilla interrupted. "The garbage bag had, other than take-out containers of food, which the raccoons were after, a smaller white plastic bag filled with disinfectant wipes upon which might be blood."

Invisible wires wound around his forehead released. "Yes-s-s-s," Nishita made a fist-pumping it in the air. Energy surged through him.

"Don't get ahead of yourself Little Ted," Camilla warned.

He snorted a laugh.

Camilla said, "It's doubtful we'll get any DNA. They are doing their best to find prints on the food containers, but it doesn't look good."

Nishita scoffed, "Come on. Food containers are full of finger-prints and saliva."

Camilla used her thumb and forefinger to make the zero sign.

"That's impossible." Nishita tried to wrap his mind around how a food container didn't have fingerprints. All the handling that goes on at restaurants and quickie marts, how was that possible? He sat back in his chair and sipped his coffee. This person was smart and knew how to cover their tracks.

"Wiping the containers, it's kinda creepy." Camilla sipped from her cup and stared off into space. "You got a theory?"

Nishita scooted his chair up to his desk, leaned forward, and rested his arms. "From the security footage I saw last night, what if Lena was killed at the bookstore? And to cover up the crime taken somewhere. Maybe with a large industrial refrigerator? Say like a clinic? The cold would mask the time of death. Then early Monday morning, her body was stuffed in her car and pushed off the cliff. The vodka bottle was planted in the car to explain the accident. Maybe they assumed the car would go unnoticed until late that afternoon. What they didn't plan for was a bike group finding the car at six in the morning."

It was the first time he'd said his theory out loud. Even to him, it sounded crazy and impossible . . . and it landed the murder squarely in the lap of the family.

"I haven't seen the footage, but can you back up that claim with video from earlier in the week?" Camilla said.

"I turned in everything I got from Gus Post for the team to check. Anyway, yesterday Marta told me she'd set up a cleaning crew to come in before the weekend. I want the name of those cleaners."

"We can check footage from the businesses around the bookstore." She pulled out her cell phone and dialed a number. Her body did a little dance while she waited for the person to answer. A smile spread across her face, and she said, "Fisher? You ready?"

His mind buzzed. Now things were falling into place. It wasn't much but it was a start. Until that time all he could do was ask the family to come in and give statements.

While Camilla spoke with Fisher, he wrote down the steps to take: speak with Dudley preferably while at the clinic, get footage of the Gemstone Conference and Dudley's movements in Las Vegas, follow up on Grant Montgomery's movements and the daughter, Anya, where was she all weekend?

Camilla lowered her cell and said, "Fisher will circle to the businesses across the street and get any security footage from the week." She picked up her coffee and sauntered out of the room.

He whispered a small prayer, "Please no ghostly headlights with unidentifiable cars." Calling Caesar's Palace in Las Vegas was his first task. He got the number and spoke with the assistant manager. It was a quick conversation. The manager said he wasn't about to surrender footage to the Santa Monica Police Department without a warrant. The manager said the order of operations was warrant first then footage and hung up.

"Snob." Nishita sighed and added "get a warrant" to his list. He looked at the spreadsheet he'd started on the footage from Gus Post. He'd barely started entering the data.

A young officer came up to his desk. "Sir, you sent me to check on Grant Montgomery," the young officer said.

"And?" Nishita asked. He hated to stop his data entry so, he didn't look up but just signaled that the officer could talk while he worked.

The young officer cleared his throat and held up a small note-pad to read. Nishita held back a small smile. At least the guy knew enough not to depend on memory and wrote down what he observed.

The officer began to rattle through Grant Montgomery's move-ments: "1630 Friday afternoon, Mr. Montgomery checked into his hotel. He attended a cocktail party hosted by the Grocer's Association in the amethyst room which ended at 2000 hours. Saturday morning at 0800 hours, the main conference began in the Topaz Room. Mr. Montgomery was in attendance until 1200 hours, then there was a break for lunch. Mr. Montgomery did not return to the hotel until his keynote speech at 2200 hours in the Jade Room."

Nishita stopped his hands over the keyboard. "Are you saying Mr. Montgomery was not at the conference from noon to ten at night?"

The officer nodded. Nishita leaned back in his chair and said, "You've got my attention."

"He was supposed to attend the evening's dinner event, which began at 2000 hours. He wasn't in the hotel or answering his cell.

He showed up just as they were about to skip his presentation. The front desk said he looked odd, disheveled. Not as put together as usual. He apologized but he said that the beautiful shoreline, people, and sunset had mesmerized him," the officer said.

The officer and Nishita exchanged a look.

Nishita stroked under his chin with the back of his hand, hearing the scrape of day-old beard and thought of the handsome Grant Montgomery and his light Southern accent.

The young officer continued, "Sunday, he attended the full day including the voting and speeches ceremony. Monday, he was at the breakfast closing ceremony. Then he used the gym and swam in the pool. Somewhere he must have heard the news about Ms. Rezenchov and turned himself in to the station by 1600—"

Nishita interrupted, "Just use regular time, okay?"

"Yes, sir," the officer said and handed him his report.

Nishita took out his notepad. Grant had said he wandered around Santa Monica after leaving the bookstore. It was a big gap in his timeline.

The officer guessed what Nishita was thinking and said, "I have the make and model of his rental car. I can see about getting footage from his route out of the hotel garage." The officer's eyes sparkled when he talked.

Nishita thought he was a detective-in-the making. He said, "The main road into Topanga from Santa Monica is the highway. I got security footage last night from the service station at the corner. Check it to see when his rental car drove up the hill and when it returned. Also, if we can track him during the day at all."

"Yes, sir," the officer said and left.

"Good work," Nishita called. The young man waved a hand over his shoulder.

The itch of more questions percolated and he welcomed the feeling. Checking the time, he noticed it was almost ten. Nothing sucks time like data entry. If he wanted to see Dudley at the clinic, he'd best get cleaned up and moving.

Locating the clinic proved challenging. Malibu, known for narrow twisty roads that end abruptly at cliffs, had cluster neighborhoods suspicious of outsiders. At one point, he saw a man watching him from the side of the road. The guy looked like an old surfer. Nishita realized the term old was liquid; this man could be anywhere from thirty to sixty. His body was thin and vigorous, but his skin was weathered by endless days in the sun. It had aged him. He'd seen many such men who lived to surf and found some way to make a small income doing odd jobs for the wealthy who lived in the hills. It seemed to work because, for sun and sand lovers, the beach was only a few steps away.

When Nishita passed the man a second time, he surrendered to being lost and rolled down his window to ask directions.

"I'm looking for the elder care clinic. Am I anywhere near it?" he asked.

The man chuckled, a deep sardonic sound and said, "Right, elder." The word elder lingered in the quiet. "Up the hill, you'll see a small gap in a line of bushes. Turn left at the tennis court and it's at the end of the driveway." The man turned away and refused further interaction.

Nishita said thanks and pulled away. Following directions, he discovered a quiet street with large frothy bushes. He could barely make out the tennis court behind a tall privacy fence. There was a small wooden hand painted sign next to a leafy bush with an arrow that said "Clinic". He found the facility at the end of a long, curved dirt driveway. Curious, it wasn't paved.

A glass-enclosed front porch protected two older women sitting in wheelchairs sleeping in the sun. The sliding glass doors opened with a whisper on his approach. The floors gleamed as if freshly buffed, and classical music played discreetly over the PA system. He passed through to the inner reception area. At the front desk, a young man shuffled papers from an inbox to an outbox. The man looked a little out of place, as he was tanned and muscular with the demeanor of a construction worker.

"Can I help you?" He stood behind an ivory marble counter.

"I'm here to see Dudley Hardwick," Det. Nishita flashed his badge.

The man pursed his lips and said, "Let me call." He picked up the receiver and spoke with someone. He held his hand over the mouthpiece and said, "Sit there." He pointed to a grouping of chairs tucked in a corner alcove.

Nishita wanted to pull rank with the young man but realized he'd best behave, so he sat in one of the stuffed chairs, and folded his arms. A small side table shaped like a cube had a white orchid resting in the middle. On the wall facing him was an oil painting. Not one of those reproductions of flowers or sunsets-by-the-sea types found in hotels and attorney's offices, this was an original. His first clue was the protective glass case, next was the small, framed card identifying the name of the piece and the date painted: 1897. He was struck by the painted flowers, trees, and a crisp blue sky. What he discovered impacted him more than he was ready for. A dark-haired family gathered around a large blanket with scattered scraps from a picnic. The people were far enough away as to be unidentifiable, giving the viewer a chance to imagine themselves as a part of that gathering. Overcome by longing, he stared at the family.

"Detective? We met last night." Rebecca said. She reminded him of Gus Post's manner. It was her familiarity in speaking that was not intrusive, but commanding and pliant at the same time. Gus had said he knew how to work with wealthy people. She had that same intuitive behavior. Tipping her head toward the painting, she asked, "You like our painting?"

"I don't know the artist," he said.

"Marie Bracquemond." Rebecca smiled. "She was one of a handful of women Impressionists in the 19th century. She had a promising career, but her husband was critical of her work. It wore her down, and she gave up."

"Oh." Nishita thought of his critical nature and his curt behavior towards Officer Fisher. He wondered why he behaved like that.

"How can I help you?" asked Rebecca.

Nishita knew gatekeepers, the ones who kept people out. In half a second these people evaluated and determined if someone was allowed access. It didn't matter if he had a detective's badge. If he was determined a threat, he'd be denied and have to return with a warrant.

"As you know, I'm investigating Lena's death." He silently said a small prayer. "I'd like to speak with Dudley for a moment."

She stared at him, and he dared not breathe. "Of course, but only for a few minutes."

"Is he better?" asked Det. Nishita. "He gave us a bit of a scare last night."

"He is exhausted, dehydrated, and his blood pressure is quite high," she said. "We are monitoring him."

Nishita considered this information. "His wife died under suspicious circumstances." Rebecca turned back to him with a questioning look. He added, "That would raise anybody's blood pressure."

She stopped walking and thought about what he'd said. "Is he a suspect?"

"I want to ask him questions about his movements this last weekend." Nishita watched as Rebecca put together what was implied but unspoken. He saw her lips press together tightly. She turned and continued to the elevators.

They did not speak while in the elevator. This was purposeful and caused an edge in the atmosphere. He glanced up to one corner of the elevator and saw the security camera. He lowered his head and figured there was no sense in getting cocky by staring at the lens.

When the doors opened, Rebecca led him along a white corridor. Each door was painted a dusty pastel color: blues, greens, yellows, and pinks. It reminded him of the painting in the waiting room. She reached a pale green door, knocked, and entered. Nishita followed.

Dudley was sitting in a large reclining chair. He was hooked up to an IV and had a blanket over his legs. When he saw Nishita his face hardened.

Rebecca took Dudley's wrist and stared at her watch. After a moment she was satisfied with the results. She adjusted the blanket and said, "I will be right outside." Nishita figured as much.

"Mr. Hardwick," he said. "Good to see you on the mend."

Dudley grunted and picked up the glass of water on the small side table. "I've always had high blood pressure."

Det. Nishita allowed himself a step deeper into the room. "May I sit?" He pointed to a chair and once he got a slight nod from Dudley pulled it up. "I'd like to ask some questions about this weekend."

Dudley's face darkened. "Do I need an attorney?" Anger bubbled in his eyes.

"I'm trying to find out what happened to Lena," Det. Nishita countered.

Dudley gave him a sidelong glance. "The husband is always the first suspect."

He had to agree, but he needed to get something from Dudley, his schedule, something he could check against what the hotel said. He decided on the most tactful phrase. "The longer I have to concern myself with innocent people the longer the real killer is out there."

Dudley nodded and waved his hand in a proceed motion. He said, "I've got nothing to hide."

Det. Nishita noted his gesture. It reminded him of a king waving to his subjects. He pulled out his pad. "When did you leave for Las Vegas?"

Dudley leaned back into his chair and closed his eyes. He said, "Thursday night, sometime after midnight."

"And you drove?"

"I bought the SUV for such trips."

"Do you remember when you arrived in Las Vegas?" Det. Nishita kept his head buried in his notebook but could see Dudley's reaction to his questions.

Dudley sighed, "I checked into the hotel around three in the morning."

Det. Nishita stopped writing. He asked, "Huh, it took you a bit. Did you stop along the way?"

Dudley rolled his eyes and said, "I met friends for a drink outside Vegas." He looked directly at Nishita and said, "Ask Marta."

Marta had mentioned she went with Dudley. He had to assume she and Dudley talked since then, but he had to ask as if he didn't know anything. "Marta drove with you?"

"Well, she slept the whole way. She was sick. We were worried at first but turned out just a bad migraine. She thought it would pass with rest, so she stayed in her room."

"Where did you stay?"

"Cesar's Palace."

Det. Nishita jotted that down and asked, "And Marta?"

Dudley grunted. "We always get rooms on the same floor." He appeared to drift off seeing the busy weekend in his mind. "She kept promising a few more hours and it would fade. Finally, I told her it was best to send her home. I arranged a limo for Sunday."

Det. Nishita checked the timeline of the weekend. "It was only one more day, she could have waited and driven with you."

Dudley let out a heavy sigh. "We debated about that. Should she stay, or should she get home and begin to unravel the receipts from the weekend? She began to feel better, but not enough to work at a convention. People think it's all fun and games, but it's a lot of work. And by Saturday night I'd procured a lot of things and asked if she'd port them back in a limo."

Det Nishita asked, "What things?"

"Priceless delicate pieces," said Dudley in an arched manner lording his wealth and rank. Nishita felt the covert dig at his place in society. "The back of an SUV can be unstable."

Nishita kept his eyes glued on Dudley. "Was it a successful

weekend?" He could always verify attendance at this conference.

"You can imagine without Marta, I had to manage all of it. The booth, the meet and greets, book signings," he said and grinned.

Det. Nishita had to begin asking the questions he'd been avoiding, "Did you speak with Lena during the weekend?"

"No, she was on a personal retreat." Dudley adjusted the blanket on his legs.

"Why not?" He probed as gently as he could.

"Her private time is sacred." He pushed air out through his lips in a dismissive tone. "Ask Marta."

This was his opening and he asked, "Anya mentioned that Lena had left town last November. She didn't tell anyone she was leaving. Marta found her in Santa Fe."

"That!" Dudley said. "I didn't know what to do. If it weren't for Marta-" Dudley stopped, his face flushed at the memory.

"Were they close? Marta and Lena?" Det. Nishita had to stop the urge to look back over his notes. Any physical movement he made could distract Dudley and stop the conversation.

Dudley stared at Nishita. "They are." He stopped. His face paled. "They were, I mean." Dudley adjusted in his seat and fumbled with the cuff of his shirt.

Det. Nishita recognized Dudley had used the present tense. Maybe there was more to their marriage than he was led to understand. "Why did Lena run away?"

Dudley looked tired. "I suppose it will all come out." Dudley took another sip of water. "Tell me, Detective, how long should someone pay for mistakes they made as a kid? How long do we punish someone for adolescent passions?"

Did he know about Lena's son? "Are you speaking of Grant Montgomery?"

"Detective?" Rebecca's voice addressed him. "It's time."

Nishita glanced and saw that Dudley had the call button in his other hand. There could be no argument; he had to leave. These questions would have to wait until he had more control over the circumstances like in a police conference room. But he had to know one more thing. Put on the velvet gloves and deliver a punch.

"Thank you, Mr. Hardwick. But may I ask about the limo you got for Marta? Did you rent it from Avis or Budget?

Dudley chuckled at the foolishness of Nishita's question, "Oh, good god no. I've been at conventions for years. I know people. I asked a friend, and he said he'd take care of it."

Det. Nishita arched his brows. This was getting better. "Who is your friend?"

Rebecca gripped his arm, "Detective? Please."

Nishita knew he was being hustled. He returned his notebook to the side pocket in his suit coat. "Thank you for your time," he said as he walked to the door.

Dudley pulled up the blanket to just under his chin. Nishita followed Rebeca to the elevator. They did not talk the entire time he was escorted out of the building.

When he got to his car, he pulled out his notebook and a business card fell out. It was Rebecca's. On the back was a handwritten note. "Will call you tonight." He never felt her slip it into his pocket. She was good.

As you awaken, you become a threat to those who fear change, growth, and life itself. Sometimes entering a room, you will trigger reactions. If, in these moments, you maintain composure when all around you lose theirs, then you will have mastered power.

—Lena Rezenchov, *Essentials of Mastery Symposium*

SEVENTEEN

DRIVING BACK TO THE STATION, NISHITA spotted an upscale grocery store. It was the same grocery store in which he and Emma had their first date. A mutual friend had set it up. They met for a simple lunch. It had a cafeteria type-buffet for busy commuters. Emma was in her final year of law school and preparing for her bar exam. He had just made sergeant and moved into field supervision. She was intelligent, funny, and beautiful. They'd sat at one of the outdoor benches and talked about law and corruption until past sunset.

A noisy stomach reminded him that he had skipped lunch, and with an afternoon of examining grainy security footage ahead, he turned into the lot. Winding through the parking lot he noted the wide variety of cars next to one another. An old beige mom van sat next to a neon green sports car. The humble parking lot proved status didn't matter; one parked where there was space.

He pulled into a spot at the far end, a habit he'd learned from his grandfather. Big Ted could complain for hours about the type of person who'd exert enormous effort to get a space at the front. In his estimation, it was faster and easier to park back a few rows and walk. He quoted his grandfather, "Everybody wants celebrity parking."

He was ready to get out of the car when he stopped. For an instant, he could smell the cigarette smoke embedded in his grandfather's clothes, the residue of oil and axel grease in the creases of his boots, and his musky hair tonic. When he and his brother laughed at his pomade his grandfather used to say, "I got to keep this mop in place," pointing to his head. As if he struggled. It was his grandmother who lovingly combed his red hair each morning.

A six-foot American serviceman and his Geisha war bride faced cold stares, exclusion from living in certain areas, and no employment opportunities. Other marriages had crumbled from less. They were the rock of his family. That kind of relationship was what he wanted but so far, it had eluded him.

Entering the grocery store, he passed by baskets of fruits and flowers, and made his way to the center area, where the self-service counters were located. Each counter provided a different style of food. There was a taco bar, salad bar, sushi bar, and a deli that sliced meats and cheeses for sandwiches.

It wasn't surprising to see suited men and women strolling the isles, given that every law firm, investment agency, and bank had offices just around the corner. Coming here offered a break to breathe fresh air rather than remain in stuffy offices, and it didn't hurt that the food was exceptional. A group of businessmen had gathered near the deli. Nishita guessed by the dark suits and flashy ties that the men were mid-level executives. He caught them eying a trio of much younger women by the salad bar, dressed in colorful attire.

He was reminded of the age gap between Dudley and Lena. From what he learned about her past, she might have had a weakness for older men. Dudley fit the criteria with his experience and success. He made a quick note to ask when they got married, was it before or after Anya was born. He then glanced back to the group of young women.

By this time, the men had joined the women and introduced themselves. There was a lot of playful banter. By their ease, it was clear they knew one another by sight but not by name. Perhaps they worked in the same building but not with the same company. The oldest of the men oozed confidence, and it worked like a tonic. One young woman smiled and leaned in. The shorter woman gushed one-word responses, her attention divided between flirting with a different man and building a salad in her white foam food dish.

Watching all the flirtatious sexual tension made him realize how much he had taken Emma for granted. He stopped treating her as special. He got smug and caught up in making detective.

Returning his attention to the group, he heard the older man mention a bar just around the corner that served the best hot wings during happy hour which, as he pointed to his fancy watch, was about to start.

Nishita hid a smile, gave up on the group, and got in line at the deli counter. He grabbed a turkey sandwich and exited. Driving to the station his thoughts returned to his former girlfriend, Emma. Embarrassed by how they ended, he told himself to grow up and congratulate her. He considered calling her, but what would he say that didn't come across as creepy? He decided email was best and set aside the phone until he got back to the station.

Camilla met him at his desk with a grin on her face. "Las Vegas sent over full security footage from the weekend and an apology from the head of security."

"Nice. We can get started. Is the AV room set?" he asked. He made it to his desk and set down his bag of food. Camilla hadn't answered. "Well?"

"Can't. The arson team has it. They'll have it for the next few days, or longer." Camilla sat in the chair by his desk and began digging in his food bag. "Did you bring me anything?"

"Hey!" He shooed her hands away from the bag. "If the Vegas footage is on the server we can begin." He pointed to his computer and rolled his chair up to the keyboard. Camilla scratched her eyebrow, a gesture Nishita knew as a sign of impending boredom.

Camilla leaned forward and said, "Have you heard about what caused the eighteen-wheeler crash the other morning on the 405?"

"Wait, what crash. "He shook his head.

She rolled her eyes. "Use your memory, Little Ted,"

"Oh, right, right. That crash. The one that called in all surrounding police personnel, so we were sent to investigate Lena's accident on Topanga," he said. "I'm with you now, go on."

Camilla leaned in as if she had the best news. "Someone tossed a towel out of their car while driving and it hit the windshield of the truck, covering it. The driver couldn't see and swerved out of control."

"Why would they do that? Do they have photos of the car?" asked Nishita.

"They're checking all angles from traffic cameras, but it might be from a limo. It was way early in the morning, around three. The footage is blurry. Anyway, that's a lawsuit waiting to happen." Camilla leaned back and placed her hands behind her head.

Nishita wondered what the chances were that this limo was the one from Gus's security footage. Limos were driven across Los Angeles twenty-four hours a day. Could the timing work out that it might be the same limo? It was crazy to think it might be connected with his case. He brushed it out of his mind and signaled for Camilla to swing her chair around so they could view the footage. "Let's start with the dull videos of Dudley and Marta at the hotel, shall we?"

Camilla grunted and moved her chair next to his. Nishita got the footage from the server and began to run it. The first section was from 4:45 a.m. Friday. It was a view of the front desk from behind the clerk. There was a line of people which surprised him. Four o'clock in the morning and there was a line to get a room in Vegas. But then again, that's Vegas. At the front of the line stood a bride and groom, or so he assumed. The bride wore a short white dress and a straw hat with a big flower and the groom was in dark pants and a pale blue unbuttoned shirt. They looked young and happy.

"Looks like a spontaneous wedding," Nishita commented. Camilla snorted with distain. Once again, he wondered. This time he asked. "Why haven't you gotten married?" She made a small twist with her lips. "No, really," he pressed. But he could tell by how she lifted her right shoulder half an inch and turned her head that she was going to lie. She began with the usual story of not meeting the right guy, then moved on to raising her son and that she didn't want some guy to mess him up, and finished with there was no time to date. Nishita knew the real answer, but she'd never say it out loud. Her heart belonged to the father of her son, a soldier who lost his life in Afghanistan. He opened the bag with the turkey sandwich and handed her half.

They munched on food and continued watching the video. Behind the bride and groom waiting in line were Dudley and Marta. Dudley wore dark pants and an aqua polo shirt. Marta had big sunglasses, a scarf wrapped around her head, and a mid-length trench coat. All Nishita could see of Marta were big sunglasses.

The bride and groom picked up their room card and she jumped into his arms. He carried her out of view. Dudley made a sour face watching the couple exit and stepped up to the clerk. Nishita and Camilla chuckled.

Dudley managed the check-in while Marta stayed behind. She kept off to the side.

Camilla leaned into the computer screen and said, "Wait. Back it up." Nishita replayed the footage at a slower speed. Camilla pointed to the screen. "Look at Marta's clothes," she said. "First, that's a Hermes muffler. Those things cost around a thousand bucks. And that trench coat!" She put her hands against her cheeks. "We need to find out who the designer is. It could be a copy, but it looks like a one-of-a-kind Dior."

Nishita looked closer at the screen. The scarf was a dark blue with light blue markings. "How can you tell what kind of scarf that is?"

"I have a girly side," she said in a defensive tone. "But look, that coat, if it's what I think it is, it costs at least five big ones."

Nishita stared at the screen. Marta was still off to the side, keeping her body small.

"You met Marta yesterday afternoon at the bookstore, right? Do you remember what she wore?" asked Camilla.

Nishita pictured Marta standing in the kitchen, the sun streaking in picture windows. "Black cotton pants, a black crewneck, and black leather flats that buckled."

"Simple, right? These things seem out of her normal style, and they look like the type of thing one would buy in Vegas, not Topanga," Camilla said.

"Maybe they were Lena's and she borrowed them," Nishita suggested. Camilla gave him a face. "What are you thinking? Dudley got these for Marta to buy her silence?"

"It's worth looking into."

"Okay, keep an eye out for that coat at the bookstore." He let the footage continue and watched Dudley get his room card and exit. Marta was left standing in line. She finally noticed he was gone and followed him.

The next clips were of Dudley and Marta in the elevator standing apart. Dudley handed her a room card, pushed the floor button, and rode facing front. They reached their floor and got out, entering separate rooms.

There was something about their demeanor that didn't sit right with Nishita, but he couldn't put his finger on why. True, Marta had said she had a migraine, which can alter normal interactions. But Dudley took little to no notice of her and was rude if not abrupt.

His phone rang and he looked at the caller. Rebecca Lopez. He showed the name to Camilla before answering.

Christopher Marlowe said, "Excess of wealth is cause of covetousness." But I think excess causes addiction. And that is a path filled with disappointments.

—Lena Rezenchov
speaking during a rehab group meeting

EIGHTEEN

At eight-thirty, Nishita pulled onto the gravel shoulder along Pacific Coast Highway. Keeping a view of the service station and Topanga Canyon Road, he waited to spot Rebecca Lopez as she arrived. She'd requested they meet inside the service station at eight-forty-five.

When she'd suggested this location, the one he had spent the night before with Gus, it concerned him. To test her, or maybe he was feeling argumentative, he offered a different location. Her fear was palatable over the phone, he agreed to meet but wondered what was behind that fear.

She told him she'd arrive first, pump gas into a red Audi, and go inside the station to pay. She said she was a regular and it wouldn't be considered out of the ordinary for her to stop and chat with Gus. Once she was inside, he was to park in the lot and enter the station.

Traffic had eased at this hour, but as a precaution, he ducked down in the seat. It was best to appear as an empty car. He stared through the steering wheel and focused on the intersection. Traffic lights signaled to empty lanes, and floodlights from the gas station spilled out to reach the vast darkness that was the Pacific Ocean. He'd met witnesses in strange places before—bars tucked in basements of factories, hotel laundry rooms crammed with bins of sheets and towels, and twenty-four-hour fitness centers, which was the most deserted of locations. Each chosen for secrecy. Still, he wondered why here.

Before completing the call, Rebecca had suggested he research her case as she wanted things out in the open. Her case was easy to find because it had made headlines and caused legal concerns for hospitals everywhere. Thirteen years ago, she was an RN working at one of the top plastic surgery hospitals in Los Angeles. This hospital was known for reconstructive surgery. Their expertise was regrafting skin on burn victims—but its reputation was built on its humanitarian efforts, donating surgery for children with cleft palates. For one week in December, the clinic set up free surgeries for any child with a cleft palate. Children from all corners would arrive for medical examinations and eventual surgery. Ms. Lopez managed it like a superstar, coordinating each event efficiently and effectively. That was until her fall from grace.

During a week of cleft surgeries when crowds were big and staff stretched thin, a large amount of Class A drugs had been stolen from their dispensary. Security footage at that time was sketchy but a figure could be seen unlocking the door to the dispensary and leaving with a full duffel bag. At that time, the locks did not have user codes; something all clinics rushed to set up after this episode.

The robber couldn't be identified, but the duffel bag was. Rebecca's fifteen-year-old son, Joaquin, had volunteered for the day, and had been seen carrying it. The footage was examined again, and it became obvious it was not a mature woman in her forties, as Rebecca was at the time, but a younger, faster, leaner figure, rushing in and exiting all in a manner of minutes. Joaquin was arrested, the duffel bag still in his possession. Rebecca was fired and her RN license revoked. It was a humiliating fall from grace and could be why she worked at the care center, not as a nurse, but as a manager.

Nishita peered through the steering wheel. At this time of night, traffic lessened with each passing moment. It would be easy to see Rebecca's car.

He spotted the red Audi turn left onto Topanga Canyon Road and then right into the gas station. She pulled up to a pump he couldn't see. "Damn," he whispered. How long should he wait? Three minutes? Four? He decided to call Camilla and get eyes on that car.

She answered on the first half ring. "Yeah, I see her. She's pulled into the far pump. Just started filling the tank."

"Where are you parked?" he asked.

"Topanga Canyon Road on the opposite side from the station. "Bout twenty feet from the station. I'm in a dark patch, no street-lights here," she said. He heard Camilla adjust in her seat. "Okay, finishing up now." She paused. "She's walking into the station. Count to sixty and go."

"Thanks." Nishita hung up. He counted to sixty, then started his car and pulled onto the highway. He parked, took a deep breath, and entered the station.

Gus was behind the counter blocking the door to his office and nodded a curt welcome. Nishita moved closer and Gus stepped aside revealing Rebecca Lopez. She looked smaller than she had the night before, perhaps because she was sitting, but Nishita noted that she was out of business attire and wore khaki pants and a dark blue parka.

"Ms. Lopez." He held out his hand. Knowing the office from the night before, he checked to be certain nothing was amiss. Gus excused himself murmuring something about making a fresh pot of coffee.

"You've read my file?" Her round brown eyes stared at him. Nishita made a soft agreement sound. "The people I work for gave me a job when no one else would," Rebecca said. "I owe some kind of loyalty."

"Why don't you tell me what you came to say," Det. Nishita said. She was stone silent. "Does it have something to do with Lena Rezenchov's death?"

Rebecca nodded and a large tear rolled down the side of her face. "I never read the news anymore. The media was rather brutal in my case. Every hospital and medical clinic used my son and I as a cautionary tale."

"I can imagine," Det. Nishita agreed. Gus entered with two cups of steaming coffee. Nishita noticed Rebecca's coffee looked prepared as if Gus knew how she liked it. She sipped, looked up and him, and smiled. Maybe there was more between them than a customer relationship. "Go on," he encouraged. Gus went back to the coffee area picked up a cup for himself and returned leaning his large shoulder against the door frame.

"I got to know Marta because of her mother," Rebecca explained. "Sophia spent weeks with us in rehabilitation after her first stroke. That must be over a year now. Marta came in twice a week to help with physical therapy. Dudley had visited the doctor long before I started." Her face changed. "I knew they had some kind of business arrangement," she spit the words. "I never put it together until Lena showed up."

Det. Nishita pulled out his small notepad. He thought of Camilla sitting in her car. She should be here to hear this. "Would it be alright if one of my officers joined us as an observer? I want to be sure to get this all correct."

Rebecca's eyes widened. She turned to Gus who moved closer.

"Are they in uniform?" she asked.

"I can ask they cover up," Nishita said.

"The fewer eyes on this, the better," Gus said. "Have them park next to your car."

Det. Nishita wondered whose eyes. He quickly texted Camilla to wear something that covered her uniform and come in. She answered she'd be there in ten. Nishita set his phone down and returned to face Rebecca. "You were saying Dudley and the lead doctor, what is his name?"

"Please understand, I had no idea that Lena had died. I don't watch the news."

"Are you telling me when you brought Sophia to the bookstore last night, you were unaware of Lena's death?"

Rebecca nodded. "Marta told me when I arrived to drop off Sophia."

Det. Nishita couldn't help but think she was afraid of her own shadow. He needed to get her to talk. He leaned back to give her room to breathe. "Tell me about the care center."

"My duties are managerial. I manage the staff, order supplies, pay the bills, and keep the center solvent," she said and wiped her mouth with a tissue. "To run a care center costs a lot of money."

"I can imagine," Det. Nishita said.

"So, when Dudley recommended a cleaning service that would work for almost pennies, I was skeptical. Dr. RJ told me to give them a trial."

"Dr RJ?"

"My manager, Dr. Hughes." Rebecca wiped her cheeks with the tissue. "The cleaners arrive at night when I'm off. I am not allowed to work nights. Still tainted by my past."

"You weren't trusted because of the drugs?" Det. Nishita asked. She nodded.

Marta had mentioned something about a cleaning service at the bookstore. In the kitchen, he'd complimented the cleanliness. She'd mentioned she had the store sanitized that Thursday before the weekend. He thought it strange she'd mention the day.

Officer Camilla entered wearing a dark raincoat over her uniform. He waved her in the office.

"Ms. Rebecca Lopez, this is my partner, Officer Camilla Leila. Officer Camilla Ms. Lopez is the managing supervisor at the Elder Care clinic. Rebecca, I appreciate you allowing her to be here."

Officer Camilla held out her hand to Rebecca. "Ms. Lopez, thank you. I'm here to assist as best I can."

Gus also shook her hand. "Nice to see you again, Officer. May I get you some coffee?"

She gave him a friendly tap on the shoulder. "You know me." Gus chuckled and went to get her a cup.

Det. Nishita pulled the conversation back to Rebecca. "Ms. Lopez was informing me of a cleaning service at the care center recommended by Dudley."

Gus had found a folding chair and set it down for Officer Camilla. He also had a cup of coffee for her. Rebecca watched every move she made.

Rebecca began, "I knew Ms. Rezenchov had a drinking problem. There were times she'd drive into our parking lot and sit."

"She'd sit in her car?" asked Officer Camilla.

Rebecca nodded. "Usually intoxicated. I'd ask if I might call someone to come pick her up because she shouldn't drive. She'd nod. Then Marta or Mr. Hardwick would arrive, get her out of the car, and take her home."

Nishita wondered about the drinking. People do a lot of things to dull pain, pain of abuse, trauma, or simple boredom. Why did Lena?

Officer Camilla's voice brought him back. "How often did this happen?"

"At first it was erratic, odd times, it seemed she knew enough not to drive far, but they became more frequent. One afternoon, as Marta picked up Sophia, she told me Lena had been arrested and sent to rehab. I was relieved, honestly. When released, if that's the term, she came in and apologized." She stopped for a moment and pulled the cup to her lips. Her hand shook as she sipped.

This was a piece about Lena he'd never heard before. "Rebecca, you work mostly during the daytime?"

Rebecca nodded. "Except when I return a patient to a family. I drive them home, as I did Sophia the other night."

"Does that happen often? That you return patients, I mean." Rebecca shook her head. "All right, so when Lena appeared intoxicated, it was in the afternoon." Rebecca nodded again. "You stated that these episodes first occurred once a month then grew in frequency."

"Mostly she showed up mid-week. Like a Wednesday or Thursday." Rebecca twisted the tissue between her fingers.

He clicked through his memory. Lena was arrested on a Thursday around four. He was ending his shift.

"Six weeks ago, Lena was parked in our lot. I went out to speak with her. She wasn't drunk this time. She told me to look into the cleaning crew. I asked her if she meant the one Dudley recommended. She nodded then drove away." Rebecca paused and stared off to her left. She seemed to go over something in her mind.

"Ms. Lopez?" Officer Camilla asked and reached forward to touch her forearm.

"Later that afternoon, as I was leaving for the day, Mr. Hardwick arrived. He went into the doctor's private office. They had a terrible argument." Rebecca lifted her hand to her lips. Her hand was shaking. "Mr. Hardwick left. That night, I hid in my car to observe this cleaning crew. I suppose I thought I'd see ex-convicts or drug addicts on the crew, people who struggle to find work. Around midnight, a truck showed up and ten women and two small boys got out and went into the clinic."

Nishita was tempted to look over to Camilla, but he knew better. It would distract Rebecca, and she might freeze. He sat still and slowly leaned in to offer silent concern. "These women were part of the cleaning crew?" he asked.

Rebecca gave a low laugh. "Cleaning crew, yeah right. I noticed the lights in the building didn't go on. Isn't that what a cleaning crew does? Turn on the lights so they can clean?" Her eyes burned with anger.

It was how she said the word clean that dug in. Things began to knit together in Det. Nishita's thoughts. He considered the video of Dudley and Marta at the hotel, the way Marta was dressed. Marta had said she had a cleaning crew at the bookstore that week. Now

Rebecca was hinting that a cleaning crew of women were at the clinic to do something other than clean.

The small office felt smaller. Det. Nishita noticed the stale air, the smell of the filled ashtray on the desk, and the perpetual odor of petrol. He had to be clear about what she was saying. "Did you suspect they were illegal immigrants?"

"More than that, yes," Rebecca said.

Opportunities are found in times of great difficulties.

—Lena Rezenchov, *Paths to Inner Power*

NINETEEN

D ET. NISHITA FORCED HIMSELF TO REMAIN still while a thousand questions raced through his mind. She'd just admitted to seeing undocumented workers at her clinic doing something other than cleaning. Perhaps some small detail, brushed aside at the time, could open up a lead.

"Can we back up?" Det. Nishita asked. "You mentioned Lena was in the habit of parking in the lot of the clinic when she drank too much."

"Yes," Rebecca said.

"And when this happened, you'd call Dudley or Marta to come pick her up. Did I get that right?" Det. Nishita kept his eyes on Rebecca.

"Correct," Rebecca answered. "I was relieved when I heard that she went into rehab."

He nodded. "About four or five weeks ago, you say she showed up in the parking lot and hadn't been drinking. At this time, she told you to check on the cleaning service used by the clinic," Det. Nishita said. "Did she ask for you to call Dudley or Marta to pick her up?"

"No."

"After telling you about the cleaning service, she drove away. Did she tell you where she was going?"

"No, of course she didn't tell me," Rebecca answered, her voice irritated.

"But that same night you parked up the hill to investigate and saw a truck or a van with what appeared to be undocumented people. They exited the vehicle and entered the clinic. Is that correct?" he asked. "What type of vehicle?"

"It was similar to all vans," she said. "No windows along the side and at the back were two doors. When the van arrived, the driver unlocked the door, and the people came out. Two of the women carried some kind of cases which I imagined were supplies. This was done in silence."

Det. Nishita considered her comment. He leaned back and said, "Silence is a funny animal. Sometimes there is a silence of respect, perhaps not wanting to disturb the neighbors. Sometimes an oppressor can create a silence of fear. Did you get a sense of which type of silence this was?"

Rebecca looked to her left. Her face changed as she seemed to be going over the events of that night. Her right hand balled into a fist, and she placed it to her lips. "Fear."

He wanted to ask her more about it, but needed information about the truck so he could do something. "Did you see a license plate? Or get a look at the driver?"

Rebecca shook her head. "It was dark, and I was too far away." Her left hand clutched her cup. She was shaking so badly the coffee was spilling.

Camilla gently took the cup away and gave her a reassuring touch. "You're doing great." She handed the cup to Gus.

"What happened next?" Det. Nishita asked.

"One of those sleek sedans pulled into the lot," Rebecca spoke very fast. "I didn't see who got out. I knew I had to get away before I was spotted. I drove away with my headlights off until I reached the main road."

Gus cleared his throat and said, "She came to me."

Nishita glanced back and forth between Rebecca and Gus.

"We tried to gather information about this truck and the cleaning service. It's one thing to suspect, it's another to have evidence." Gus spoke with reassurance, but his eyes signaled concern.

"Did you think that if Rebecca called the authorities, it would be obvious she was the source?" Nishita asked. He noticed Rebecca still clung to Officer Camilla's hand.

"The people in the van would be in the biggest danger," A flash of emotion raced across his face. He got himself under control. "Rebecca and I didn't know if Lena was involved with the cleaning service, or Marta or Dudley or all three. We knew Dudley was associated with the owners of the clinic in some way but anything more than that and we were in the dark."

Det. Nishita's ears perked up. He remembered Dudley owned an import-export business. Anya had said Dudley traveled to London and Cairo, that he brought rugs, silks, and statues back to sell at the bookstore. What else did he import?

Det. Nishita asked, "Have you watched for this van during these last months?"

Rebecca nodded and said, "As much as I could without drawing attention."

"Good. I don't want you in danger. When you did see the van, did you notice the same people came to clean the clinic?" he asked.

Rebecca shook her head. "I never found a record of invoices from any cleaning service. I asked about payment and was told not to bother with that. The one person I could ask was Lena, but she'd vanished." Rebecca said. "When she returned, she was constantly traveling. Marta said for book tours."

Gus broke in and said, "I kept an eye out for a white van. Every night, I'd watch the security footage from that day. Do you know how many white vans drive along PCH?" Gus asked in exasperation.

"Did you discover anything?" Det. Nishita looked over to Rebecca. She appeared to have calmed. Perhaps it was Officer Camilla holding her hand, perhaps it was Gus with his protective nature, but it was clear her nerves had been soothed.

"Not really. I have some footage of several light-colored vans driving towards Malibu. My security footage doesn't give me that clear of a picture," Gus said.

"What about this sedan?" Det. Nishita asked. "Ever get any footage of that?"

Gus shook his head.

His comment made Nishita appreciate his cool thinking. Just because a van drove toward Malibu didn't mean it was _the_ van. "It's possible they took a different route and headed north," Det. Nishita said. "Are there any other security cameras that might have footage of this van and sedan?"

"That would be under your jurisdiction, not mine, Detective," Gus said.

"Camilla?"

"On it," she answered and picked up her phone. She began to text.

"Who are you calling?" Rebecca said rising in panic.

Officer Camilla said, "I know an officer with the Malibu police. He's worked in Malibu for years and knows how to be discreet. I'll ask him to check on security cameras along that route." Camilla patted Rebecca's hand. "We need to check routes of regular deliveries. If we know the normal times we might identify the odd one and find yours."

Rebecca sat quietly. She looked up at Gus and he gave her a reassuring wink

"Rebecca, you have helped this investigation greatly," Det. Nishita said. "But I have to ask, when Dudley was brought in last night, what was his demeanor?"

"Dudley didn't speak while I drove him to the clinic. One of our night staff met him at the door and I left. When I arrived the next morning, he had been put in the green room."

"Do the colors of the room signify things to the staff?"

Rebecca listed each room and used her fingers to count. "Pink is watched with care. Blue is stable but needs quiet, yellow can be discharged when awake. The green rooms are for patients that need light care."

"How many green rooms do you have?" Rebecca lifted four fingers. "When you arrived, this morning, were you concerned?"

"Not at all. I took his vitals; his pulse was normal as was his blood pressure. I did my best to make him comfortable and continued my day as usual."

Det. Nishita remained still as he asked, "Do you think Dudley had something to do with Lena's death?" He kept his focus on Rebecca. He felt Gus hold his breath. The room held one of those silences.

"I never got the impression he had that hard of an edge," she said. "He was a salesman."

That was his assessment of Dudley, a gregarious man wanting to make his mark. But everyone has a breaking point. Det. Nishita had to hear the coroner's report before he made any judgments. He looked at his watch. It was nine forty-five. Coroners in Santa Monica often worked late into the night if a case demanded it.

Rebecca folded her hands in her lap and lowered her head. Nishita thought she looked lonely and wondered what happened to her son after stealing drugs. At his age, he must have been sent to juvenile detention. He could only hope her son didn't make the wrong type of friends there.

"Rebecca, would you like a break?" Officer Camilla handed her the cup. "Did you get dinner tonight? I'm sure Gus and I can arrange for something." Gus nodded vigorously.

Accepting the cup, Rebecca nodded. Officer Camilla helped her up from her chair and they moved to the center of the station. Rebecca made her way to the far hallway which Nishita assumed was a bathroom.

He held his phone up and gestured to Gus, "Will you excuse me for a moment?" He walked to join Camilla. "I'm going to call Dr. Boyd and see if he has anything."

Officer Camilla nodded, then turned to Gus and asked, "You think I could get a second cup of coffee?"

Nishita watched as Gus and Camilla moved to the coffee area. Before he dialed the coroner's office, he remembered the first autopsy he ever witnessed. Autopsies are challenging. Sometimes they have clear images as to how the person died; sometimes all they can answer is the person has died and nothing else. He hoped Lena's autopsy would shed new light on her death. He dialed the coroner's office.

"Boyd," the strong doctor's voice answered.

"Dr. Boyd!" Nishita's voice cracked. "This is Detective Nishita, I'm checking on Lena Rezenchov." He spoke quickly, knowing how lucky he was to speak with Dr. Boyd himself.

"I'm writing my report now. I should be finished with it in about forty-five minutes," Dr. Boyd said.

Nishita always suspected Dr. Boyd was slightly hard of hearing. Maybe decades of using high-pitched drills and saws to cut bones had eroded his hearing. But he was the best coroner in the county and the oldest, at seventy-five. He'd said more than once the only way he'd retire is if they carried him out feet first.

Nishita said, "I can be at your office in thirty minutes. Will you be able to go over it with me at that time?"

"Thirty minutes. If you are not here by then, I'm out the door," Dr. Boyd said and hung up.

Nishita pumped his fist in the air. He turned and saw Gus giving him a questioning look, Camilla smiled knowing something good had happened in the case, and Rebecca stood with a grim expression. "I need to return to the station; will you be comfortable speaking with Officer Camilla?"

Rebecca shot a furtive glance at Gus, who gave a reassuring nod. Nishita thanked Rebecca and acknowledged her bravery. He asked her to come into the station and get her statement on record. Fear flashed across her face, but she agreed. It was what had to happen eventually. Camilla gave Rebecca a look like a proud mother to a brave daughter.

As he left the station, he wondered more about the connection between the clinic and the Goddess Garden Bookstore.

"Let us beware of saying that death is the opposite of life. The living being is only a species of the dead, and a very rare species.

—Friedrich Nietzsche

By the time I was 6, I was able to talk with spirits. I thought everybody did. What made me so special? I grew up outside Atlanta and my grandmother took me to visit the Military Museum of the Battle of Chickamauga. Two young boys who fought in that battle spoke with me. They were delightful. I saw other spirits that day, but they snubbed me. Perhaps they don't believe in the living.

—Lena Rezenchov, *Beyond Death and Dying*

TWENTY

NISHITA FACED THE EMPTY DESK CHAIR in Dr. Boyd's office, his heart pounding. On the drive over, he got trapped behind an accident and lost precious time arriving at the morgue. When he parked, it was 8:58, which left him two minutes to race to Dr. Boyd's office at the far end of the building. As he ran down the corridor, Dr. Boyd-having just exited the men's room boomed, "Don't run, Detective. That's a newly waxed floor; you could slip." Dr. Boyd then pointed to his office. "I will join you presently."

Not Nishita's finest first impression.

There were stories, whispered in the locker room, about Dr. Boyd. The favorite was the one about a hotshot detective who thought he knew more about how his victim died than the doctor. Dr. Boyd pulled him into the morgue and went over the cadaver inch by inch until the detective turned green and vomited. That detective got what officers called a Boyd-itude Adjustment. Nishita did not want to slip up in any way. He sat quietly surveying the office while he waited.

The wall behind the desk was filled with framed diplomas, awards, and citations for distinguished service with the Navy. It appeared Dr. Boyd was a corpsman during the Vietnam War. One framed photo was of a young Dr. Boyd next to a man Nishita recognized as the young Honorable Judge Robinson. He saw a partial hull number on the side of the ship and wondered if that was enough to find out which ship it was.

By the awards and citations, Dr. Trent Boyd had some stories to tell—and he would love to hear them. The citations were for his distinguished service record in the Navy and Dr. Boyd had had a long and illustrious career, but an apple and slice of cheese resting in the center of a crumpled piece of wax paper spoke volumes. That simple snack revealed more about him than his degrees and awards.

"Detective Nishita," said Dr. Boyd as he entered his office. He was a tall man with a full head of cropped silver hair. Nishita extended his hand to greet him. "Sit," ordered Dr. Boyd. He carried a manilla folder filled with papers. He set the folder to the side and settled himself in his chair. Picking up a Swiss Army knife, he held up the apple and asked, "Have you eaten?"

Nishita realized he hadn't, not since that half of the turkey sandwich he'd shared with Camilla. He'd planned on grabbing dinner, but things like food tended to slip his mind while on a case.

"Detectives." Dr. Boyd chuckled. "Some forget about themselves until they drop." He unfolded a blade from the knife, cut a slice of apple and handed it to Nishita. "As I've aged, I find I can no longer eat large meals as it upsets my system. I always stock a little something in my office."

Nishita accepted the apple slice and out of the corner of his eye spotted a small refrigerator. Soon Dr. Boyd handed him a piece of cheese. "Don't make me eat alone."

It felt surreal eating apple slices with Dr. Boyd. It reminded him of the time when he and his brother saw the actor from the Batman films at McDonald's. At first, the two of them were thrilled and starstruck. His brother had no fear and went up and asked for his autograph. Nishita couldn't move from his seat. He felt invasive watching a celebrity do something normal. It didn't bother Allen, and he returned with the autograph with a big smile on his face.

"I have the report on Ms. Rezenchov," Boyd said and wiped his fingertips on a small napkin. He handed the report to Nishita. "That's your copy."

He reached for the paper, but the doctor made a noise in his throat, stopping him.

"We can go over the photographs, or I can take you downstairs and we'll go over the body. Which do you prefer?"

Nishita set his half-eaten apple slice down. He'd been at autopsies before, but never with Boyd. Choosing to follow the hierarchy of the moment he said, "I would like to see the body, but please finish your food first."

Boyd studied him. A half smile filled the right side of his face. "Let me go over the photos, and then if you still want to, we can view the body." He made a gesture with his right hand implying Nishita should take the folder. "When you first saw her body in the car, what did you suspect?"

Nishita cleared his throat and chose his words carefully. "Sir, when I approached the car, it was still in the ditch. With no dents or broken windows to suggest a crash, I suspected the car had been pushed. When the car was towed from the ditch and Ms. Rezenchov removed, I noticed the lack of blood in the car or on the victim. Her legs were cold, possibly suggesting she'd been there for hours. She had bruising along the side of her jaw and the side of her head was dented. The injuries to her head were inconsistent with hitting the steering wheel. I was curious as to how she got that head wound."

"What did you suspect was the cause of death?" Boyd asked as he fingered a piece of cheese before playfully popping it into his mouth.

Watching the doctor, Nishita suppressed a smile. "Head trauma."

Boyd nodded and gestured for him to read the report.

Nishita opened the top cover. He quickly scanned the list of injuries. It listed bruising around the neck, back, knees and elbows. The bones of her hand were broken. He searched for the time of death. "Undetermined." His heart sank. He was hoping against hope that Boyd might be able to give an approximate time of death. "You can't determine time of death?"

"No, she was kept cold, and I can't determine it."

He flipped through the pages and looked at the photos of Lena's injuries. The bruises along her jaw were small round marks, suggesting fingers. When he looked at her hand the bruises completely encircled her wrist, and the report stated that two fingers on that same hand were broken. His breath stopped when he saw the bruises on her back. They covered the top half of her neck and shoulders and were in a crisscross pattern. He caught Boyd's eyes.

"Any drugs or alcohol in her system?" Nishita asked. Boyd shook his head. "Any usable DNA on her body?"

Again, Boyd shook his head. "No liquor or drugs present. I discovered faint traces of disinfectant present under her knees and armpits. You will see that in my report. Also, her fingernails were trimmed, as were her toenails. There was no blood in her hair. I suspect it was washed after her death."

"Washed?" Nishita repeated. He flipped through some of the pages with photos of her injuries. "What happened?" he asked running his hand through his hair.

"That's your job, Detective," said Boyd in a world-weary tone and stared at him. "What questions do you have for me?"

Nishita studied the photos. He concentrated on one of her broken fingers. "It takes a lot of strength to break hand bones. I can't imagine these bones on the side of her hand broke from a fall."

"This part of the hand," Boyd held up his hand, pointing to the outside of his palm, "isn't used to break a fall. The wrist bones are the ones that try to stop the fall." He held up his hand with the wrist at an angle suggesting stopping. "At the side of the hand," he mimicked squeezing the first hand, "the bones break when someone grabs it. Also, it happens in a bar fight when fists come out." Boyd made a fist and took a swing in the air. He pointed to the outside of the hand. "These bones break. But you may have seen that as a patrol officer."

Nishita remembered breaking up several bar fights, and once the fight was over, one man sat on the curb, holding his hand, and moaning in pain.

Boyd continued, "The distal phalanges break under pressure, as in squeezing. That is an injury I see mostly in females fighting off attackers."

"Did these bruises happen near time of death?" Nishita asked.

Boyd nodded. "Once her head hit something hard, a rock, or counter, she'd go into the death rattle," Boyd said. "The body convulses and shakes as it dies. But someone had to do a lot of work to clean her and place her in that little car. That takes strength and agility."

"Do you think more than one person was involved?" Nishita asked.

There was no way the doctor knew about the footage from the service station, or what Grant Montgomery told him about seeing someone on the third-floor window of the bookstore. Boyd leaned forward on his elbows and stared at Nishita.

Boyd said, "My job is to determine how death occurred. Who is working with you on this case?"

"Officer Camilla Leila," Nishita said and went back to study the photos.

"No other detective?"

Nishita shook his head. "I was the detective available that day."

Something shifted on Boyd's face. "I am the last person to hear the dead. Their body tells me about their life and death. I see the chronic effects of a bad diet, the toll of heavy drinking, and the destruction of drug addiction. Lena's death suggested several things to me, but if you ask me to swear to this, I won't. Understood?"

"It stays here," Nishita said and placed his hand on the desk.

Boyd leaned back in his chair and began, "This speaks of an argument that escalated to a fight. Perhaps she tried to strike someone, and her hand was grabbed in defense and squeezed until it broke. She fought back and perhaps a second person tried to separate the two. Lena was pushed up against something with this pattern." He pointed to the photo of Lena's bruised back. "That person began to choke her, but the person who choked her didn't have the same strength as the one who broke her hand. See along her neck, the bruises are not deep. The body puts up a fight when faced with death. Lena fought, possibly kicked the person choking her. She had a small bruise on her right big toe. Then perhaps a struggle and she fell and hit her head."

Nishita picked up the thread and said, "The killer or killers cleaned her body and washed her hair to cover the crime. Then put her someplace cold to mask the time of death. It's unusual to spend that kind of time. Killers want a lot of distance once a crime has been committed." He picked up the pictures of the bruises on Lena's back and studied them. The pattern looked familiar, but where? He thought about the wrought iron fence at the front gate of the bookstore. He'd have to go back and take pictures. He'd have to photograph every inch of the bookstore and the clinic. "Lena was five-foot-one and weighed one hundred and five pounds, and two people went after her," Nishita said studying the photo of the bruises on her back.

"You met her before?" Boyd asked.

"I was in the office when she was arrested," Nishita muttered. "Must have been eight months ago."

Boyd rolled back in his chair and reached down to a lower drawer in a metal filing cabinet. He lifted a bottle of bourbon. It was a simple bourbon, not one of the new boutique spirits. Boyd reached behind him, grabbed two empty mason jars, and poured a shot in each. He handed one to Nishita, and they clinked the glass jars. "You'll figure it out."

While they sat and enjoyed good conversation and sipped bourbon, the night slipped away.

TWENTY-ONE

NO ONE ELSE WAS AS DEDICATED to the bookstore as Marta was. Under her management, it rose to an oasis of rejuvenation, revitalization, and renewal. Not to mention the A-list clients with their endless stream of friends willing to spend lots of money. She was the only one who cared. Dudley didn't, not with his current business dealings.

Marta ended the call; her mind raced while she stared out the third-floor window of her mother Sophia's bedroom. It was just after ten. The sun cresting over the hills. If she left now, in forty minutes she'd arrive at Anya's neighborhood and see for herself what was going on. It was imperative to make sure Anya hadn't set up some legal foolery, some way to cut her out.

Dudley would never doubt his golden girl, Anya. Marta had caught Anya stealing from the store—twenty dollars from petty cash here, a piece of jewelry there. Marta had found a pair of pearl and diamond earrings sold by Anya on eBay. And what thanks did Marta get when she pointed these things out? The ice-cold atmosphere around the bookstore was more than she could bear. Anya was shipped off to a boarding school in Ojai, then up to Berkley for college. She only returned to their lives when Lena completed rehab. That entire night of apologizing, crying, and asking for forgiveness disgusted Marta. It made her sick to her stomach. Why don't people get over it and get on with it?

She glanced at the clock by her mother's empty bed. Best to get moving considering she had to do everything. No one was thinking rationally these days. It fell on Marta's shoulders to figure things out as usual.

Flying down the marble steps to the first floor, she made a quick check at the cashier's desk to see if there were messages. None. Business had been slow since Lena's death. Slow was one word for it, extinct was better. The cashier was let go yesterday. If business didn't pick up, they might be forced to close the bookstore and turn exclusively online. It was the trend of the future. Well, that was a conversation for another day. She went to the front door and turned the sign to "closed" and set the locks. Made one final glance out the glass doors, sighed, and picked up her pace past the elevator and to the kitchen.

Morning sun sparkled through the large glass windows brightening the chrome countertops and highlighting the refrigerator doors. Her mother and caretaker weren't at their usual spot; the corner booth soaking in the sunshine and sipping weak tea. It was sad to see the kitchen so empty. The kitchen had always been her mother's domain.

Before her illness, Sophia had made delicacies for customers. Salads decorated with edible flowers, hand rolled pasta with herbs picked from the garden and crumbled feta cheese. Nothing but the finest ingredients for Sophia, balsamic vinegar from Spain, and extra virgin olive oil from Italy.

It was her desserts that brought return customers: lemon and ginger cookies that melt in one's mouth, raspberry meringues that looked like pink and white clouds, mulled wine chocolate cake with fresh figs, plums, and blackberries. Everything was served on exquisite China plates to make people feel like royalty. She'd talk with them for hours while she baked, chopped, and sauteed. The kitchen was the hub, the place of activity, voices, and laughter. But all that stopped after Sophia's stroke.

Dudley had tried to find a substitute chef but had no luck. It tugged at Marta's heart to see the kitchen empty and silent. Small tears formed at the corner of her eyes, but her mood shifted to irritation seeing the blinds open. With a huff, she lowered the ones along the outer wall. The afternoon sun would raise the temperature ten to fifteen degrees and the air conditioner would kick on causing an astronomical electric bill.

But where was her mother? She didn't have time to deal with any distraction from an inept caretaker who barely spoke English and wasn't old enough to wear a bra.

"I'm going out. I've locked up and closed the store," she called out unconcerned if anyone heard or not, and collected her purse, keys, and jacket. She skipped down the back stairs to the underground garage but at mid-step slowed. Her back burned with fear and she turned searching this way and that. Was someone behind her? Was that stupid healthcare girl following her? There was nothing. Once satisfied, she rolled her shoulders to calm herself. She was a little over-emotional. What did that doctor tell her, learn to ride the wave of emotion? Ride the emotion, what an idiotic thing to say.

She opened the entry door into the garage. Meager light came from sunlight streaking in through gaps from under the double garage doors. Musty stale air filled her senses. She detested that odor and covered her nose. The empty spot she dreaded was there. The dove gray sports car wasn't in its corner. Lena was gone.

She pushed the button, thinking, *Stay on target.* It seemed interminable, waiting for the doors to creep upward. She drove out, making sure she pressed the remote to shut the door. Her mouth hardened and she thought, *no sense in making it easier for neighborhood hoodlums to steal what isn't nailed down.*

By the time she turned into Anya's neighborhood, the sun had burned through the morning haze and exposed a cloudless blue sky. Marta parked in a spot that gave her a view of the coffee shop across the street from Anya's apartment yet remained hidden behind a large SUV. Her lip lifted with a sneer of disdain seeing the Royal Herbs house. The apothecary was on the ground floor of the painted blue house. Anya's apartment was on the top floor. As the accountant for the bookstore, Marta knew to the penny how much money the owners of Royal Herbs made from renting that horrid apartment and selling herbs to the Goddess Garden Bookstore. It wasn't only from herb sales but from illegal items Dudley imported. That connection allowed Anya to live in the upstairs apartment for pennies. Anya never understood the ins and outs of business. She did understand, having been raised in the school of hard knocks.

A car pulled up, and the burly man behind the driver's wheel stared ahead. "Anya saw me last night. She may have called the police."

"I thought you were the professional," Marta grilled.

"Look she's smart, probably took some stupid self-defense class in college," the man said, "I've got to hire new guys."

Marta knew where this was headed: more money.

The man turned his face away from Marta. He dug into something on his passenger's seat, pulled up a file, and held it out to Marta. "Report on that detective. He has weaknesses." Marta smiled a cat-like smile and held out her hand. The man jerked the file away from her. "Not so fast."

She nodded, held three fingers up, and stared back. The man countered with a short jerk of his thumb upward speaking the universal language of "higher." Marta pursed her lips and held up four fingers. The man twisted his head in a dissatisfied gesture and held his hand up then added his thumb. Marta gritted her teeth but nodded in agreement. Without further conversation, the man pulled away.

Outrageous, charging five thousand dollars per day to follow someone, she thought. It's not as if Anya were dangerous. Actually, who cared what she did? The tracker on Anya's phone was the best source of information, and perhaps that made the five thousand payment worth the price. It was against the law somewhere, but she didn't care. Daily she received a report of Anya's movements and when she made calls and to whom. That was golden information. But honestly, did that guy just sit in his car and eat all day? She bristled.

She was trying to protect Anya, save her from who knows what Dudley could think up. When it all came out, as everything does, the police and everyone else would see her generosity and compassion.

Anya stepped out of the house and entered the street. Instinctually, Marta ducked. She watched Anya's dark hair weave through parked cars as she made her way to the rustic coffee shop down the street. Feeling perspiration along her neck, Marta clutched her necklace, kissed the amethyst crystal, and whispered a small prayer of thanks that she hadn't been spotted.

The man had told her Anya was meeting Grant Montgomery today. Police must get a warrant to see phone records, but her guy used hackers and got the information as it happened. Seeing Anya, Marta's senses heightened. She heard distinct engine sounds from cars as they drove past, the click of high heels, and the flap of tennis shoes striking cement sidewalks.

Two tall, thin men approached the coffee shop, one clean-shaven with dark hair, the other sandy-haired with a trimmed beard. The dark-haired one was Grant; Marta knew because Lena had changed her will to include him. That was the first time Marta had heard about Lena's past. It was the first time Dudley had heard about it as well. What a night that was. Divorce became a constant discussion.

Did Lena realize how dangerous Grant was? He was the one who'd screamed at the window and broke the geranium pots last Saturday. Marta had feared for her life seeing the rage in his eyes; what would have happened if Lena had answered the door? What would he have done? It was too frightening to think. As if she had been submerged underwater, all sound became muffled while she pondered that question.

In the middle of the journey of life, I came to myself in a dark wood where the straightway was lost.

—Dante Alighieri, *The Divine Comedy*

Lies are short-term solutions to deeper problems. When I completed rehab, I thought my life would be heavenly. After all, I wasn't drinking. I followed the steps, found humility and grace. Like a slow-moving landslide, the lies surrounding me began to unravel. Each lie exposed, I remember thinking, a drink would taste so good now.

—My best, Lena Rezenchov

TWENTY-TWO

LAUGHTER ECHOED AROUND HIM; HE KNEW they were laughing at him. Opening one eye, he could make out blurry shapes of uniformed officers. He sat back against his chair, moved his arm and electric sparks raced down his spine.

With care, he rubbed his neck. "Talking in my sleep?" he muttered. Scattered laughter was the response and the group dispersed. A large cup of coffee was placed on his desk. He looked up to see Camilla wink. The last thing he remembered was Boyd calling an Uber to drive him home. He didn't go home. He came to the office.

"It's a bad habit to sleep at your desk," Camilla said. She sipped her coffee, watched him, and pushed his cup closer.

His right arm was still numb, so he used his left to grab the cup and holding it under his nose, smelled the bitter aroma. Temporarily his mind cleared. He asked, "What did I say?" No answer. "Cam?"

"Something about waves," Camilla said. She sat in the chair aside from his desk. "Were you surfing?"

"I wish." He wasn't one to take stock in dreams and the communication of the subconscious mind. Some say dreams predict the future or are a warning. His dream faded into disconnected images of Emma and ocean waves. He rubbed his scalp to wake up and returned to the massive pile of papers on his desk, all concerning Lena's murder. "Thanks." Nishita sipped the hot liquid.

"How'd the autopsy go?" Camilla asked. "Did you impress Boyd?"

"Friends for life," he said. After the autopsy, he and Boyd had talked. Nishita couldn't remember how long it had been since he'd had a relaxed conversation over a drink. Boyd stirred memories of late-night chats with his grandfather. For years, he'd hoped that his father would unwind and speak with him, but his father had an iron spine. Nishita's therapist told him that this can happen when a parent buries a child. It was best to give him time and gentleness.

Boyd told a few stories of his time in the service and why he became a coroner. Nishita admitted to his concerns about permanently being single. Boyd chuckled at that and told him of his two divorces and how the right woman would show up when he was ready and not before.

He returned to the office to file his report on the autopsy and fell asleep around four. Now he was hungry and hungover.

Camilla said, "Well, best get cleaned up, word circulating is the chief wants to speak with you this afternoon. We've placed bets on his velvet glove speech."

Nishita's head pounded. Not the velvet glove speech. "Great. I'm a mess. Look at this." He gestured to his suit jacket wrinkled from using it as a pillow.

Camilla asked in her get-to-business tone, "Got a clean shirt? In your desk or locker?"

"Yeah." Nishita slipped open the lower drawer of his desk and lifted a white shirt wrapped in dry-cleaning packaging. "But my suit, it won't matter if I have a clean shirt with this." He held up his suit coat unraveling the sleeves.

"Oh my god, you complain like my son. Come on." Camilla stood up and gestured for Nishita to stand. "Off to the locker room. Shower, shave, and brush your teeth. I'll find a one-hour dry cleaner and get this," she tugged at the suit jacket, "pressed." She started to rummage through the front pockets.

"Hey!" Nishita stopped her. "Cut it out." He grabbed his suit coat and pulled out a handkerchief from his breast pocket, a utility knife, and a cell phone from his side pocket. Camilla's eyebrows shot up seeing the cell. "Private phone," Nishita said. "I'm allowed." That reminded him of the papers he went over last night. He handed Camilla a stack. "This was on my desk. Grant Montgomery's cell records."

Camilla read through the text messages from Grant to a cell with only a number as identification. He watched her face cycle through emotions from irritation to a gentle look with her hand over her heart. She said, "Aw, she had a nickname for him, how cute." She flipped a page and kept reading. Nishita felt her move from concerned to confused.

She lowered the paper and said, "It sounds like a mother talking to a son." Camilla's brow wrinkled. "Has it been confirmed that this number belonged to our victim? Does this match with the records we got off the cell from her purse?"

"Dudley blocked releasing the records to his and Lena's phones. His attorney advised him," One more warrant to get. "This number doesn't match the number from the cell in Lena's purse." Camilla and Nishita exchanged glances. He pointed out the last page of the text. "She stopped answering on Thursday. Here." Nishita pointed to the bottom of the page.

Camilla read slowly and studied the page. "He keeps texting her."

"Exactly." Nishita pointed to the bottom of the page, "Here, he said he's landed and checked into his hotel, confirmed their appointment at the bookstore for Saturday at noon, and repeated that he's looking forward to meeting her. This number never responds."

"We need to get phone records," Camilla said. She sat across from him placing the paperwork on the desk. "These texts go back for weeks. If she had an unknown phone, one she kept from

Dudley, she could communicate with Grant privately. Anya mentioned her mother kept secrets."

"According to Anya, Lena and Dudley had started divorce proceedings. We need to contact the attorney who represented Lena," said Nishita. "We could ask Anya and get the name."

Camilla said, "Fisher will know, or know how to find out without tipping off Dudley. Give Anya one more day to herself."

Nishita stood, his intention to walk to the locker room, but soon was defeated as his knees became liquid. He sat back down. He could feel his face flush, whether it was from embarrassment, hunger, or last night's bourbon he couldn't tell. A long cold shower would help.

"Best medicine for a hangover is junk food. Specifically, French fries," said Camilla. He gave her a questioning look. "I wouldn't know personally, naturally. I've been told by others." Nishita guffawed and she punched him on the shoulder. "Wise guy. Hey, get your pants off, I need to get them pressed as well."

He protested, but she shouted out to the bullpen if anyone had extra sweatpants or running shorts for Nishita to borrow. No one answered, so Camilla called out, "Hey Gaston." A six-foot-three dark-haired hulk of a uniformed officer slowly turned around. "Yeah, you. Pretty boy. You got extra sweats in your locker?" The officer nodded. "Get "em. And while you are out, there's a homeless guy sitting outside the front door, goes by Malcolm. Give him this," she handed a ten-dollar bill to the tall good-looking officer and put on her sweetest smile. "Tell him Cam wants a ten-piece with fries and a soda."

The officer held the bill between his thumb and finger and shot a glance to Nishita as if to ask is this for real? Nishita gave him a hard blank stare and the big guy relented and turned to take the stairs down to the first floor.

"Oh, and Malcolm knows he gets to keep the change," Camilla called out. By her body language, Nishita knew she was flirting, and a smile spread across his face. She caught him and snapped her fingers. "Get out of those pants before Gaston returns."

"That's not his name." Nishita chuckled while he hid behind his desk, unbuckled his pants, and handed them to Camilla.

"It is now."

He watched her exit the bullpen. While he was stuck behind his desk in his underwear, he figured it was a good time to start on a report on his conversation with Rebecca and Gus. The cleaning crew of undocumented workers would have to be located. He couldn't hide what he was told, but his concern was that this would disrupt the investigation into Lena's murder. He'd ask for time to dig deeper into how these "cleaners" were connected to both businesses, knowing that the moment he submitted his report an investigation would begin of the clinic. Rebecca would be fingered as the whistleblower. She'd need protection and he wondered how long she could continue working without drawing attention.

Asking the chief for a few more days before sending a truckload of ICE officers was his best bet. A mistake in judgement could be forgiven but incompetence was unthinkable.

"A civil war is the worst of all wars. Its passions run highest. Its hatreds last longest. A civil war is no less a war when it is fought in words and not blood."

—King Edward VIII at the time of his abdication in 1936

When I heard about the king who gave up his throne for the love of a woman. *I thought it was so romantic. A man would rather not be king, with all its wealth, power, and privileges, then lose the love of his life. But I couldn't understand why he was forced to choose. Wasn't he a king? As in all endeavors, the truth was laced with obsession, secrecy, and betrayal.*

—Lena Rezenchov, *Healing Emotional Wounds*

TWENTY-THREE

NISHITA KEPT HIS HEAD DOWN AND focused on the computer screen. It was lucky his desk was in the far corner of the Santa Monica Police station. It gave him the ability to cover he was sitting in his underwear waiting for two things: Camilla returning with his suit neatly pressed and Officer Mateo with food and sweatpants. His attention was divided between the door and the grainy security footage playing on his laptop.

The section of Dudley and Marta leaving the hotel late Sunday intrigued him. Dudley, in dark pants and a light shirt, pushed a luggage cart loaded with boxes to the curb. Marta had on the same raincoat and scarf covering her head. Nishita examined the footage frame by frame hoping to catch something.

Then it hit him: the limo. He leaned in and examined it. It was an older model with faded paint on the roof and a scratch by the rear fender. The driver never got out to assist Dudley. That didn't fit with how wealthy clients are treated. It would seem there were a few cracks in the façade.

A paper bag was plunked on his desk. Next a pair of navy blue sweats, neatly folded, were set alongside. Glancing up, he saw the tall officer with a scowl on his face. The guy was imposing, just as one wants for a law officer. Nishita leaned back in his chair and said, "You're Mateo Russo, right?"

"Teo," he corrected, "I go by Teo. But yes, Detective." He folded his arms across his chest.

It was clear Camilla got under the guy's skin, but not by calling him Gaston. It was the "pretty boy" comment that left a mark. Nishita picked up the sweats and held them in a gesture of thanks. "Don't let Camilla get to you. She was the only girl in a family of brothers. Four. All older."

Teo snorted a laugh of understanding, turned, and left.

Nishita moved slowly. He pushed his chair back from his desk, swung his feet around, and leaned forward to step into the sweats. He vowed never to drink again, at least not on an empty stomach. That reminded him of food, but his stomach flipped with the thought. "Not just yet," he muttered.

He got the sweats on by standing up quickly and lifting the pants over his butt, and he noticed how big they were. Two of him could fit inside. Well, he was not moving from his desk until Camilla returned with his suit. His desk phone rang. "Nishita," he answered.

"Sir?" the young officer said. "There is a woman here for you. Name of Marta Stannis."

His mind raced. He had to see her, but not like this. "Ask her to wait, I'm in a meeting, and I'll come out as soon as possible," he said.

"Yes sir," the voice said and hung up.

Marta. Here. Now. He picked up his cell, and while he walked to the locker room dialed Camilla. She picked up, "What?"

"Marta is at the front desk. Now," he said. Camilla inhaled a gulp of air. "I need you to keep her busy while I clean up. Do you have my suit?" His voice shook. It was probably remnants of his night with Boyd.

"Be there in two shakes, suit in hand." She hung up before he could say anything.

He made it to the locker room, grabbed a towel from his locker, set the shower to cold, stripped, and stepped in. The shock woke any part of his body still asleep. After the shower, he shaved, brushed his teeth, and combed his short black hair. He had to re-wear the same underwear and socks from the night before. Swearing as he pulled a sock on, he decided to keep extra socks, underwear, shirts, and a clean suit in his locker from now on.

"Detective?" Nishita turned and saw Teo standing at the doorway of the locker room holding the pressed suit, "Got your suit."

The newly pressed suit was on a hanger and written on the paper protecting the suit was the store's motto: "Making your clothes camera-ready since 1994." Teo passed it to Nishita with a sly smile. By that smile, Nishita knew Teo had made peace with Camilla or at least teased her back to even the score. "Cam—er, Officer Leila said she'd take the witness to interrogation room three."

What did he know about Marta? She was divorced and had a few speeding tickets but nothing extreme. He put on the suit, checked himself in the mirror, then made his way to the interview room, stopping briefly at his desk to grab a notepad. Officer Camilla and Marta were chatting inside room three. Marta appeared comfortable with a cup of tea, the tag hanging out of the side of her cup. She stood as he entered. He noted her clothing, simple dark pants and a deep maroon silk shirt—expensive and elegant.

"Thank you for seeing me on such short notice." Marta lifted her hand to shake and held his eyes. "As I mentioned to Officer Leila, I wanted to know how the case was progressing. Do you have any leads?" she asked.

It wasn't her question that stopped Nishita but her calm demeanor. Again, she reminded him of a movie star from old films with the practiced modulation of voice, the stillness in her body, and the direct eye contact. Det. Nishita sat across from her and said, "I appreciate you coming in. We've made some progress. We've discovered the identity of the man who broke your planters: Grant Montgomery. Is that name familiar?" It wasn't necessary to tell her that Grant turned himself in after hearing of Lena's death. Information like that he kept close to his chest.

Marta fiddled with her cup. "I don't know a Grant Montgomery. Is he an associate of Dudley's?"

Det. Nishita opened the notebook and looked for a pen, but he'd forgotten to put one in his suit pocket. Camilla silently handed him a pen. "Mr. Montgomery said he was Lena's son. Can you tell me anything about that?"

Marta leaned back in her chair and steepled her hands together touching her mouth. "A son? Are you sure? When someone becomes a celebrity, all sorts of people come out of the woodwork to claim they are long-lost relatives or people who knew them back in high school. They ask for money. A little something to help get through a rough patch or some such nonsense. It's always about money." She adjusted in the chair.

Det. Nishita got the impression that under her calm exterior, she had a lot of energy. He glanced over to Camilla and asked, "Has that happened before? Someone claiming family ties?"

"Of course." She lifted a small handbag pulled out a lace handkerchief, and wiped away tears that ran down her cheek. "Lena trusted too easily."

"You asked if he was an associate of Dudley." Det. Nishita let the implied question linger.

"Well, Dudley is from London and Grant Montgomery sounds English, doesn't it?" Marta asked. She gently dabbed her nose replaced the hankie in the bag and picked off a puff of lint from her sleeve.

Det. Nishita noticed Marta press her lips together. He considered the next question carefully. "Marta, you told me you always went with Dudley to Las Vegas for conferences, but it sounded as if you didn't travel with him when he went overseas, is that correct?"

Marta nodded and kept her eyes cast down.

"Did Dudley keep secrets from Lena?" Det. Nishita asked almost in a whisper. Officer Camilla remained still.

Marta stood. "I shouldn't have come. I only wanted to check on the investigation." She picked up her purse and moved to the door.

Officer Camilla opened the door to the investigation room, giving her the freedom to leave or stay.

Det. Nishita said, "Marta, please help us. Is there something you know that will guide us in the right direction?" He wanted to say that Lena deserved it, but that could alienate Marta and he needed her to see him as a friend.

"Dudley Hardwick was formerly Darian Harkness from London," Marta said. "He left a string of broken hearts and stolen dreams there." She gestured for Camilla to move aside and exited.

Det. Nishita got up and followed her. "Are you saying Dudley is not who he says?" Marta did not stop and moved with speed, threading in and around the officers along the hallway and steps. "Thank you for coming. I will look into it," he called after her, but she was gone. He made eye contact with Camilla. "Darian Harkness," Det. Nishita said. "Let's make some calls."

While attending a conference in Las Vegas, my senses were seduced. Brilliant neon lights hypnotized me, and upbeat music beguiled me. Displays filled with top-of-the-line clothing, Jewelry, and electronics beckoned. On one of my midnight strolls, a pretty woman passed me. While she moved, the skin on her face peeled away revealing rust-encrusted bones. Her face mutated into a distorted skull. I found a large column to dart behind and bumped into a tall man wearing a cowboy hat. He glared. Muttering an apology, I noticed under the brim of his hat, a child's skeletal hand crawled down the side of his neck. I swallowed my scream and went straight to the bar.

—Lena Rezenchov speaking at group session in rehab.

TWENTY-FOUR

Nishita fired off an inquiry to Interpol for information on Darian Harkness in London. He needed to give his height, but while Dudley's driver's license said he was 6'2". Nishita estimated him to be almost two inches taller, so entered that he was 6'4". He used Dudley's birthdate and approximate birth year. Everyone remembered their birthday; mentally, that would be hard to give up, but fudging on a birth year was pretty common these days. If what Marta said was true, Dudley might have changed his birth year, shaving off a few to make himself younger.

"Darian Harkness, Dudley Hardwick." Camilla said both names as if she were tasting each letter. "He kept the same initials. That's interesting."

An automatic response popped up from Interpol, thanking him for his inquiry and stating it would be answered in a timely fashion. He chuckled and wondered if they noticed a detective from the States was behind the inquiry, would the timely manner shorten? The time difference between Los Angeles and London would make it eight o'clock at night there. He decided to give his inquiry twelve hours before following up. He turned to Camilla. "How's research on Hardwick's Imports Export? Any word from Border Patrol on exporting illegal items?"

She shook her head. "Clean."

Nishita wondered why.

Teo arrived at his desk. "Detective? Captain Cooper wants you." Nishita stole a sideways glance at Camilla and saw her eyes light up. Teo nodded and left. Nishita felt the pull between Teo and Camilla, but he didn't see any hope for the pair. He was no relationship guru, not with his past. He did think coworkers shouldn't date because it rarely worked out, and when the relationship failed, work environment got messy.

A worry passed through his mind: Rebecca Lopez and the undocumented workers at the clinic. If the chief contacted INS, that might undermine his investigation. His prime suspect was connected to the center. Nishita rose and collected his notebook.

Camilla leaned in slightly and using her best attempt at an inside voice said, "Teo, er, Officer Russo and I have a bet. I say you will get the glove speech. Teo says no. I've got five dollars riding on it, so, you know," she moved her hands in a circular motion as if to say, 'encourage the chief.'

Nishita said, "Officer Leila, are you suggesting I manipulate the outcome?"

Camilla rolled her eyes. "Don't get all holy on me, Little Ted." She punched his upper arm.

He stifled a laugh and made his way up to the chief's office. The door was open. Captain Cooper, holding a phone to his ear, gestured for him to enter. An imposing man at six-foot-three, with a shaved head and in remarkable shape, Nishita calculated he was in his mid-fifties. When the call ended, Captain Cooper sat and made a note. Without looking up, he said, "Ted Nishita, my young hot shot detective. Tell me about your case."

Right to the point, Nishita thought. "Our victim is one Lena Rezenchov. I met with Dr. Boyd last night and—"

"I know about her injuries and where she was found. What can you tell me about the husband, Dudley Hardwick?" There was an irritation in the chief's voice. He was an honest man who could look you in the eye and see inside your head. It was both admirable and frightening.

Det. Nishita cleared his throat and said, "We have a lead on a possible alias: Darian Harkness from London," Det. Nishita began but was interrupted by Captain Cooper holding up his hand.

He squinted slightly as he stared ahead. "I've spent most of the morning fielding calls from a city councilman, an attorney representing Mr. Hardwick, and a business owner of the Royal Herb Apothecary. They called to tell me of the remarkable impact Mr. Hardwick has made to the community. I expected to get calls from the media asking about the investigation, but I haven't. What do you make of that?"

Det. Nishita paused and pictured the news report he'd watched with Gus Post. The group of mourners in the background looking more like hired actors than real people. At the time it puzzled him, but to hear of no media interest in Lena's death was odd. "I can't say, sir."

"You are suggesting Mr. Hardwick might not be who he says he is."

"I received an informed tip and am in the process of verification." Det. Nishita shifted in his seat.

"Good." Chief Cooper stood and paced behind his desk. "In your report, you mention that Mr. Hardwick is connected to this clinic in Malibu and may have used undocumented workers?"

"Monday night he had an anxiety attack and used the facilities for rest and observation. I believe there is a deeper connection, perhaps financial," Det. Nishita said.

Cooper folded his arms across his chest and stood legs apart. "You suspect he's connected to these undocumented workers?" He stared down at his desk. "If there are undocumented people and possible underage children, legally I have to contact INS."

Det. Nishita drew in a breath. Rebecca would be in danger. He itched to text her or Gus a warning. "Yes, sir."

"You know what I detest more than anything?" Cooper asked.

Det. Nishita shook his head. "Being strong-armed. And that's what I suspect the calls concerning Mr. Hardwick were about. Telling our investigation to back off." He sat at his desk and typed something on his keyboard. "I'm going to hold this report for twenty-four hours. Find something that connects your case with that center." Cooper fluttered his hand in the air in a dismissal gesture. "Get on it."

Once out of the captain's office he took a deep breath; he had twenty-four hours until INS learned about the center. It'd take a few days for them to set up surveillance and gather evidence, but with the possibility of children being exploited, the process would speed up. Rebecca had made it clear not to call her personally. His best avenue was to pass the information through Gus Post. While in the elevator, he searched his phone for Gus's number. It went to voice mail. "This is Detective Nishita. Give me a call as soon as you can. Thanks," he said.

When the door opened, Teo stood before him, blocking the sunlight. Nishita wondered if a man that big ever realized his size. He guessed Teo was about twenty-four and probably was a big kid in school. Big kids get picked on just as much as little ones. Teo must have both inflicted and suffered a few bruises growing up.

Officer Mateo said, "Officer Leila said to get you. Room two."

"Who is in there?"

"Rain Sahota and Anya Hardwick," Officer Mateo said.

Curious, Nishita thought, *first Marta and now Anya*. Most family members call to check on the investigation. A visit signaled the need for personal contact. He noticed Teo was waiting for an acknowledgment. "The sweats did the trick; I made it to the locker room without offending anyone."

Teo winked in response. For a moment, Nishita thought about warning him. Camilla was flirtatious and friendly, but she pushed away any guy that had serious relationship stars in his eyes. Camilla's son was her world. All her attention went into raising him. It was how she dealt with emptiness. He knew that feeling. It was what strengthened their friendship. She'd lost a potential husband; he'd lost a brother. Grief has no timeline.

He knocked on the door to room two. As he entered, the charged atmosphere warned him to tread softly. Unlike the friendly banter between Camilla and Marta hours earlier, this room was filled with hushed voices and a tissue box that had exploded on the table. Anya clutched a wad in her right hand, and Rain sat next to her holding her left hand. Small bottles of water were left unopened on the table.

"Good afternoon," Det. Nishita said taking time to connect with each woman. He sat across from Anya and folded his hands on the table. She looked as if she hadn't slept or eaten for two days. With her rainbow-dyed hair and bangles up and down her arms, Rain was indeed the woman he'd seen on Pacific Coast Highway singing at the top of her lungs.

Rain reached out, shook his hand, and blurted, "Anya is being followed."

Det. Nishita looked over to Anya, who avoided contact.

Rain started, "As you can imagine, sleeping has been nonexistent." Anya mumbled agreement. "So, I pulled the sofa around to face out the front window. It gave us a chance to see the full moon. I spotted a man in a car parked across the street. Around four in the morning, a different car pulled up. That guy got out and approached the first car. The two talked for a bit, then the first car left, and the second guy got back in his car and stayed."

Det. Nishita asked, "You said it was around four in the morning?"

Rain nodded.

"Was this second man there all night?"

Rain shrugged. "I fell asleep around five-ish. I woke at daylight and saw no sign of either car."

"Could it be a security guard for one of the retail stores or a fan of Lena's?" Rain shook her head. The mood shifted in the room. He felt Anaya's fear and Rain's anger.

"We'll send a patrol," he said and made eye contact with Camilla.

Anya set the wad of tissues aside and cleared her throat. "Grant said he spoke with you." She said it as a statement, but her eyes asked the question. "Grant Montgomery? He said he came on Monday."

She hadn't mentioned Grant when they first met. It piqued his interest that she mentioned him now. He didn't expect her to volunteer information at that time. He decided to take it slow in questioning her. The last thing he wanted was to cause her to shut down. "What can you tell me about him?"

Anya turned to Rain, and they connected the way old friends do; silence filled with meaning. "He is my half-brother. My mother had him when she was fifteen and had to give him up." For the first time, Anya looked at him directly. "So much made sense after hearing that."

Secrets choke the life out of a family and leave a film that builds year after year, layer after layer until it has to be dealt with. He asked, "Can you say more?"

"I had a troubled childhood." She folded her arms across her chest.

"That's putting it mildly," Rain scoffed. Her eyes darkened, but she pressed her lips together and signaled to Anya to continue.

"My mother had post-partum depression after I was born and couldn't . . . she couldn't touch me. Sophia took over and became my mother. I suppose that caused the trouble with Marta because she and I fought constantly. It spiraled out of control, and I was sent away to boarding school." Anya furtively glanced to each person. Her shoulders relaxed and she said, "It was for the best. I got away from the crazy environment, focused on my studies, and got a full scholarship to Stanford." Anya sat up for the first time in the interview, and her eyes sparked at her accomplishment.

"And then Lena, I mean Ms. Rezenchov, went into rehab," Rain said.

Anya flushed and repeated the words in a flat voice. "And then rehab." Fine lines raised to the surface of her face. "Family week. Have you ever been to one?"

Nishita shook his head. Years after graduation, an acquaintance from high school went to rehab, or rather he was given the choice of rehab or prison. He chose rehab. He called to ask if Nishita would attend family week. Remembering the teasing the guy dished out to him in high school, he declined saying he was in the final week of police academy and couldn't take time off. He never heard from that guy again.

Anya tipped her chin upwards. "No addictions in your family."

Det. Nishita noted the challenge in her voice. He attempted to lighten the mood. "None with a support group." He wondered if she was jealous or envious, they are similar emotional responses but have different outcomes, "What happened at family week?"

"I learned about the overdressed lawyers pressuring her to sign an NDA, and the money she was paid not to prosecute the father for statutory rape. When she gave birth, the doctors declared her dead and left with her son. If it weren't for two attending nurses unwilling to let her die, she wouldn't have been revived. When she was able, she ran away to Santa Fe, New Mexico." Anya stopped. "It was a lot to take in." Her skin paled, and her eyes dimmed from within. She faced Nishita. "Like I told you, my mother kept a lot of secrets."

"That must have been a shock," he said.

"It caused a rift between my parents. It must have been six months later, my mother asked to stay with me."

Divorce affects both parents and children. Even adult children aren't free from the trauma. He asked, "Did you know Grant and your mother were to meet?"

"Yes," she whispered. "Saturday. I assumed it went well and she and Grant were bonding. When you told me of her death, I called her hotel and found out she checked in on Thursday morning but never returned." She and Rain exchanged a glance.

As Rain stroked her hand, Det. Nishita got the impression Rain was like family to Anya. He asked, "How did you connect with Grant?" hoping to hear of a second phone.

"My mother's attorney had already set up a meeting for her, myself, and Grant to meet. Given the circumstances, we thought it best to keep the appointment," Anya said, "He and I met in his office."

Rain said, "After that meeting, we regrouped at the coffee shop across the street from her apartment. Then Grant's husband spotted a man watching us. He said we should report it."

Officer Camilla leaned in and asked, "Mind if I ask something?"

Rain and Anya nodded. Det. Nishita noticed they moved as one.

She asked, "Did Lena have a second cell phone?"

Anya placed her hand against her mouth while she considered the question. "I don't think so. I never saw one. It wouldn't surprise me."

"If you find an extra cell phone, will you turn that in?" Det. Nishita asked.

Anya pushed an envelope towards him. "This is her unfinished manuscript. It might have something useful."

There was a knock on the door, and Officer Camilla got up to answer. Det. Nishita saw the edge of Tao's face. He and Officer Camilla spoke, and when finished, she returned. She said quietly to Nishita low, "Fisher is here for you."

He acknowledged the message and excused himself, thanking Anya and Rain for coming in, and asked them to describe the man to Camilla and as many details of the car as possible. With that, he slipped out. When he returned to his desk, Officer Fisher was there, wearing nitrile gloves, a large folder in his lap.

"What do you have for me?" Nishita asked.

From the manilla folder, Fisher lifted out a stack of photographs and photocopied newspaper clippings and articles. Spreading the materials out on Nishita's desk, he assembled what appeared to be a timeline for the Topanga area hillside. The first photo was of an old, broken farmhouse with a for sale sign attached to the front steps. It was the same location as the bookstore; the difference to what it looked like now was remarkable. In the photo, the area was barren. A thin one-lane roadway separated the farmhouse from the Wagon Wheel Bar. There was a meager dirt lot for parking and none of the surrounding businesses. "Is this?" he didn't have to finish his question, as Fisher murmured agreement.

He grabbed gloves from his desk drawer and flipped the page of a newspaper article with a photo of a young Lena, Marta, and a vibrant older woman who must be Sophia. All had big smiles, and each woman held between them a deed. "Anyone else besides you touch this?" Fisher shook his head.

Nishita turned on the desk lamp, spreading light on the materials. A collection of remodeling and construction photos were next. He noted a grainy picture of a younger Dudley wearing a hard hat and ordering several men. The title of the attached article stated, "Ground Broken." He assumed it was about the new bookstore.

"When did Lena purchase the property?" Nishita asked.

"1991. Things were grim. The big Hollywood studios were sinking, and set designers and craftsmen were laid off. It was bad." Fisher kept his eyes downcast.

Nishita returned to the packet. There was a ribbon-cutting ceremony at the bookstore. However, the wrought iron fence and garden were absent. What was present was an "Open for Business" sign. Following that photo a series of ribbon-cutting celebrations of surrounding stores—the French bakery, the ceramic store, and the silk fabric store. Next, a spreadsheet outlining the financial boon the bookstore had made the area.

Someone was making a point.

"Who gave you this?"

"It was in my mailbox," Fisher looked directly at Nishita. Seconds ticked by as they stared at one another, but he broke contact and stared down at his hands. "Maybe one of the businesses I asked for security footage from the weekend, but I don't know."

"Is that what you think?" Nishita asked.

Fisher shook his head. "I know these people; we're like family. But who else would do this?"

Nishita picked up his desk phone but before dialing the forensics department asked, "Did you tell anyone else about this?"

Fisher shook his head.

Contemplation Card #23

"A lie runs out as it is overtaken by the truth."

—Cuban Wisdom

Lies are curious things. Some lies are like papercuts, painful but bearable. Some bounce from person to person igniting communities. A lie will take hold until exposed for what it is: a lie. I can only give you this: Every lie has an expiration date.

—My best, Lena

TWENTY-FIVE

NISHITA ESCORTED FISHER CARRYING THE ENVELOPE to the lower level of the Santa Monica Police station where forensics resided. They briefly spoke with Luis. Collecting all the pieces from the envelope, Luis dusted it. The envelope, the most promising due to the tactile material, revealed several prints. Luis said, "I'll submit the results to AFIS and when I get a hit, I'll call." Like many brilliant people, he had a wicked wit and short temper. Nishita considered warning Fisher, but sometimes it's best to stand aside and allow people to learn.

"You expect to find something?" Fisher asked wide-eyed about being in the lab.

"Someone who does things like this," Luis pointed to the envelope, "hand-delivering and not sent through regular mail, will have been involved in other questionable activities. So, yeah, I'll find a trail." Luis looked at Fisher while he spoke. Fisher's cheeks flushed.

Nishita's cell vibrated, and he saw the call was from Gus. "Yeah," he answered.

Gus said, "Got your message, you saw Dudley's announcement, right? A memorial for Lena, tomorrow at the bookstore."

"Tomorrow?" Nishita sought Fisher's eyes, but the young officer returned a blank stare. "Hold on a minute." He lowered the cell from his mouth and asked, "Did you know about the memorial?"

"What you are you talking about?" Fisher held firm in innocence.

Nishita returned to Gus. "When did the announcement come out?" He turned back to Fisher.

"Check your phone, see if you find any hits for Lena and the memorial."

"It went out just a few moments ago," said Gus.

Fisher went to work and found several posts and reposts of a video announcement. He turned the volume up on his phone and held it up. Dudley and Marta stood on the porch of the Goddess Garden Bookstore with Sophia sitting in her wheelchair. Marta, wearing black, held a white handkerchief near her face.

Dudley spoke, "Dear, dear fans, customers, and clients of my lovely wife Lena Rezenchov. Sophia, Marta, and I have been in mourning. Through our grief, we heard your request. You have waited patiently, and we shall deliver. Tomorrow at four o'clock, right here at the Goddess Garden Bookstore, we will honor and celebrate the life of Lena. Please come." The video ended.

Nishita heard his heartbeat in his ears, then broke the silence and watched the video again. This time, he absorbed every detail, where Dudley stood, the absence of Anya, the perfect framing of the bookstore in the background, and the seemingly warm light surrounding Dudley and Marta. This was no quick video setup with a cell phone camera. This was a work of art. When was this filmed? And where was Anya?

"Detective," Gus's voice echoed from Nishita's phone, "you there?"

Nishita had to regroup. "How did you see it?"

"TV news at the station," Gus said. "I thought that's why you called."

Why did he call? Rebecca. He had to warn her. With an impromptu memorial taking center stage, Dudley must feel pressure. He had to hand it to the man, distractions were a smart strategy. This would cut into his time to research the clinic. He'd have to do that tonight. Holding the phone up he said, "Rebecca told me not to call her directly. Will you tell her to be careful at work?"

"She just called. One of the patients passed away this morning and she's been dealing with the mortuary picking up the body, closing patient files, and gathering personal items to return. She should be ending her day soon," Gus said.

Nishita grunted and then checked his watch. It was coming close to six o'clock. There was a lot to do before the memorial. He went back to his phone. "Tell her to call me when she is able."

Hanging up, he faced Fisher, "Did you know anything about this?"

Fisher shook his head.

"You never saw a crew on the lawn of the bookstore filming at any time?" He leaned into the younger man's face, but he shook his head. Nishita had to contact Dudley. He dialed his number.

Dudley picked it up on the first ring. "Detective! How wonderful to have you call." He spoke over traffic sounds in the background.

Nishita didn't need to put his phone on speaker. Both Fisher and Luis could hear him and the rushing traffic. He said, "Sir, I saw the notice for Lena's memorial. Have you set up security and crowd management?" He didn't handle that well, just stepped right into it and didn't prepare.

Dudley scoffed. "I have. And hired an independent security firm."

Nishita noticed an edge in his voice, a slight petulance that he had been questioned. Nishita kept his voice calm. "I'll see you there." He hung up before Dudley filled his lungs to protest.

He turned to Fisher. "Do you know what security firm he is talking about?"

"I can't think of a security team. There were the men that set up the CCTV cameras for the strip mall and the bookstore," Fisher said.

"Well, call them. Find out if they're working the memorial or if they know of anyone who is. Get me a name."

Fisher stood up straight and said, "Yes, sir." He moved to the side and got out his phone.

Luis had been quietly watching. He smiled at Nishita and said, "This case gotten under your skin?"

It was hard to admit, but it had. Why was he so easily upended? This was the first case in which he felt he knew his victim, deeply knew her. He'd met her at the station and saw her kindness for the women in her cell. When she was in rehab, did she see things in Dudley she'd avoided for years? Dudley had faked an anxiety attack and retreated to the clinic to avoid speaking with him. He asked Luis, "Do you know anything about Lena? I mean, have you read any of her books or cards?"

Luis said, "My sisters have her—meditation, no that's not it. Contemplative-"

"Contemplation cards," said Nishita.

"That's the one. They read one to each other every morning." He chuckled. "Whatever floats your boat." He blinked, perhaps seeing something on Nishita's face. "It's not my cup of tea, is all I'm saying."

"I didn't think it was mine either." He thought of Grant, the son she surrendered, and Anya saying Lena had post-partum depression after she was born. Lena had surrendered her to Sophia's care and turned to alcohol. Her public persona and private life were on a collision course. But what tipped it over? He said, "I can't get a solid lead on where or why she died."

Luis pointed to the envelope and materials he was examining. "This will give you something. I'll work it myself and call you with results." Luis placed his hand on Nishita's shoulder and gave a reassuring squeeze.

It was the first compassionate touch he'd felt in a long time. He didn't realize how much he needed it until Luis's hand warmed his shoulder.

"A case gets under a detective's skin. They get frustrated that they can't find the one piece of the puzzle that will tip the scales in their favor. It happens. You've got a long career ahead. Don't let this one break you."

"Thanks," said Nishita.

Contemplation Card # 143

"Compassion hurts. When you feel connected to everything, you also feel responsible for everything. And you cannot turn away. Your destiny is bound with the destinies of others. You must either learn to carry the Universe or be crushed by it. You must grow strong enough to love the world, yet empty enough to sit down at the same table with its worst horrors."

—Andrew Boyd

The story of my life, if it is ever written, is familiar. Someone who had to learn to defend without inflicting damage and not perpetuate a cycle of revenge. But how does one do that? The best advice I was given was this: be in the world but not of the world. In other words, develop a moral compass able to steer away from false arrogance and toward empathy.

—Love, Lena

TWENTY-SIX

FAMILY MEMBERS OF MURDER VICTIMS COMPLAIN. They say the investigation isn't moving fast enough or it isn't following up on possible suspects. So, it was strange to get a packet filled with praise for Dudley and his positive impact on the community as if protecting a family member. But Nishita wondered who were they protecting?

He looked away from Luis, Fisher and Camilla and stared at the packet of materials. He couldn't shake the impression that it all began at the Royal Herbs store. Currently, Anya lived on the top floor of that business. She had mentioned the birth of Dudley's business was importing roots, dried leaves, and tree bark for the store. Before that, he was in construction. Once he and Lena were married, Dudley became the go-to importer, traveling to Egypt several times a year bringing in herbs, crystals, brass tea sets, statues of gods and goddesses, and jewelry.

Nishita still couldn't wrap his head around the fact that Dudley had never been flagged by border police. He tried to picture Dudley entering the country with imports of teas, herbs, and tree sticks cocooned in plastic and labeled. The agents would be looking for contraband; hashish, heroin, and prescription drugs things dogs are trained to detect. But what if he brought in things that didn't smell? Dudley brought in all kinds of rock crystals. Crystals don't smell, and if hidden deep enough would pass border inspection. However, crystals don't bring in the kind of money and influence Dudley had gained so quickly and easily. What could? He closed his eyes to think.

An incident in 2007 tickled his memory in which an under-cover operation arrested two men secretly selling uncut diamonds at a gem show in Arizona. Suddenly, Dudley and his gem show connections clarified. Raw diamonds look like rocks or crystals, don't smell, and can be smuggled without detection. The crystals and gems sold at the Goddess Garden Bookstore started to make sense it was cover for illegally importing raw diamonds and other precious stones.

What if Royal Herbs was complicit in this illegal smuggling? He could check if the store had dealings with the police before, maybe a robbery or break-in from a misunderstanding of what type of herbs they sold. He'd put Camilla on that. But it still left a gap. Royal Herbs, the Goddess Garden, and the Elder Clinic were miles apart in both distance and function. When he opened his eyes, he saw Camilla, Fisher, and Luis staring at him. "What?"

"You all right, Ted?" Camilla asked and stepped closer. "Have you eaten today?"

"Breakfast, remember?" he said.

"That was hours ago." Camilla gave him an incredulous look.

Nishita waved off her protest and began, "I need deep research on Royal Herbs. See if they've ever had any dealings with the police or bad marks from the Better Business Bureau, Chamber of Commerce, anything. Also, dig into the files of both the Elder Clinic and Royal Herbs and get business documents, a DBA or LLC. Check the names on the forms and see if any show up on both."

"Brilliant. We can link them up that way," Camilla said. "What else?"

"Fisher see if that security firm Dudley hired for the memorial has some office or web site. Maybe we can speak with previous clients," Nishita said.

"Right," Fisher said and pulled out his phone and dialed. Someone answered and he said, "Rain, is your father home? Can I speak with him?" He turned away to cover the sound of his call. Fisher returned with an odd look on his face. "Sir, I asked Mr. Sahota, Rain's father, he owns the ceramic tile shop there. Anyway, I asked about the security cameras along the strip mall. He said a friend of a friend of Dudley's installed them at a hefty discount. Mr. Sahota got a funny feeling from the guy and declined."

"Is that why his camera is the only one that recorded the road?" Nishita asked.

"Could be," said Fisher.

"Security firms pop up and disappear faster than door-to-door salesmen," Nishita said.

"Door-to-door salesmen?" Camilla chuckled. "Ted, that's ancient history."

Nishita leaned back in the chair and said, "My grandfather used to tell me stories of men that traveled from small town to small town selling all kinds of things--hairbrushes, bibles, encyclopedias." He smiled, thinking of his grandfather telling stories of the olden days. The memory wrapped around him like a soft blanket.

"That would never happen today," said Luis. "People don't open their doors to strangers anymore."

Fisher cleared his throat in a way that asked for attention. "Detective, Mr. Sahota gave me the security guy's name and number. Should I call?"

"It's probably a dead lead but might as well," Nishita said.

Nishita offered to order pizza. With that they moved to his desk, and each took possession of a nearby laptop or computer and searched police records for photographs and announcements of the three businesses.

Camilla found the first link from 2003. An herbologist, Dr. Ralph Hughes at Royal Herbs, was arrested and given a five-year sentence for using a form of speed in his weight loss tonics. Digging deeper she also connected a Dr. R. J. Hughes as one of the physicians connected to the clinic when it opened in 2012.

"Could be the same guy. He did a few years at Central, and when he got out, shopped around for a new gig. Work in geriatrics might make it easier to hide an illegal past," Camilla said.

It reminded Nishita of Rebecca's son stealing drugs which caused her to lose her RN license and led her to take the job at the clinic. He didn't ask her at the time, but it seemed important now: did she apply for the job or was she sought out?

It was almost ten o'clock when Camilla surrendered and said she had to get home, to at least say good night to her son. Fisher was willing to stay as late as needed and pick up where she had left off, but Nishita told him to go home. It would be a hard day tomorrow. They shut down computers, stretched stiff joints, and went to their cars.

Nishita watched the two drive away and sat for a moment. He was wound up and thought a night drive along the coast might help.

The roads were clear, and with the hum of the engine and streetlights whizzing past, his mind calmed. Before he realized it, he'd driven past the service station where Gus worked, its lights spilling onto the street. Gus was probably mopping the floor or making a pot of chili. Nishita considered stopping, but he decided against it and pressed forward. He continued north on the highway and turned on the road that led to the Elder Clinic. He pulled off the road onto a dirt fire lane about six hundred feet from the center's driveway. There was a large bank of Jasmine bushes, and he tucked his car as close as he could and parked. In the quiet, he questioned the wisdom of being here alone. What did he think he'd see?

He turned off the interior lights, opened the door, and slipped into the cool night. With no streetlights, behind the fences, an ambient glow from landscape lighting gave the area an eerie feeling.

Silently, he moved to the side where the center's driveway met the road and found a large eucalyptus tree to stand behind.

He figured he was about a hundred feet from the center's long driveway, close enough to hear yet far enough away not to be discovered. Discovered by whom? What was he concerned about? But then he heard men speaking and ducked low behind the tree. He couldn't make out what language they spoke. It had a Slavic ring to it, but didn't sound Russian, perhaps a dialect of some kind. Car doors opened and shut, expensive car doors, the ones that make an elegant thwomp sound. He wanted a better look but didn't see any other place to move unless he walked across the front yard of a neighbor. In this part of town, he had to assume security floodlights would flash. He glanced across the street and noted the privacy fence of that home with no cover for him to duck behind. He'd be out in the open, but it might be worth the risk. He took a step toward the fence.

"Don't." A man's voice spoke from behind. Said in a hushed tone, Nishita barely heard it He turned around and saw a figure in the shadows.

"Don't." A man's hushed voice said from behind. Nishita barely heard it. He turned around and saw a figure in the shadows.

"Don't," the man repeated and stepped closer. He was the same man Nishita saw days ago, the tall, lean older man who looked like a surfer. He whispered, "We've met, Detective." The man smelled of wood fires and dirt. "These are not good men. Your badge won't stop them. Come back prepared." The man turned back, slipped into the shadows, and left.

Headlights covered the driveway of the center and car engines spooled up. They were leaving. The words, "don't," rang in Nishita's ears, and he ducked behind the tree and waited. Two dark sedans exited and eased onto the road. He wanted to lean out and grab a license plate number, but he heard male voices in the driveway. Some had stayed. He took shallow breaths and listened.

Cigarette smoke filled Nishita's senses. The men spoke in low tones, teasing one another while smoking. When they finished, he heard the building doors open and close. The outside lights were turned off. Nishita made his way to his car. He waited for another twenty minutes before easing out of his spot and retracing his route.

"Silence like a cancer grows."

—Paul Simon, The Sounds of Silence

From a young age, I was told to listen and never disagree with men. When I broke that rule, the punishment was swift and harsh. One might suppose, now that I'm older and a public figure, I'd have no trouble in any circumstance to express myself. And yet, I have felt a cancer of silence grow within.

—Lena Rezenchov, *Perseverance*

TWENTY-SEVEN

WHEN HE ARRIVED BACK AT HIS apartment, he kicked off his shoes and lay across his couch. Thoughts and fitful dreams wrestled for control of his mind, and he woke every twenty minutes with aches and pains. Around four-thirty, he rose and paced across his living room. By five, he went on his computer and wrote a report for Captain Cooper outlining the previous night at the care center, the number of men, the two sleek sedans, and the strange man with his warning. In his report, he asked the chief to notify ICE and begin an investigation. At six, he texted Gus suggesting Rebecca call in sick for the next few days.

He arrived at the station at eight and fired off an email to Boyd asking if he knew of Dr. Ralph Hughes who worked at Royal Herbs. In less than thirty minutes, Boyd called. Their conversation was brief and to the point. Dr. Ralph Joseph Hughes was an herbologists, not a medical doctor. Nishita could feel the burn in his voice as he complained of a Ph. D.s using the title of Doctor to confuse people. He went on to say Ralph Hughes was sentenced to four years for selling herbal tonics flavored with Dexedrine. Nishita laughed and repeated the word flavored and shared a story of a notorious doctor during the 1930s who gave movie stars vitamin shots for weight loss flavored with amphetamines.

Boyd had said, "Some things never change."

The biggest connection came from the efforts of Officer Fisher. Following the contact Mr. Sahota gave him yesterday, he had dug through the twists and turns of phone numbers, and name changes, until he found a John T. Towel living in Las Vegas. Mr. Towel was Marta's ex-husband and owned a limousine service working outside of Vegas. Nishita remembered Marta had said she was divorced but brushed it off saying it happened a long time ago. "Fool me once," Nishita said when he heard that news and then told Fisher to locate Mr. Towel.

It was close to two o'clock when he and Camilla headed out to attend the memorial service. Topanga and Chatsworth police were called in to manage crowds and traffic—which Nishita thought strange. Dudley had said his private security firm would handle the event. Perhaps what he meant to say was his firm would handle his safety.

Camilla pulled into a fast-food drive thru. "What do you want?"

Nishita brought himself out of his thoughts and noted the type of fast-food Camilla had chosen. "A number eight and sub onion rings for fries."

"Don't get onion rings; get the fries." Camilla gave him a sidelong glance. "Your breath will reek of onions during the memorial."

He made a guttural sound. "Fries, then." It didn't really matter what he got; he ate it so fast he barely tasted it. At least it provided energy.

By the time they reached Topanga Canyon Road, traffic crawled. Vans filled with fans clogged the main roadway. As they neared the spot where Lena's car was found, Nishita heard music and recognized the same group of musicians he'd seen that first night. The congestion was a gapers' block as people had pulled off to the side of the road to hear the music. The group sang old hymns, voices rising and falling in harmony. Passersby sang along. The leader of the group, the thick man with the guitar, welcomed each voice to the prayer. Nishita's throat tightened and the corners of his eyes burned as he watched.

Once past the singers, the road cleared and in a few quick turns the bookstore came into view. Colorful banners and signs directed participants where to park. Nishita thought it looked less like a memorial and more like a carnival. People meandered across the road carrying paper plates overloaded with food. The bookstore, decorated with purple flowers and twinkling lights sparkled. A traffic cop, dressed in a vibrant yellow vest and helmet, directed Camilla to park at the far side of the Wagon Wheel Bar and Grill. The closer they got to the restaurant the more intense the aroma of meat sizzling on a barrel pit filled the car. Nishita's mouth responded and he noticed numerous cooks and a line of hungry customers. The French bakery had a blue and white striped cart selling espresso and pastries, and next to that was a yellow and white striped cart which offered sodas, water, and fresh-squeezed lemonade.

They parked alongside the ambulance. Officer Camilla waved to Steve, the EMT who had helped remove Lena's body from the accident. "Why are you here?" she asked.

"Precaution." Steve sipped on a large cup of lemonade.

"Quite a memorial," Det. Nishita said.

Officer Camilla lifted her hands and said, "Best get started."

They crossed the street toward the bookstore, and for the first time Nishita got a view inside the underground garage. Two tables covered in dark cloths barricaded the entrance. One table was dedicated to selling volitive candles to be used for the formal part of the ceremony. The second table sold ceramic tiles in which a person could etch their name. Those tiles would be placed along the walkway in the succulent garden. Both tables were staffed by young women. Nishita guessed the women might be eighteen, but without them using the usual distraction of cell phones and chatter an eerie feeling came over him. It was probably enhanced by the music as a group of violinists played light music near the open garage.

Both he and Officer Camilla gravitated toward the tables. It appeared only one of the young women spoke English; the others had to be directed what to do.

Officer Camilla said in a low voice, "I'm going to check this out and see if I can find out where they're from."

Nishita let her wander. He wanted to get a view of the front of the bookstore, as that seemed to be the focal point for the ceremony. The last rays of sunlight dimmed and the bookstore, despite surrounded by sparkling lights, looked ominous. The night air cooled and standing propane heaters were ignited offering warmth. He decided to stay in the background and observe.

The first thing that caught his eye was Rain Sahota and her rainbow-colored hair. She was in a friendly chat with Grant Montgomery.

The crowd gravitated toward the front of the bookstore. Two men were setting up a microphone on the front porch. A woman was brought out in a wheelchair. Her eyes showed intelligence and Nishita realized this was Sophia Stannis, Marta's mother. She was placed to one side of the microphone by a female healthcare worker wearing a blue smock. This woman matched the young women at the tables in age with similar facial features.

Marta Stannis exited the front and with staccato movements of her hands directed the worker to step back. Dudley Hardwick followed Marta and waited for his moment to speak. Anya Hardwick slithered out and stood behind Sophia as if her wheelchair could protect her from the crowd. Rain and Grant moved in but stayed to the back.

Nishita turned his attention to Sophia. He could see the effects of her stoke. The right side of her face drooped. However, the left side was sharp and searched the crowd. It was obvious, even in her fragile state, that Sophia ruled. Dudley turned to her, and she gestured with an infinitesimal proceed motion. Seeing that gesture, Nishita wondered whose idea it was to hold the memorial. All this time he'd suspected Dudley.

Dudley stepped up to the microphone. He spread his arms out and lifted his head upward, closed his eyes as if in prayer. The crowd leaned in. Nishita observed a strange silence. It was as if the entire crowd waited for what Dudley would do. He lowered his arms and said in a big voice, "Thank you for coming tonight. To see your kind faces means a lot to us." He turned and looked at Marta. She stared back at him. Dudley returned to the mic. "Lena was a visionary. She inspired us to do better, to reach higher and welcome challenges."

The crowd murmured.

Dudley acknowledged eyes that met his. "Through her books, seminars, and teachings, she made an impact." His voice rose as he spoke. "Lena wanted people to believe in their creative power. People responded to her love and guidance."

Nishita noticed Sophia staring at her palm resting in her lap. He'd seen his mother do that exact gesture at his brother's funeral. It was how she controlled grief. Public displays of large emotions were frowned upon in his family. As he grew up, he'd wished his mother would wail like the mothers from stories of ancient rituals, release it from her body—but she never did.

He glanced at Anya, huddled next to Rain. Grant stood behind as if to catch Anya should she fall. He wondered if she was doing her best to remain in control. The crowd, went eerily still, waited for Dudley to continue.

Dudley opened his arm to his side, hand open. Marta snapped her fingers at the woman in the blue smock. She reached in her pocket and pulled out a small white candle and offered it to Dudley. Without acknowledging her, he accepted the candle and lifted it up for the crowd to see. "Let us light our candles together, to honor Lena and her devotion to others. She said the best life was serving others. We love you, Lena." Then he covered his mouth with his hand. Marta put her arm around his waist. Dudley became a soldier with eyes front and shoulders back.

Marta said, "Light your candles for Lena." She snapped her fingers to the woman in blue. Marta's behavior made Nishita wonder if this woman was a healthcare worker or an assistant. The woman picked up a tray of candles and lighters. Marta selected a candle and lighter. The worker went to Dudley next. He appeared to pause before selecting a lighter. He licked his lips and finally chose one. Finally, Anya and Rain were last to get candles. Marta lit her candle and held it up. At her signal, each lit the white stick candle.

The crowd followed suit and held their candles upwards. Soft music began, and Nishita saw the string trio had moved to the front yard below the porch.

A woman standing next to him asked, "Don't you have a candle?"

"Sorry, no. I arrived late," he said. It wouldn't work to tell her he was a detective. That would give him undue attention.

"Well, you can always purchase a ceramic tile and write your name on it for the herb garden as a way to honor Lena," the woman said with derision in her voice.

"Is that what that table is for?" he asked. The woman pursed her lips and nodded. "Good," muttered Nishita. He glanced over to the walkway to the garden.

There was a blood-chilling scream from the middle of the crowd. The sound shot up his spine. He touched his gun along his hip and began to move. Nishita spotted, under one of the heat lamps, people gathered around a woman. There was a great deal of muttering, then a woman's voice cut through the night, "I saw her. Lena! Up there."

There was a whooshing sound from the crowd, a quick intake of a collective breath. All eyes looked up to the bookstore. He was tempted to check the reactions of Marta and Dudley, but his immediate concern was the woman. He pushed his way through to the area, wondering if she needed help.

He tried to reach her, but others also rushed and blocked his path. Holding up his police badge, and shouting, "Police, let me through," helped. People slowly moved aside. Camilla had entered from the other side. They made eye contact. She was on her radio, ordering the ambulance.

The woman was on the ground, her head cradled by a man. The man looked just as distressed as the woman.

Det. Nishita wondered if they were married. "Are you all right mam?" Guessing the woman was probably in her early fifties, he repeated, "Mam, are you alright?"

Her eyelids fluttered, and she muttered to the man holding her. "I saw Lena, in the top window," she said.

"Comin' through. Please step aside." Steve carried his gear through the crowd while his partner pushed a gurney.

Nishita backed away to give Steve and his partner time to assess the situation. The woman kept muttering that Lena was in the window while Steve checked her pulse and lifted her lids. Ever gracious, Steve never disagreed with the woman telling him she had seen Lena in the window. He asked if she took medications. Once satisfied the woman was physically fine, he escorted her to the gurney and told his partner to take her to the van and rest.

Det. Nishita asked. "Is she okay?"

Steve kept his voice low and said, "Tired, dehydrated. She and her husband drove twelve hours straight from Santa Fe to get here for the memorial. She's a little emotional." Steve whispered, "Don't repeat that."

It occurred to Nishita there might have been times when paramedics were called to the bookstore. He asked Steve, "I realize this is slightly out of left field, but I was wondering if you knew about any emergencies in which one of the family called 911?" He gestured at the bookstore.

Steve stood still and looked as if he were picturing past events. "Come to think of it, we were called when Sophia Stannis fell. Must have been last summer."

"She fell? Where did she fall?" Nishita asked.

"In front of the elevator in the hallway. Ms. Stannis was still lying on the floor when we arrived. Marta couldn't move her. We got her to the hospital pretty fast. I suspected it was a stroke. Doctors confirmed it," Steve said. His partner waved and Steve responded. "I'd best get going."

"If you remember anything else, call," Nishita said. Steve gave a salute and walked back to the van.

Things were more stressful in the household than the public was allowed to know: Lena's DUI, her time in rehab, then her disappearance. Curious there was no record that the police were called.

Camilla tapped him on the shoulder and said, "I'm going to walk across the street. See what's happening." She pointed to the Wagon Wheel Bar and Grill.

Most of the crowd had left the bookstore and wandered over to the bar. The restaurant owners must have prepared because Nishita saw corn on the cob, turkey drumsticks, hamburgers and hot dogs on paper plates clutched by hungry customers.

He turned back to look at the front porch of the bookstore. Dudley, Marta, and Sophia had vacated. Anya was speaking with well-wishers. Rain was busy managing the long line of people waiting to express condolences. He walked up the steps and slipped into the bookstore.

Once inside, he saw customers carrying shopping baskets filled with candles, books, and gemstones to a cashier. Nishita couldn't get his mind around it. They were attending a memorial service. Didn't they realize she was murdered, or had that part of the story been suppressed and the drunk driving story had taken hold?

Dudley and Marta's voices could be heard in the kitchen. He walked slowly towards that area but stopped in front of the elevator. A large marble staircase was to one side of the elevator. The cage was empty. Perhaps Sophia had been taken upstairs. The grate of the elevator sparkled under the spotlights. The grate was iron in a woven pattern sprayed gold. He walked up to the grate and touched it. Pressing his face against the grate he tried to get a view of the bottom of the shaft. Raised spikes were along the diamond pattern. He must have pressed against it too hard because his cheek stung. He pushed the palm of his hand against the metal cage. He pushed harder and then lifted his palm. The indents matched the pattern of bruises along Lena's back.

All sound stopped.

He stared at the elevator and over to the marble steps. He examined the creases where the marble sections met. There were pale stains in the grout.

He reached for his badge and held it up. He shouted but his voice sounded muffled. "Police. Everyone out of the bookstore. Now!" He barricaded his body in front of the elevator. He could barely hear himself speak. He shouted, "I am Detective Ted Nishita. Leave the bookstore, now!" With his other hand, he picked up his cell and pushed the speed dial for Camilla. As soon as she answered he said, "Cam I'm in the bookstore, I need you." He heard some response and hung up.

Dudley and Marta peered around the corner from the kitchen. "What are you doing, Detective?" Dudley asked.

Det. Nishita commanded, "Do not come any closer unless you want to be arrested for obstructing a police officer in the line of duty. Exit the building. Now." Heat rose in his neck as he glared at Dudley. Dudley lost all color, his mouth tightened, and he lifted his hands in a sign of surrender and backed away.

"There are more things in heaven and earth, Horatio, than are dreamt of in your philosophy."

—Shakespeare, *Hamlet*, 1.5 165-66

I was once told that reality was a series of collective agreements and because I went against the collective in seeing spirits, my path would be difficult. I wouldn't trade what I've seen and heard and experienced for an undisturbed life.

—Lena Rezenchov, *Perseverance*

TWENTY-EIGHT

OFFICER CAMILLA'S VOICE CUT THROUGH THE din, demanding people move out of her way. When she came into view her hand was on her hip holster and eyes alert. She paled when she saw him. Immediately she scanned the few remaining gawkers, some recording the event with cell phones.

Satisfied the people weren't a threat, Officer Camilla moved in. "Are you okay?"

Nishita nodded, ears ringing. His voice sounded miles away as he said, "Call Luis." He wanted to tell her this was the crime scene, but there were too many eyes watching, and way too many cell phones. He suspected Dudley, standing just around the corner, was recording as well.

"You're bleeding." She pointed to his hand.

Glancing down, he saw the blood pooling where he had pressed it against the grate. Blood seeped from thin wounds like tiny papercuts on his palm stained the cuff of his shirt. Out of his top suit pocket he retrieved a handkerchief and pressed it against the wounds.

"Your face, too. What happened?"

He touched his cheek and saw blood on his fingertips. This is insane, he thought and said in an intimate tone, "Secure the area.

We need a warrant. Call Judge Robinson. Tell him I have reason to believe I've discovered the crime scene. He pointed his thumb behind his shoulder, the golden cage of the elevator glinted under the spotlight.

The tiniest smile crept across Officer Camilla's face. She nodded, turned and addressed the crowd, "Okay, show's over. For those filming, please capture my good side. She posed and said, "It's this one."

A woman holding a basket of items, complained that she wanted to buy books and candles. A few other voices chimed in. Officer Camilla told them to line up at the cashier and purchase what they had in hand, but for now they couldn't continue shopping. There was more grumbling. She suggested, "You could purchase these things from the bookstore's website and have them delivered to your door and wouldn't that be lovely." A big man in the crowd chuckled and somehow that dissipated dissention.

With his handkerchief, Nishita wiped his cheek. It was odd because he didn't remember Lena's back having cuts. Bruises, yes, but no cuts. Was she wearing a heavy jacket and the grate didn't make it to her skin? When he found her, she wore black linen pants and an aqua and purple silk shirt. If she died here, the killer had time to hide or dispose of bloody clothes. It would take a miracle to find those.

Officer Camilla managed to keep people away from the hallway with humor and a no-nonsense manner while handling a call on her cell. Det. Nishita heard voices filled with impatient curiosity asking Officer Camilla for information. She smiled and gave them none. It would only take one disgruntled loudmouth to twist a peaceful situation to an ugly one. Somehow, she kept the peace.

He tightened his jaw and widened his stance. Derailing solving Lena's death wasn't an option for Nishita. This case had to move forward with precision. Most murders are disorganized messes. That's what was so baffling about this one, it was too organized.

There were too many dead ends, too many alibis validated through video evidence. It was the cover up he'd spent the last week trying to dismantle, and with the stain along the grout, he could find out. The why was key.

Dudley, with cell phone in hand, appeared from the kitchen and shouted "Detective! This is a memorial for Lena. You are ruining it!" Marta stood behind Dudley, blocking the kitchen doorway.

"Mr. Hardwick, I'm sure you and your attorney, and say hello for me, know the law verbatim. I have found probable cause to search here," Det. Nishita said his voice under control. He circled his arm to illustrate the hallway. He didn't want to draw attention to the elevator shaft.

"My lawyer will be here soon," Dudley shot back.

"That is your right. You should know, I've reached Judge Robinson. The judge was in the process of issuing a warrant for your wife's cell phone records. This," he said and circled his arm, "is an easy addendum."

Dudley gritted his teeth. "This is a witch hunt. You've already decided I'm guilty and you're searching for anything to validate that assumption." Dudley turned and brushed past Marta. She followed him into the kitchen.

Officer Camilla finished a call and leaned in. She whispered, "Judge Robinson has left for the day. It's his wife's birthday, and he's taking her out to dinner."

Nishita sucked in a big breath.

Camilla lifted her hand to calm him. "We've left messages on his phone and a black and white, with the new warrant on their phone, is on their way to the restaurant."

"How long?"

"Maybe fifteen," Camilla answered.

His stomach caved. *Stay calm* he told himself. He looked to his right and stared at the faint stains in the grout. Marta had told him they had had cleaners over the weekend Lena was away. But just how deep a clean? If they used regular cleaning products, blood would still be present, and they'd get a solid sample. If they used bleach, then he was screwed.

Fifteen minutes would test every ounce of his patience. He let out a slow breath. His scalp prickled with the release.

Camilla's cell rang. She listened, briefly spoke, and then hung up. "Fisher says they're packing up the tables outside. Closing down the memorial."

"I guess I did ruin it," said Nishita. He'd attended other memorials, but nothing like this with tables for fans to purchase books, and candles and write their names on tiles to be placed in the garden. This was more of a sales event. He wondered about the young workers sitting quietly. Were they connected to the cleaners at the clinic? Is that how Lena knew to warn Rebecca? "Camilla? Did we get the make and model of the vans that arrived?"

"I'll get Fisher on it," Camilla said. She turned and made the call.

Nishita took a moment to scan the surroundings. The bookstore had emptied. He heard hushed voices in the kitchen area. By the sound of it there were four different voices. Dudley's deep voice was the only one he recognized.

"In the beginning, the taste of power is sweet, savored on the tongue, like fine wine. It whispers promises in your ear and pretends to be your friend. It is easy to become addicted to this feeling."

—Rahma Krambo

The athletic, the smart, and the popular teenagers extorted tremendous power at my high school. Excluded from these groups, I adapted until something happened that changed my status. It had to do with my after-school job at a grocery store. The owner selected me for a marketing campaign. Wearing my apron and name tag, I was photographed helping a customer. These photos were used in advertisements in local newspapers and flyers.I became a celebrity. The attention filled me like helium. I began to seek revenge against those that had snubbed me.Seeing my personality change, my grandmother sat me down to set me straight. She said everything from businesses, to countries, to celebrities rise and fall.How well you treat people as you rise will soften your inevitable fall. Little did I realize, my fall had already begun.

—Lena Rezenchov, *Spiritual Freedom*

TWENTY-NINE

HOW LONG COULD HE BLOCK THE hallway? How long could he grip his cell phone? He relaxed his hand. If Dudley and his attorney presented a legal defense before the warrant arrived, Nishita would have to leave. Evidence around the elevator shaft would vanish. It was a gamble he had to take. What if Judge Robinson wasn't located? What if the officers couldn't get him to sign the search warrant, what then? Dr. Boyd was a close friend of Judge Robinson. Could he? Dare he?

Nishita texted Boyd: I need help. Need Judge Robinson

to sign off on a warrant for my case. We can't locate him.

Boyd texted: Funny, I'm sitting next to him. I'll ask, but you owe me.

Nishita texted: Agreed.

From the top of the staircase, he heard light footfalls. "Please?" a soft female voice asked.

Looking up, he saw the healthcare worker in the blue smock. Gesturing with her arm, she was asking if she could walk down the steps.

Marta came out from the kitchen and faced the woman. The healthcare worker stopped. In the same soft voice, the woman said, "Miss." She lowered her head. "The bus."

Marta faced Nishita and demurely folded her hands in front of her chest. "Detective, may she come down?" She tilted her head to the side.

There was something about Marta's manner that raised the hairs on the back of his neck. She was back to her submissive behavior; Geisha Marta had returned.

Maybe if he played it right, she might soften. Nishita bowed at the waist hoping she'd see it as deferring to her authority and said, "Of course." Turing to face the woman he said, "Keep to the far side of the stairs." He used the hand that gripped the bloody handkerchief to point where the woman should walk. She saw the blood and recoiled. He tucked the cloth in his front pocket.

The woman tip toed down. Marta stopped her once she got to the bottom of the steps and held out her hand. The woman bowed her head. She fumbled, unbuttoning the front of the blue smock. Her nervousness mounted until she finally succeeded. She slipped out of it and handed it to Marta. The woman waited, head bowed, while Marta inspected the smock for stains or tears. Marta grunted approval. The woman bowed and shuffled into the kitchen. Nishita heard Dudley speak but couldn't make out the words. A small exchange and the back door opened. There were more voices and the back door closed.

He picked up his cell and texted Cam: Who's leaving?

She answered: Driver taking workers away. Got license #.

When he looked up Marta was staring at him. "I'm not leaving your side."

"I appreciate the company. It is a little lonely here," Det. Nishita said. He wondered what happened to Geisha Marta.

"If you get the urge to plant anything, I'm here," she said. She leaned against the far wall and crossed her arms in front of her.

"You have security cameras. Three have a solid view of this hallway," he pointed to the camera at the top of the landing, the one on the left corner and one in the bookstore facing him, "and have recorded my every move."

Marta held her stance. Geisha Marta was long gone, and Cold Marta had taken over. His cell rang. The screen said Miles Robinson. He took a deep breath and answered. "Detective Nishita."

Detective," the judge began, "you do realize it is my wife's birthday."

"Your Honor, I apologize. I wouldn't intrude if it weren't vital," he answered.

"Oh yes, vital," he said lengthening the words. "I've already been called by Mr. Hardwick's attorney."

Det. Nishita swallowed. "If I could say."

The judge interrupted and spoke plainly. "I don't like to be hounded by detectives on my off hours, but I like it less from pushy attorneys twisting the law as if I don't know it word for word."

Nishita heard his heartbeat. He reminded himself to give the judge time to process. If he interrupted him, it showed disrespect. The judge might turn adversarial. That wouldn't work for the case or his career.

"I will agree to this: You may have one technician to search the area for blood residue. You will not search for the victim's cell phone. At this time, it is not a useful piece of evidence. We are already requesting the cell records."

"Yes, Your Honor. I understand. If I happen to find a blood trace that connects to the bottom of the elevator shaft, and I see the cell phone, what then?" he asked in his most acquiescent voice mimicking his Geisha grandmother.

"Only search the elevator shaft if the blood trail leads you there. All you are to find is blood. Nothing more. Understand?"

"Yes, Your Honor."

"Now, I have signed off on your warrant with my changes and it will show up on the police computer system. If you don't mind, I'd like to get back to my dinner celebration" Judge Robinson hung up.

Nishita couldn't stop the smile spreading across his face. He got his warrant. His cell buzzed. It was Camilla.

She texted: Got warrant.

As he put his cell in his front pocket, he couldn't stop smiling. Lifting his gaze, he met Marta's. Her eyes glared red sparks, and her face mutated into a pasted-on smile. She pushed her body forward with her shoulder and walked into the kitchen.

His scalp prickled. Cold Marta was formidable. Would he ever see Geisha Marta again?

Camilla entered the bookstore with the warrant on her cell screen. "Here we are."

Nishita accepted it and scanned it quickly. It had the hallway and the elevator grate included in the blood search. Now to contact Luis. "Call the station and see when we can get a technician here," Nishita said.

"Way ahead of you."

"You already called?"

Camilla smiled and gave a slight nod. "I knew we'd get the warrant, so while waiting I called," Camilla whispered. "Good thing I did, because Luis was just leaving," She kept her voice low. "I promised him dinner for two at the Steakhouse if he'd get here as soon as he could."

Nishita's jaw dropped. That was the top restaurant in Santa Monica and beyond expensive. "Who's going to pay for that?" Nishita asked.

"Well, he didn't go for it." She tisked her tongue. "Something about trying to lose weight. So, I did the next best thing: I begged. He'll be here in about ten."

Dudley turned the corner, his cell phone in hand. "Detective, I heard you've gotten your warrant. When will we be forced to suffer a parade of technicians?"

"Parade?" Det. Nishita repeated.

"Should I say army? With their dirty boots tracking in this house. My house." His voice rose in pitch. "You push in here just like you pushed your way into the clinic at all hours. And what did it get you? Nothing. You will find nothing here." He leaned in close to Nishita.

"And if that happens, I will apologize for the inconvenience," Det. Nishita replied. He stood firm keeping his gaze fixed on Dudley who finally grunted and turned away. Nishita noted the man still had his phone in hand. He could be recording their conversation. Perhaps he was trying to goad him, get some kind of reaction or evidence against him? Turning to Camilla, he asked, "Do you have your body camera on?"

Nodding, she snuck a furtive glance to the kitchen. Voices were heard echoing in the stainless steel kitchen, but words were difficult to distinguish. Dudley huffed and walked into the kitchen closing the door behind him.

"Good." He wanted to say more but held his tongue.

Camilla's shoulder radio beeped. "Yeah?" she spoke quietly into the microphone.

Nishita turned back to the hallway to study how Lena had died: pushed up against the elevator grate. Being pushed and choaked would explain the bruises on her back. She fought. Was that when the side of her hand broke? She didn't die of strangulation. Was she pushed, or did she slip and fall against the edge of the marble steps? That might explain the shape of her head wound. There was no way the steering wheel of her car made that dent on the side of her head.

"Luis is here," Camilla said.

"That was fast." He stepped away from the hallway when he saw Luis' big frame wearing a blue forensic suit. In gloved hands, he carried a black case.

Nishita handed over the scene. Camilla stepped in to assist and put on nitrile gloves. She got out the yellow tape and sectioned off the area. Luis set his bag on the outside of the tapped area. He pulled out a camera. He slowly and methodically took pictures of the entire area. Voices from the kitchen hushed. The click-whirr of the camera was the only sound.

Luis stared at the rim along the edge of the steps. He asked Camilla to hold the camera and got down on his knees. He took out a mirror from his belt and checked under the lip. Putting the mirror back on his belt he took out a prepared vial and what looked like a scalpel. He scraped under the rim of the step and tapped the particles into the vial. Luis looked back to Nishita. Holding out his blue glove, dark flakes were on the tips. He removed his gloves and placed them in a small baggie. Then he put on new gloves.

Watching him focus on the layout of the hallway Nishita could see him work through the same questions. Luis returned to his bag, retrieved luminal spray and a handheld black light wand. He gestured to the bank of floodlights. "Is there a way we can shut these off?"

"Checking," said Camilla. She walked over to the cash register area and found a bank of switches. Testing each, she located the correct one to turn out the floodlights over the hallway.

"Turn them back on for a moment," Luis said. She turned the lights back on.

Nishita wondered if the switching of the lights might bring in Dudley and Marta, but they made no noise in the kitchen. Were they even there?

Luis sprayed the floor and along the base of the steps and the elevator grate. Surprisingly, he sprayed the walls. He signaled to Camilla. She shut off the lights and the room went black. He switched on the black light wand.

A bright blue glow illuminated the grout between the marble tiles like a checkerboard. Luis moved to the elevator, sprayed and the light showed tiny blue specks in one small round area along the crisscross pattern. Luis went to the wall next to the bottom of the steps and small blue dots lit up along the baseboard.

Sadness filled Nishita.

He should feel triumphant—he'd gotten what he was looking for—but he didn't feel anything. A wave of regret washed over him. He should have done this when he was here six days ago. His eyes burned.

"When you find no solution to a problem, it's probably not a problem to be solved, but a truth to be accepted."

—Unknown

My problems were of my own making. I fashioned them brick by brick. Each time I spent more money than I had, I culled the clay. Each time I spoke out of anger, I forged the bricks. Each time I drank to avoid feeling, I assembled the walls. Secure in the illusion I was protected, I never saw the flaws until it all came crashing down. Fantasy and reality collided. Reality won.

—Lena Rezenchov, *Courageous Love*

THIRTY

"WHEN CAN WE GET DNA?" ASKED Nishita.

Luis packed the black light wand in his case. With a heavy voice he answered, "3-6 months."

"Come on," Nishita said, "this is a top priority case."

Luis let out a long sigh and his shoulders slumped. "All detectives say that. I answer the same thing: It's not my call."

Wishing he could take it back, Nishita said, "You're right." He stopped and looked at Luis noticing dark circles under his eyes. He was here as a favor to Camilla. "You've really helped us out," he said and decided to send the restaurant gift card to Luis anonymously.

"What's with the blood?" Luis asked pointing to Nishita's side pocket.

Looking down, he saw the bloody handkerchief spilling out of his pocket. "I pressed my palm against that grate and I got these little cuts." Nishita lifted his hand to show Luis. "They bleed like crazy."

"I'll need a fresh sample from you to eliminate your DNA," Luis said. "It looks like one area was your palm because of the position and height, but on the other I found a long dark hair. Did your victim have any cuts on her scalp?" Luis pointed his finger to the back of his head.

The late-night meeting with Dr. Boyd felt like months ago. He had drunk a lot that night but that's no excuse not to remember any points from the autopsy.

Luis wore a sly smile. "You worked with Dr. Boyd?" He chuckled when Nishita nodded. He said, "It's past eleven. I'm going to finish up here and get back to the station."

"Sure, sure, sure," Nishita said. "Thanks, again." He looked him directly in the eyes. Luis gave him a thumbs up and went back to his work.

Punching his fist into his hand, Nishita walked over to Camilla. "What's next?" she asked.

Nishita was ready to say they should arrest Dudley but seeing Camilla's shoulder camera he bit his tongue. He said, "I'd like to get Dudley and Marta's statements on record. Blood evidence is enough to ask them to come to the station." Polite, not too pushy.

"It's been quiet back there. Let me check." Camilla made her way to the kitchen.

The bookstore was empty. He glanced from security camera to security camera and wondered if the cameras recorded that fateful night. If so, they had probably been erased.

"Ted, they're gone," Camilla shouted.

She sounded as if she were outside. Nishita jerked forward, "Say again?"

"Gone. Dudley, Marta, and the men with them. Gone," She ran into the main area, and was out of breath. "No cars in the driveway."

He hustled into the kitchen. The smell of coffee brewing caught his senses. He noted the used coffee cups on the counter, but the room was empty of people. He went to the back door and looked out into the vacated driveway, and his thoughts raced. He assumed Dudley left because his attorney advised him to do so. Nishita called him. It went straight to voice mail. "Hey Dudley, this is Detective Nishita, give me a call, doesn't matter what time, just want to go over what we found on the search."

Think Ted, he told himself, *where would they go?* "What if they went over to the bar?" he asked.

Camilla said, "Let me check." She got on her shoulder com and buzzed Fisher.

The shoulder mic beeped and Fisher answered, "I'm at the restaurant with Anya and Rain. No sign of Dudley or Marta."

"Are their vehicles in the lot?" Camilla asked.

"Checking," Fisher said.

She looked over to Nishita and bit her lower lip.

He asked, "Do we know the name of Dudley's attorney?" She looked blank. "Wait, Judge Robinson spoke with him on the phone. He told me he didn't like pushy attorneys." He checked his watch. By now it was close to midnight. He couldn't call the judge at this hour—but it was strange. The attorney had never spoken with Nishita. It was the usual play to protect a client; separate them from the investigation. He'd have to it do first thing in the morning—at best eight hours from now. If Dudley had run, he had a massive lead, but there was no lawful reason to detain Dudley. There was too much footage of him in Las Vegas.

"Ask Fisher to detain Anya," Nishita said.

"What are you going to do?"

"If she is agreeable, I'll bring her to the station and get her statement."

"You think she'll go for it at this hour?"

"If I've read her correctly, she will." In his first interaction with her she seemed ready to spill all she knew about her parents and their relationship. Unfortunately, he'd been pulled away. He was ready to get over to the restaurant and speak with Anya, see if she had had contact with Dudley.

Camilla snapped her fingers. "Sophia Stannis is all alone. We can't leave her. She's an invalid."

"Right," Nishita answered and glanced upwards. "Anya can look after her but then I won't get her statement."

"I can try social services. See if they can send someone to look after her for the night," Camilla said.

Nishita said, "Let me speak with Anya first, see if she knows where they are." It was a little surprising that Marta would leave her mother.

Camilla gave a thumbs up. "I'll stay. You go."

Nishita went out the back door and followed the dirt path by the side of the house leading to the road. As he got to the garage, which was set under the bookstore facing the road, its double doors were open. Its lights cut into the dark night. He glanced into the garage. It was empty but had room for two big cars. In the far corner, he saw the base of the elevator. He wanted to go in and look for the cell phone, but Judge Robinson was crystal clear that under no circumstance was he to do any deeper investigation. It would tarnish his case and his reputation with the judge. He took a deep breath and continued walking.

The restaurant was at the far end of a strip of businesses across the street from the bookstore. The store fronts were elegant, crisp, and the sidewalks dotted with potted plants. That spoke volumes given that this part of Topanga was carved out of the rough hills notorious for snakes, tarantulas, and rockslides.

The Wagon Wheel Bar and Grill fit in perfectly. It was a throwback to the restaurants from the old sprawling ranch days. Based on the life of cowboys, it had hitching posts and mock antique wagon wheels at the front door. Why people glorified the slow crossing of dusty countryside staring at the backsides of cattle, he never understood. Fantasies die a slow death.

Fisher stood at the front door waiting for him. "Detective," he straightened his posture when he spoke, "Anya and Rain are sitting in the back booth."

Catching the familiarity in Fisher's voice when he said her name, Nishita asked, "Tell me again, how long you have known Anya?"

"Met her in first grade." Fisher saw Nishita's reaction and answered, "Topanga is a tight-knit community. The bookstore was a dilapidated farmhouse when Lena bought it, and as Anya grew up other kids teased her about being poor white trash. They never let her forget her beginnings."

Nishita had dealt with his own brutal teasing in school, so he could relate. Those wounds never fully heal.

"When major remodeling of the bookstore began, it's like they got rich overnight. Mr. Hardwick said it was Ms. Rezenchov's best-selling books and high-end clients that caused the success."

"You didn't believe him?"

Fisher rolled his eyes. "It's not that I didn't, but it seemed too good to be true. Things like that take time. My father used to say any overnight success started with a long night."

Nishita thought about ways to spot corruption. He remembered hearing that when something consistently goes against the odds, then something else is present and often that is cheating. Each corruption case takes tenacity and steel nerves to break apart. Is that what Lena did? Crack the façade of success?

"Did you ever investigate Dudley's business? Hardwick's Import Export?" Nishita asked.

Fisher shook his head. "Unless someone files a complaint, our hands are tied. And no one, I mean no one, ever did."

"Curious." He made note of that. It would seem Dudley Hardwick was as well-funded as connected.

Fisher leaned in and said quietly, "Something happened when Anya was in seventh grade. She ran away. Twice." He grew silent and seemed to argue with himself over what to say next. "She was one of the smartest kids in school."

"Do you know what happened?"

Fisher shook his head and said, "I can guess it had something to do with Marta. Those two fought constantly. There were times I'd see bruises on her arms and shins. She never told me, and I was too shy to ask but who else would have done it? Finally, Anya was sent away to boarding school." Fisher opened the door to the bar and stepped aside for Nishita to enter first. "I was glad she got out."

Upon entering the bar, a collection of men and women were scattered throughout drinking and playing darts. *Friendly*, he thought.

Anya and Rain were sitting in a round booth in a back corner. There was a large plate of French fires and what appeared to be plastic tumblers filled with cola. Rain swirled several fries in a plate of ketchup. People forget how hard memorials are for family members. The long lines of well-wishers, listening to them express their sorrow for your loss and not caring one bit about you. At least that was his experience when his brother died.

He said, "Thank you for seeing me at this hour. May I sit?"

Rain, with a mouthful of fries mumbled her approval. Anya, with arms folded in front, only stared.

He slipped into the booth and set his phone on the table and took a pause to connect eye to eye with Anya. "How are you holding up? Any more trouble?"

Rain had just consumed a mouthful of fries and couldn't speak; Anya was silent and didn't speak. Both Anya and Rain shook their heads. He turned his attention to Anya. "Are you eating, sleeping?"

Rain spoke up. "She's not." She pushed the plate of fries closer to Anya in an effort to get her to eat one. "They're your favorite." Anya brushed an errant hair off her forehead.

Deciding it was best to start he said, "I'd like to ask you a few questions. Do you mind if I record our conversation?"

"It's okay," she said. She pulled her tumbler closer and sipped.

"Have you spoken to your father or Marta in the last hour?" Anya shook her head and tightened her arms around her stomach. "He's not at the bookstore. I've tried calling, and it went straight to voice mail. I say this because Sophia is alone, and Camilla will need to call Protective Services if we think she is in danger of being uncared for."

Anya and Rain stared at one another. Anya said mostly to Rain, "Marta takes care of all that."

Rain said, "I'll go." She grabbed a few more fries and got up. Anya put up a bit of a fuss, but Rain shooshed her. "Meet me over there when you're done." She walked through the bar and waved to several people. Some waved back and a woman rushed to her and listen to Rain explain what was going on. Tight-knit community indeed, Nishita thought. That woman would surely pass along any tidbit to her friends . . . but to get them to talk against one of their own to police was tricky.

He turned his attention back to Anya.

Her face gave away a building worry and she got her cell out. She dialed, listened and then said, "Dad, call me when you get this. We can't find Marta and Sophia needs care for the night." She hung up. "Voicemail," she said flatly.

"Do you know where he is?"

Anya shook her head. "It's not like Marta to leave without setting something up."

"Did she use a service? Can we call them?" Nishita suggested.

"We never hired anyone not connected to the clinic." Anya pressed her lips. "Marta never paid for anything unless forced."

It would seem Anya knew Cold Marta. By her response did she ever see Geisha Marta? "Can you say more about that," said Nishita.

"Marta and I clashed for years," Anya muttered.

"Was that why you ran away?"

Anya lifted her head and peered over Nishita's shoulder. She said, "Scotty Fisher tell you about my volatile youth? Or did you look it up yourself?"

He didn't answer.

"Ah, yes, my case would be in the juvenile file section. You'd have to get a court order to see those," Anya said. "I'm guessing it was Scotty."

He let her draw her own conclusion and waited to see if she pressed for an answer or moved on to the next conversation.

Anya fingered the moisture on the outside of her plastic tumbler. "My parents adored Marta. Well, my father did."

"Did that cause trouble with your mother? His and Marta's closeness?"

Anya chuckled. "Dad met Lena through Marta. When my mother and Sophia bought the farmhouse it was Marta that found

Dudley to do odd jobs and repairs. But Dad wanted to marry Mom. Marta eventually married one of the construction workers. They didn't stay married. Marta and my father shared the love of building the business and making money. They liked spreading it around to curry favors." She let that last accusation dissipate.

"What do you mean spreading it around? Spending it?"

"Everything went into the bookstore. Rewiring, plumbing, painting, all the pristine display cases, modern kitchen, and bathrooms. My father always carried cash for tipping. Taxi drivers, restaurant servers, hotel staff." She finally took a sip of her drink. She noticed the moisture on her palm and wiped it on the napkin next to her. "All this success and I still had to buy my clothes at the second-hand store. Marta wouldn't allow me to buy new things."

"Marta was in charge, above your parents?" Nishita asked. "That'd get under my skin."

"My mother and Sophia were on publicity tours or leading seminars. My father was traveling all over the world, and Marta and I were to hold the fort," Anya said. "Hold the fort," she whispered. She leaned back against the booth cushion and closed her eyes. "I couldn't wait to get out."

Nishita paused. He wanted her to trust him. "You mentioned Marta never paid unless forced. Can you tell me more about that?"

"Did you know she only allowed volunteers at the bookstore? They could get "free" readings from my mother in exchange for work at the bookstore."

"What did she have them do?"

"Work in the gardens, clean the kitchen, answer phones, stock shelves, or do errands."

"What was your father doing?" Nishita asked.

"Gone mostly. He traveled to other countries and brought back an assortment of things to sell at the bookstore. There was a time when he brought home Persian rugs. I remember wondering why a bookstore sold Persian rugs," Anya said.

Her cell chirped. She read it and said, "Rain said Camilla helped settle Sophia in bed." She leaned back from the table.

Nishita could tell she was getting tired. If she said she was done talking he'd have to stop. "Just one more question and I'll escort you home," he said.

"You don't have to do that," she said. "I know the way."

"Fair enough. I didn't mean to imply you were incapable. Officer Camilla is at the bookstore, and I should check on what's happening with Sophia."

"So, you're not a nice guy?" she teased and toyed with a limp French fry.

He laughed. "Should we get some fresh food? Those fries look sad."

"Let's go back to the house. Rain is an awesome cook. She'll whip up something wonderful," Anya said with a smile.

They stood. Nishita put his phone in his top chest pocket and kept it recording. "Did you ever suspect your father might have brought back other things not for the bookstore?"

"Are you asking me if my father was a smuggler?" she asked.

"Did you ever wonder?" Nishita pressed.

She put on her sweatshirt. "He traveled to Egypt, Turkey, London, and Mexico eight times a year. All were shopping expeditions for the 'bookstore.'" She used air quotes when she said bookstore. "I wasn't allowed to unpack the boxes when he returned from a trip. Marta and Dudley did that alone in the garage. Marta said it was because they needed to document the inventory and I would distract them. Now that I'm older," she drifted off.

"You wonder?" he finished. She didn't answer.

I obsessed over the slick and glossy images of celebrities. Could I be famous too? When fame graced me, life sped up in ways for which I wasn't prepared. Days, weeks, and years spun out of control. The more people bowed and scraped the more erratic I became. Who was going to stop me? I was the main attraction, the breadwinner, the star.

—Lena Rezenchov, *Courageous Love*

THIRTY-ONE

FISHER HELD THE DOOR AS NISHITA and Anya stepped out of the warm bar and into the cool night. Saying goodnight, Nishita caught the look of longing Fisher hid. Watching Anya smile in that special way that said, I like you just not *that* way, he cringed inside. He'd seen that same look heading his way often enough and gave Fisher a reassuring smile.

Fisher signaled for him to move closer. "Got intel on the license plates on the vans. They're from stolen cars in Las Vegas," he said.

Nishita whispered, "Okay, thanks."

The night air was cooler than expected and Anya zipped up her hoodie. The street was dark, empty and they walked in silence. There were no homes close to the bookstore, no streetlamps. The only light was from the neon sign above the bar which cast an orange glow.

As they got closer to the bookstore, he noticed Anya rubbing the side of her face. It looked like a habitual movement. Nishita wondered if it was a gesture of thought or the remembrance of a past event.

"Detective." She stopped when she reached the edge of the driveway and took a moment to take in her surroundings. "Are you going to arrest my father?"

It was her first direct question. "He's a person of interest. What that means is I need to get his statement on record."

Anya walked like someone familiar with the terrain. She never looked down. It surprised Nishita because the gravel was uneven along the side of the road—remnants of rockslides.

She slowed her steps and appeared to admire the imposing bookstore. "My father loved being the only man in a house full of women. He was the center of our world. He never raised his voice or hand to anyone."

He'd seen this before. A child, even a young adult can't imagine one parent harming the other. He had to move carefully. "What was it like growing up here?"

"Are you asking why I ran away from this idyllic place, the celebrity lifestyle?"

"I'd never assume anybody's life was idyllic," he answered . . . not with the secrets his family kept.

He saw the pain in her eyes and hoped she saw compassion in his. She combed her fingers through her hair and continued the movement until her hand wrapped around her neck, the same side she touched a moment ago. She stared up into the black night.

He started slowly, keeping his voice soft. "How was living with Marta? By that I mean when you two were left alone."

Anya chuckled lightly. "I rebelled. She retaliated."

A world of memories passed across Anya's face—choosing what to say or what to leave out. Nishita thought of the interaction between Marta and the healthcare worker—the fear in the woman's eyes while Marta checked the smock for damage. The two faces of Marta: Cold Marta and Geisha Marta.

She said, "Sometimes I'd run into the hills just to get away and breathe. Once I moved out, I never looked back."

"I've only spoken with Marta on two occasions. Granted it's a stressful time, but she does swing hot and cold."

Anya laughed. "I used to call her Manic Marta. Rain dubbed her the Kray twins." As she spoke, tears ran down her cheeks. Nishita reached for his handkerchief, but once he saw the blood stains, decided against it, and stuffed it back in his pocket.

He had to ask. "The Kray twins? Weren't they the gangster twins in London? Beat people up to get their way?"

Anya said, "Yeah."

"I imagine you'd be the last person Marta would call to leave instructions on her mother's care." He let that thought linger.

"She wouldn't even think of me. Check my phone if you like."

They stared at one another. He didn't know if seconds passed or minutes. Somehow, he had to find Marta and Dudley. An inkling of an idea flashed across his mind. It was weak, but if he could get backing from Anya, it might work—but it had to be her idea. "Sophia has been left alone in that big house. Do you think Marta will return anytime soon?"

"I don't know."

He had to deepen the urgency. "Sophia will need a lot of care. Do you feel you are prepared to provide that?"

She looked at him, then glanced to the top floor of the bookstore.

He continued, "Let me put it this way, do you feel you have been informed by Marta as to Sophia's medications and physical needs?"

Anya thought about the question and then said, "No."

"Did she leave a contact number to call to bring in professional help?" He emphasized the word professional. He didn't want her to suggest she'd take over. He had to locate Marta before she slipped through the cracks.

"Where are you going with this, Detective?" she asked.

"It's clear that Marta and your father are gone and have left no word on their return. Would you agree?"

More tears ran down her cheeks and she nodded unable to speak. She wiped her face with the sleeve of her sweatshirt.

"The only legal avenue you and I have to find them is Sophia." Det. Nishita watched her reaction. Anya made a slow nod. "Marta hasn't called you with instructions or a time when she will return, correct?"

"True," she said.

"There's a law against abandoning seniors who need care. It's the Elder Justice Act. It mostly covers facilities, but Sophia is cared for at home and as far as you know, no future support has been set up for her."

He figured Marta and Dudley were on their way out of Los Angeles. It was anyone's guess which way out. He knew they couldn't get on an international flight until late tomorrow. If he hustled, they'd contact all departments in the southwest. It was a long shot, but it was all he had.

"Could you use this law to stop Marta?"

"With your approval, I'll send out a BOLO to all surrounding police departments and airlines. In case they are trying to fly out of the country."

"Out of the country?" Again, she rubbed her jaw. Anya straightened up and her eyes flashed. "Do it."

She has fire, he thought. *Good. She'll need it*. His shoulders eased. He always relaxed when there was action to take. "I'll get Camilla to call Protective Services. We won't get a nurse at this time of night. At best one will arrive tomorrow morning. Can you hold out that long?" he asked.

"Rain will help."

"Rain?" he said trying his best to keep his opinion to himself. It didn't work, she gave him a sidelong glance.

"Don't let the hair fool you. That girl is a genius." Anya smiled.

Nishita thought it was the first genuine smile he'd seen on her. His cell phone rang. The ID said Barstow PD. "Excuse me." He answered, "Detective Nishita."

"Detective? This is Officer Norwood from Barstow PD."

His mind raced. Barstow was a city on the I-5 freeway—the one people take to Las Vega. His heart jumped. "What can I do for you Officer."

"Twenty minutes ago, we got a 911 call from the Chevron Truck Stop."

"I know the one."

"A cashier taking out the night's trash found a woman behind the dumpsters. She'd been severely beaten. She told the EMT to call you."

"Me? Did she give her name?"

"It took her several minutes to remember her name. But she said, Marta."

"Marta. Last name Stannis. What happened? Is she all right?" Connecting eye to eye with Anya, he noted she'd lost all color. He could read her thoughts. She was worried about her father.

Officer Norwood said, "She was sent to the ICU." He lowered his voice and said, "She'll be there a while."

"Was there a man with her? Dudley Hardwick?" Nishita asked.

"No one was with her. We're checking security footage to see if we can discover when and how she was left."

Nishita shook his head and mouthed that there was no sign of Dudley. Relief fluttered across Anya's face . . . but if Marta and Dudley left together, where was he? Everything he'd suspected about Dudley's business flooded his thoughts. He was smuggling illegal items. If it was drugs, he was a transporter, but Nishita got the feeling Dudley was smuggling something far more profitable. Whomever he was working for had kept him and dumped Marta. Was that a good sign or not?

The hair on the back of his neck tingled. He looked back across the street to the bar. It was so dark he couldn't see anything except the neon sign. The porch lights of the bookstore blazed behind him. Instinct told him it wasn't safe to stay outside.

Holding his cell to his chest he said, "Anya, we need to get inside." Instinctively she rebelled. "Come on, now." He held out his hand for her. They hustled down the back path to the back door.

"Detective?" Officer Norwood's voice called out to him from his phone.

Entering the kitchen and locking the door he answered, "Yep, I'm here. Send me a copy of the security footage. We've got the license number of a white van in which Marta was last seen."

Camilla and Rain entered the kitchen. Rain positioned herself as if to protect Anya. Camilla asked without speaking what happened.

"I'm going to pass you to my partner, Officer Leila. Tell her what you told me. She can give you the details of the van." He passed the phone to a curious Camilla. Nishita then turned his attention to securing the bookstore. He couldn't answer why exactly, but somehow danger felt very close. "Is the front door locked? Are the security cameras on?"

Anya stood frozen to her spot. She seemed to have lost the ability to speak. Rain whispered, "I'll go." Rain moved to the front door. "What is this all about?"

"Precautions," Nishita called to her. He checked on Anya. Her hand shook as it moved to her mouth. She lost what little color she had and began to fold in on herself. Nishita rushed forward. "Come over here," he said and guided her to a chair next to the table.

"Anya!" Rain rushed to her side.

He still needed to secure the bookstore. Rain had gotten the front door, but he turned out the lights in the main part of the store. The garage door standing open flashed in his mind. He opened the grate to the elevator shaft and got in. Locating the floor buttons should have been a snap, but he didn't realize that he had to set the crossbar. Once in place the control panel was revealed. He pushed the button with a worn "B".

No one could accuse the elevator of speed. The thing bumped and rattled and shook side to side as it crept down to the lower floor. He kept his balance as it shimmied its way down to the garage. With a thunk, it stopped. He stepped out. The main floodlight was still on, and he searched for the control panel. He finally spotted it on the left side of the garage.

He switched the light out and got a clear view across the street into the Wagon Wheel's parking lot. The bar must have closed as people were sauntering to their cars. One by one, the cars started. Headlights brightened and cars entered the street and turned left or right. The outer lights of the bar turned off. The street went black.

He should lower the garage door, but something stopped him. The distinct sound of a truck accelerating from the bottom of the hill rose in the quiet of the night. Its headlights turned off before it made the last rise of the hill—a dark truck with a push bar slowed as it approached the bookstore. Nishita stepped out of the garage and onto the driveway blocking the entrance. This was the truck on security footage. He was sure of it. He unclipped his gun holster keeping his hand on his gun. The truck slowed and stopped. The windows were completely black. Nishita readied. An indistinguishable face appeared in the driver's side window.

His ears rang as he stared across the dark road. He had the feeling that the man in the truck was sizing him up. The truck sped up and turned around, driving over the rough terrain of the shoulder and drove back down the hill. Nishita released his gun and reclipped the holster. He took out his bloody handkerchief and wiped the sweat off his palms. Back in the garage, he found the switch to close the garage door and pushed it, watching the door rattle and close.

When the elevator reached the first floor, Camilla was waiting for him and handed him his cell. Distracted by the glare from the kitchen, he ordered, "Turn those lights out and check the back doors. And lower those blinds."

"I need light to cook," Rain complained.

Anya muttered, "Just do it." Rain groaned but turned the bank of lights off and rechecked the bolt on the back door. She then lowered the blinds of the windows that faced the back. "Can at least have the light over the stove on?" she asked.

Nishita waved his hand permissively, then pulled Camilla close to him. "Get Fisher over here."

She nodded, turned, and made the call from her cell.

A new set of motives surfaced. If Marta was beaten and Dudley had vanished, what did that tell him? Dudley beat Marta. He couldn't see that. Dudley was more of a desk jockey type, not the muscle. But what about the other men? That was possible. How could he find out about Dudley's business?

Rain had begun whipping eggs in a large bowl. Anya sipped on a cup of coffee. He could tell by the look on her face that she wondered if her father was alive.

Nishita addressed Anya, "I don't have to tell you that with Marta in the hospital, this case has changed. I need to know everything about your father's business."

Anya turned her head away from him and took a moment. When she looked back her manner had changed. She looked determined, more in charge of her situation. She rose and signaled for him to follow. She led him past the elevator hallway and past the cashier's station. There was an oak door. It opened to a small office. "This is Marta's," she said. "She usually keeps it locked, but seems she left in a hurry."

Clean and organized, there were chrome shelves filled with copies of Lena's books filed by color of the front jacket. On lower shelves were boxes clearly labeled with the names of gemstones. Atop a simple chrome desk was a computer, printer and three monitors. It seemed excessive to him that there were three monitors. He was itching to get into her computer, but that would have to wait for a warrant. "Too bad we can't get in."

"I can't hack it, but Rain can," Anya bragged. He must have looked shocked because Anaya said, "I'm still part owner of the bookstore. They're my files, too." She noted the confused look on his face. "My parents' divorce didn't finalize. She, she died."

"She was changing her will?"

Anya sighed, "Dudley was given the bookstore. Sophia was to get all royalties of her early books. Grant and I were to get ownership of the books and contemplation cards she'd self-published."

"Marta was left out?" Nishita said.

"Dudley was still her boss. Sophia got income from book

royalties," Anya said. "Nothing changed except I would have been released from the bookstore."

Marta might have expected to get Anya's slot. A change in the will could trigger an argument. "Were you upset?"

"This place makes my flesh crawl." Anya checked her emotion and said, "The will was to be finalized when the divorce went through. But that didn't happ—." She stopped, took a deep breath, struggled with what to say. "Anyway. I'm still part owner and can access the accounts." She turned to enter the kitchen to speak with Rain.

Rain put up a bit of a fuss, said she'd made omelets for everybody, and they needed to be eaten while hot. "Whatever is on the computer will stay there for the next ten minutes," Rain insisted. They sat in the kitchen. Anya, Rain, Camilla, Fisher, and Nishita and ate.

After plates were cleared, Camilla said she was going to check on Sophia briefly and excused herself. Fisher went to check the grounds.

Anya, Rain and Nishita moved into the office. Anya was correct, it took Rain three tries, and she got the computer open. She dug around and found five folders. "Lena 1", "Lena 2", "Clinic", "Goddess Garden", and "Do Right".

"What's the 'Do Right' file?" Nishita asked.

"Let's see," Rain said.

Once opened, there were numerous spreadsheets. Rain opened a few and sorted them on different monitors. Files were distinguished by years. Egypt 2009-14, Turkey 2008-18, and so on. Nishita thought it was Dudley's travel expenses. Lines were color coded, but he couldn't figure out what color meant what.

After a few moments Rain sat back in the chair. "You're going to need a forensic accountant to look over these. If I'm understanding correctly, the yellow line is an item and the red, green, and blue lines are people. I'm sure it's in code. The yellow line is an item with an invoice number. But the others are names in code. See? The numbers have a spacing, so each number is a letter. Look on the blue line. 18 then space then 5 space 5 space then 4. Name of Reed. It's an easy code, way too many people use it. They think they are being clever. But check here." She pointed to one line. "You can see there is an item on the yellow line. Number T5492 dated two weeks ago. It looks like some kind of auction and each highlighted line is a person bidding for T5492."

Camilla said what everyone was thinking, "What are they bidding on?"

Myths stir the imagination. Good versus evil, a hero betrayed, and the sacrifice of the common man who saves the world. Countless stories have been woven from these. Beware the dark side when myth is presented as fact. Facts do not require belief to function. Gravity is a fact and will work whether you believe or not. Requiring belief, myths have been used to poison hearts and close minds.

—Lena Rezenchov, *unfinished manuscript*

THIRTY-TWO

NISHITA STARED AT THE SPREADSHEET WITH row upon row of columns, yellow highlighted invoice numbers, green highlighted product numbers, and blue budget numbers. As always math turned his stomach. Math was connected to his older brother's disappearance. In sixth grade, math was his last class of the day. It was the only time he had to search for his brother. If he skipped math class, he could go out on his own. During that precious time before he had to race home and care for his despondent mother, he checked every gas station, mini mart, and strip mall up and down the streets of Santa Monica. Hoping by showing his brother's picture someone would remember seeing him. He failed math and never found Allen. Looking at the files on Marta's computer dredged up memories. He blinked and caught Anya staring at him.

"Detective you, okay?"

"Oh, yeah, I'm good." A wave of exhaustion swept through him. He addressed Rain in the desk chair. "I'll need a copy of those files. If that is all right?"

Anya nodded, and Rain opened the side drawer and using her fingers shuffled through the items in the drawer. Easily enough, she found a thumb drive and began the process of copying. Rain hummed while she worked, her voice light and pleasing. Her confidence was a glimmer of optimism, something Anya would need in the coming weeks.

Turing back to the monitors, he wondered why Marta had three. It seemed excessive for a family-run business. He reread the names of the folders. Lena 1, Lena 2, Do-Right and Clinic.

"Can you open the 'Clinic' folder?" he asked. "With your permission, naturally." He made eye contact with Anya.

Camilla walked in and mentioned Sophia was sleeping soundly. Anya lifted a pale face and asked if she was snoring. "Yes, she is," Camilla answered. The answer made Anya smile, but her eyes remained vacant.

Watching Anya, he knew that blank stare and decided he and Camilla would give her a chance to unwind. If it was possible for her to sleep and not churn with thoughts all night. He never could. But if she was bone tired, as he suspected, she might get a few moments.

Rain opened the 'Clinic' folder, clicked on the file inside, and all three monitors lit up. She let out an exclamation. Anya cowered. Camilla and Nishita flinched. Each monitor was filled with multiple views from security cameras. There was a street, an outer wall of a building, and a parking lot with a driveway. One entire monitor was filled with views of hallways, hospital rooms and office spaces. Rain leaned in muttered, "Is that smoke?"

Nishita examined each separate video. "Is this live?" Smoke began to pour out of hallways, covering the cameras. Flames licked the walls crawling upwards to the ceiling. An office with a desk and bookshelves exploded in front of them. Both Rain and Anya cried out in surprise. Smoke covered the lens from the office camera.

Anya said, "It's the clinic." She held her hands over her mouth.

Rain stared at each video and pulled Anya into a hug and said, "Don't even think that. I'm sure he's not there."

From the street view, a group of people gathered outside wearing pajamas and robes. Lights flashed in the dark night and trucks turned into the driveway. Firemen got off the trucks and moved quickly. One man held back the gawkers. Several unwound hoses, and three began to adjust their face masks and gloves. A patrol car entered the parking lot.

Nishita's mind swirled. "Are any patients in residence? Any staff, cleaners, or night crew?" The question came out harsher than he expected. His eyes remained fixed on the screen. A few more cameras blackened over, consumed by smoke and flames. The cameras in the driveway and walkway were clear and he followed the movements of the firemen entering the building. He couldn't wrap his mind around why Marta had a live feed from the clinic.

Energy shot up his back, and his mind went to the truck that had slowed as it passed the open garage door earlier. "Anya, it is normal for the garage door to be left open, as it was this evening?"

Rain chimed in, "I noticed that and thought it was strange. I don't ever remember seeing it open ever. I mean, people can get into the family's part of the house from there."

Nishita and Camilla locked eyes. Whoever burned the clinic was still connected to the bookstore and the files on Marta's computer. Lena's murder was interwoven with a long tentacle of smuggling and possible trafficking. The list was getting longer.

The question flew out of his mouth before he could stop. "Any reason Marta would have video surveillance of the clinic?"

Rain piped up. "Insurance?"

"You mean, blackmail?" Nishita arched his brows.

She nodded. "I think she wanted to make sure the center paid her. If I'm reading the files correctly, these invoices for cleaning services are not just at the clinic. See, here's a list of invoices for an investment firm downtown. There is a CPA group, and I believe this is a law firms office. It's crazy. Marta did all the books. She had to know exactly what was going on."

He couldn't hold back the smile. "You'd make a good PI."

Rain leaned back in her chair and giggled. "Maybe I should start my own YouTube channel: Finding Fraud for Fun."

Camilla did her best to suppress her laugh and failed. Nishita hid his grin with his hand. But Anya clutched her shirt over her chest and appeared to be gasping for breath.

Rain immediately got up and put her arms around Anya. "Honey, I didn't mean anything about your family." Anya made little sobbing sounds and hid her face in Rain's shoulders. Rain looked over to Nishita, "I'm going to." And led Anya out of the office and back towards the kitchen.

After Rain and Anya turned the corner, Nishita sat in the main chair. He watched the video of the firefighter wrestling with the blaze. It was difficult at this stage to determine who was winning, the men or the fire.

"Are you thinking what I'm thinking?" Nishita looked over his shoulder at Camilla.

"Arson?"

He leaned forward, placed his elbow on the desk and rested his head on his fist. "I wonder if Lena threatened to expose all this." He waved his other hand towards the monitors.

"What do you think has happened to Mr. Hardwick?"

"Could be holed up somewhere in a mansion, or on a plane to parts unknown."

Fisher made his way into the small office, his face filled with curiosity.

Nishita turned to him and said, "Dudley has the resources to disappear for a long time, am I correct?"

Fisher couldn't answer.

Camilla sat on the small chair at the edge of the desk. "What if we asked Anya to make a statement speaking to Dudley. Appeal to him as her father, tell him she misses him and loves him and wants him back. That way we can show his picture and not have to declare any charges he might face."

"Good idea. We can do it first thing in the morning. Send it out to all the stations, post it on all social media channels." He began to rise.

She stopped him. "Let me. I'll appeal to her as a daughter that understands difficult fathers." Camilla looked at him and arched her brows.

"Done," Nishita agreed. "Well, Fisher, we've got a long night. I spied some comfortable couches in the front room. We can take turns."

"No one gets a free ride. By that I mean we will all be pushed and prodded, tempted, and tested. When these things happen don't you just want to run, scream, and hide? Remember: In times of darkness find the light."

—Lena Rezenchov's opening remarks for the
Winter Solstice Ceremony
at the Goddess Garden Bookstore.

THIRTY-THREE

IT WAS TWO IN THE MORNING and the bookstore felt wrapped in mystery. He'd love to search the mansion from top to bottom, check through closets, dig inside desk drawers, and investigate attic rooms. His inner kid imagined all the magical swords, wands, and crystal balls he'd touch. Maybe he'd find a ring that gave him super intelligence or a cape in which he could walk back and forth through time; he'd solve cases with a snap.

Dismissing his thoughts, he returned to looking out the bay window. The strange man had warned him of ruthless men surrounding the elder center. No wonder Rebecca was frightened.

He stared into the black night, if any van drove up the hill, he'd see it. In a way he was proud, he'd done exactly as Captain Cooper had instructed: take the gloves off, dig deep and reveal who's protecting Dudley. But he might have pushed too hard and too fast. Marta, beaten and discarded, the clinic on fire, and there had been an implied threat to the bookstore. Dudley had vanished. The list was growing.

The muscles in his neck tensed. His former girlfriend had said he was a people pleaser, and it would give him ulcers. Standing in the dark, he wondered if he held himself to unrealistic expectations.

Anya and Rain were resting on the third floor with Sophia. Camilla was in the office checking Marta's computer. Fisher had claimed a spot in the kitchen watching the backyard while sipping strong coffee. Nishita heard movement by the stairwell, turned and spotted Camilla moving past the suits of armor, the floor creaking with each step.

She kept her voice low. "I love the sound of creaking floors, very haunted house." Before reaching him, she searched out the far bay window. Satisfied it was currently calm, she stood next to him.

He said, "Any word on Dudley?" Camilla shook her head. He said, "Still early. We might get something at daybreak. Anything new on the computer?"

"A couple of things, but more interesting is what I haven't found." She eyed him. "Marta wore a scarf and a trench coat in the footage we got from Vegas, right?" she waited for him to nod. "I haven't seen it anywhere in the house."

With all the distractions, he'd forgotten about that footage. But it also jarred his memory about Marta's ex-husband and the limo service. With the scarf and coat missing, it was one more tick suggesting Marta and the woman in Vegas were not the same. "You've checked everywhere?"

She tipped her head toward the staircase. "While upstairs, I offered to look in Marta's room in case there were medications for Sophia," she said in a tone that sounded like justification. Nishita hid a smile. "I did a sweep, then another in Sophia's room. Before I came down, I wandered around on the second floor. It's Dudley's office, bedroom, and sitting room. Elegant in that royalty from days gone by kind of way." She sighed with a tinge of envy. "Then I checked Marta's office. No scarf, no coat."

He wanted to compliment her work, but the words got stuck. Nishita remembered he wasn't assigned another detective to work with. He'd asked for her and how that landed with Captain Cooper—but Camilla had been right next to him all along, suggesting actions to take and following up before he asked. Officer

Fisher, who set his teeth on edge, had worked with the community, gaining information Nishita would have been locked out from. He'd have not gotten this far without either.

"Camilla," he began.

"Oh-oh, this is serious," she said.

"It is." He took a breath faced her squarely and folded his arms across his chest. "Make peace with Captain Cooper. Apologize, bow and scrape, whatever is needed. Do it. Ask to take the detective test again and pass with flying colors." She began to protest but he interrupted her. "Stop. Just stop." He let those words fill the room. She turned away and stared out the window. "It's time."

With the back of her hand, she wiped along her jawline. He knew she was wiping away tears. She tried to speak but had no voice and eventually she merely nodded. He wanted to slap her on the back but checked his impulse and held his hand to his side. They looked out the window and Nishita wondered if they were looking out at the same night, or was she mentally composing her apology? He decided to give her some space and check on Officer Fisher.

In that instant, the floor rose up and fell. His first thought was an earthquake. His knees buckled and he was hit with a deafening boom, as if he'd been smacked with a baseball bat. He fell backwards. Destruction surrounded him. Glass shattered, wood beams collapsed, and thick dark smoke poured up from the elevator shaft. He reached Camilla on the floor. Loud ringing in his ears muffled all sound.

Nishita clutched his handkerchief, the blood-stained one from his suit pocket to his mouth in an effort to block the smoke. "Cam!" he shouted. His voice was drowned out as the siren in the hallway rang. She had fallen backwards and lay as if asleep behind him. He got to his hands and knees and crawled to her, keeping his head away from the smoke. He touched her and she moaned.

Slowly she sat up and touched the back of her head. Bringing her fingers forward they were covered in blood. "Dammit! That stings," she said.

"Can you get up?" Nishita held out his hand to help her.

"Don't!" She took a breath and said, "I'm fine." She moved to her hands and knees.

With a dishrag against his mouth, Fisher ran out of the kitchen, keeping to the far wall to avoid the flames that engulfed the stairwell. A second blast rocked, and Fisher fell.

Noise overwhelmed Nishita, glass cases shattered, metal groaned and the stone floor rumbled. He had to get them out before the second floor toppled down on them. A wall of heat hit Nishita, and his eyes burned. "Fisher," he yelled. Fisher popped his head up and gave him a thumbs up, signaling he was good and crawled to him. Nishita pushed Camilla and pointed her to the broken front door. The three crawled out to the porch and once there gulped clean air. Nothing ever tasted so sweet.

Eyes stinging, he scrambled to his feet, got out to the front yard and checked the rest of the house. The garage doors had been blasted open and fire filled the entire space. He could smell gas fumes. Camilla caught his attention and pointed up to the third floor.

Rain waved her arms and shouted out the window. "We're stuck!"

The fire doubled in size before his eyes. "How long until fire trucks arrive?" he asked.

Fisher coughed, rubbed his eyes, and answered, "Ten-fifteen? They come from the lower hill." He looked up and pointed at Anya in the window and said, "I know a back way."

"Go!" Nishita said and the three raced around the side of the mansion, past the kitchen door and around to the back of the building. Next to a large bush, a small door in which one had to walk down a few steps to use appeared.

"It's the old servants' entrance." Fisher lightly stepped down to the door. It was locked but Fisher pulled out a set of lock picks and got to work. In a few seconds he'd opened the door. He had to push against the door with his shoulder as it stuck like it hadn't been opened in years. But after a moment, the door slid against the cement, and they entered. An old wooden stairwell curled up to the higher floors.

"Do I need to worry about you?" Nishita asked.

"I'm a licensed locksmith. Besides, I told you, I watched them rebuild this house ever since I was a kid. I know every brick."

He looked up the stairwell and began climbing the steep steps. Camilla and Nishita followed. They reached the second floor and a large metal door closed off the entrance. Fisher signaled for them to keep going. They reached the third floor and the same type of metal door denied access. He got to work picking the lock, struggled but finally got it opened. A smoke-filled hallway greeted them. He signaled them toward the front of the house and Sophia's bedroom.

"Rain! Anya! It's Detective Nishita," he called out. Smoke was billowing up from the elevator shaft, and Nishita heard the flames building in the lower floors. They had to act quickly.

Rain appeared in the hallway a look of relief mixed with panic spread across her face. "We can't get Sophia to move." Camilla rushed ahead and went into the bedroom first, Nishita and Fisher behind.

Sitting on the edge of her bed, Sophia held her hands over her face and appeared to be weeping. Anya, arms around Sophia's shoulders, sat next to her.

Camilla moved slowly to the bed and, keeping her voice soft said, "Hi Sophia, we're sorry to wake you like this." The woman gasped in short breaths in an effort to speak but couldn't make words. Camilla faced Sophia and lifted her right arm, the limp one, and wrapped it around her neck. Sophia smiled and got her left arm in place and gripped her wrist. They both rose to standing. "We need to go out the back way. You know that way, right?" Sophia made an agreeable sound. Camilla said, "Wheelchair."

Rain wheeled it in. Camilla gently lifted Sophia and in one graceful move had her in the chair.

The fire sounded louder, closer, alive. "Cam, we need to move," Nishita said.

Fisher led Rain, Anya, and Camilla pushing Sophia in the chair. Nishita, at the end, did his best to observe each detail of the bedroom and the third floor. Was there anything that caught his eye, perhaps out of place? But thick dark smoke rose from the stairwell filling the hallway with every passing second. Arriving at the back staircase, it was obvious the wheelchair wouldn't fit in the small passage or be taken down the steps.

"Camilla, get Rain, and Anya out. Fisher and I will carry Sophia," Nishita said doing his best not to cough. Then he pointed for Fisher to grab Sophia's legs while he lifted her from under the shoulders. She fussed, but Nishita said in her ear, "I've got you." She surrendered to his arms and the three began an awkward move down the steps.

The staircase had been unreliable before they had to carry an invalid woman down it. Now the stairs took on a dangerous quality as smoke billowed up from the lower floor. He heard Camilla order Rain and Anya to cover their mouths and keep going. Fisher cried out. "We've got to cover Sophia's mouth. She'll choke on the smoke."

"Set her down." Nishita lowered Sophia on a step and standing behind her held his knees against her back to stabilize her. He pulled off his jacket and gently held it under her mouth wrapping the arms around her neck. Once satisfied it was secure, they picked her up again and step by step lumbered down. Fisher coughed, and Nishita's eyes stung. As they got lower and lower, the sound of fire intensified.

Camilla called back, "We're out. But the basement hallway is on fire. You have to hurry." There was a loud whoosh, and flames shot out along the bottom floor. "The stairs!" she shouted.

The lower set of steps caught fire. Even if they hurried, they wouldn't make it now. The fire was consuming the dry wood at remarkable speed.

"Back up, back up," he shouted to Fisher. And they retraced some steps to the second floor. The metal fire door was locked. Nishita took Sophia in his arms while Fisher worked his locksmith magic. The stairwell crackled from the fire and part of the steps collapsed.

Fisher pushed the door open, and they entered into a dim hall-way. Nishita, holding Sophia to his chest, looked into her eyes. She nodded to let him know she was good. Nishita's chest ached, and his throat burned from inhaling smoke. Glancing toward the front of the house, he saw large flames of fire eating away at the main stairwell. A small room was to his left. As far as he could tell it was free from fire. He gestured for Fisher to follow. They got inside, and it was a white-tiled bathroom. Nishita set Sophia atop the toilet. She grabbed onto a rack to her right and coughed.

Fisher found a light switch, and the size of the room revealed itself. It was larger than expected with a free-standing porcelain tub with gold-painted feet and gold faucets. On one wall, a floor-to-ceiling mirror was surrounded by large open drawer type cabi-nets. Towel racks were filled with expensive white towels.

Fisher grabbed two of the towels, soaked them in water, and placed them along the floor of the door.

It was smart to keep as much smoke out of this room as pos-sible. There was no way of knowing how much time they had until rescue arrived. Nishita had to do something. Scanning the room, he saw a reinforced bubble glass window above the tub. It was small, compared to modern windows of today. He figured it was a holdover from the original building. He tried to open it, but it was painted shut. "We've got to open this," he said, "the firemen need to know we're up here."

Fisher began to search under the sink for anything that might break the glass. Nishita turned to the drawers, pulling them out and frantically searching. At the back of one of the drawers he found a safe. It was the type homeowners were advised to place important papers in to keep them safe from fire damage. What would Dudley keep inside? He lifted it towards him by the handle and pulled it out. It was solid and heavy but easy to handle.

"Cover yourself and Sophia," he ordered. Fisher grabbed more towels and huddled next to Sophia and lifted the towels over their heads. Nishita stood in the tub and slammed the safe against the window. The glass cracked, but with the wire reinforcement, it didn't break. The crackle of fire sounded outside the bathroom door. He hit the window again, and the wooden cross bar broke but was held fast by the glass. Fragments had hit his face and he felt something warm along his knuckles. Shards tinkled into the tub by his feet.

Nishita gulped air, and his chest burned. He figured the window had one, maybe two more hits, and it would release. He lifted the safe again, but his feet wobbled in the slippery tub and when the safe met glass it was a weak punch. Nothing much had changed. "One more," he said. Using both hands in a push motion, he threw it against the glass, pushing it as far as he could out the window. By thrusting it so far out the window, he lost control of the safe, and it crashed outward and glass shards along the bottom edge of the window sliced the underside of his upper arm. But sweet air filled the bathroom, and he drank it in.

Sirens echoed in the hills followed by blue and red lights flashing in circles around the white tiled room. Camilla yelled up to him, "Ted!"

"Here," he bellowed out the window. He glanced back to Fisher and Sophia. They were smiling. "We're good." His knees gave out and he slipped down the side of the tub while Fisher wrapped his arm to stop the bleeding. His head spun as the room faded to blackness.

THIRTY-FOUR

T HE BEEPS SET HER TEETH ON edge. She hoped they'd fade to the background like white noise, but the beeps echoed in the hospital room. A collection of jumbled smells intruded, nurses that slithered in her room interrupted with pricking needles, and that constant beeping infringed on any peace and quiet. It was reason enough to escape. Could she? Dare she? Marta had to think about that. In her current condition she'd never get far—but what was the option?

She moved to one side and electric pain shot through her leg to her ankle, the side of her head pulsed, and her left arm throbbed. She sucked in air through her teeth and let out a slow breath. *"Breath through pain Marta and pleasure will fill your body."* Her father had said many times. He was right, pleasure and pain are connected.

Could she stop the memories floating through the medication? Things she wanted to forget but couldn't. That last argument and what she was forced to do.

"Fame and Glory—that's what you said you wanted. Fame and Glory—I gave you that—I did," She remembered her voice shouting.

And Lena screaming in front of the elevator. *"This? This is not glory—this is greed—pure evil greed—"*

Marta shut her eyes to stop the memory, but it was no use. Lena and her dramatic outbursts happened once a week, why was this one any different. She'd had these before when she felt stressed over planning a lecture or seminar. Sophia would reassure her, remind her of her incredible abilities. Eventually, they'd move to the kitchen and drink martinis. Once Lena calmed, they'd talk about something like her next book or a comment from a fan. She was different after rehab. Sophia was in a wheelchair and couldn't cajole. There were no more martinis or settling down. Lena argued about stupid things. But that night, Marta fought back.

She pushed against the memory, but it was no use. It played on repeat. Night after sleepless night. She, Dudley, and Lena, entangled against the elevator, arms wrestling, and tugging. Lena hit Marta scratching on her forearm. Marta fought back twisting Lena's hand until it broke. Lena screamed. Dudley pulled Lena and Marta apart. With one hand lifted Lena up. There were too many arms and legs jumbled in a small space and Lena fell backwards. With a horrifying sound like a falling pumpkin, it was over.

Marta had to find a way out. The beeping intensified.

"Beware the person who stabs you and then tells you they're the one who's bleeding."

—Jill Blakeway

Bullies fight with cruelty. Faced with combative behavior, I play peacemaker. Lately, I've wondered if that works, or if it reinforces aggression.

—Lena Rezenchov, *unfinished manuscript*

THIRTY-FIVE

IT WAS STILL EARLY, JUST PAST seven. Careful not to move his right arm, Nishita checked the number of views Anya's video had gotten from overnight. Recording it, he'd told Anya they needed to get a photo of Dudley out to the public ASAP. Two days since it was posted on YouTube, and it became lightening in a bottle. Anya, pleading for her father to come home, was a stunning reversal from a father asking for information on a missing daughter. This was a daughter pleading for a father's safe return made all the more urgent as his business partner had been found dumped behind a gas station in Barstow.

Merely sitting caused each of his thirty-four stitches to pulse. The gash under his arm had severed his artery. Luckily, Fisher knew first aid and had cared for him until he was carried out of the burning mansion by firemen. With glass exploding in his face, he was lucky glass shards didn't get in his eyes, but he did get a number of small cuts on his face.

His mother wept when she saw him in the hospital, and his father tried to melt into the wall. Losing another son would devastate them. When he was released, his mother made her Earl Grey Tea cupcakes with Lavender Buttercream frosting for the nurses and staff. It was quite the sendoff.

At the hospital, he was told it'd be six weeks for a complete recovery. Fisher bounced back effortlessly. Sophia, with her age and weak condition, got a chest infection from the smoke. Rebecca was hired to care for her.

Speaking with Marta's doctors, Nishita got approval to see Marta. He'd called Camilla immediately, and while he waited, gathered evidence. With what was discovered in the burned-out building of the clinic, this case had turned a corner.

But he couldn't stop himself from viewing the twenty-year-old security footage of his brother's car leaving the strip club by the LA airport and the truck with the push bar following him. It was grainy with no sound and the frames skipped every few seconds . . . but was it the same truck that faced him in the roadway of the bookstore? His memory played the rumble and guttural sound of engine. His grandfather taught him to distinguish the sounds of engines. How each engine has its own voice, tone, and timbre unique unto itself. He only had to listen and remember. That truck, he'd remember.

"Ted," Camilla called out to him.

He glanced up from his computer. Camilla had inhaled a lot of smoke from the fire as well. Today was the first day she was back to her old acerbic self. "So ready for a trip to Barstow?" Nishita teased.

She handed Nishita a stack of papers. "Crime stoppers reports. Don't get your hopes up, most of these are guys that want to date Anya."

"We knew that was going to happen," Nishita said. He ruffled through the stack.

"One you should see. It's from Interpol. They answered our inquiry about Darian Harkness. A woman had filed a complaint against Darian twenty years ago. He, allegedly, embezzled £30,000 from her, then vanished."

Nishita whistled. "How much is that in dollars?"

"$56,000, give or take. It'd be more these days," She sat in the chair next to him. "The woman said he was so charming and sweet and temporarily short of cash. He implied he needed a position.

She ran an investment firm and hired him because he claimed to be royalty. Claimed he was, Sir Darian Harkness."

Nishita rolled his eyes. "Does that work?"

"I guess. We found passports in the fire safe you so recklessly tossed out the window," Camilla said.

He grunted and peered over at Camilla who smirked. "Anyway, he had a string of aliases."

"Dudley was a womanizer?" Nishita said. "I never got that vibe."

She shrugged. "A con is a con. I think he's always been after money. We have an alert to the Met in London, but they haven't spotted Dudley." Camilla smiled but wasn't completely happy. He could see it in her eyes.

Nishita said. "We'll get him. It's just a matter of time."

"What of the undocumented workers? What do we have to help them, or even find them? Who knows where he is now?"

"One case at a time," Nishita said. "Did you ever wonder why Anya was working on a report on human trafficking? I think Lena suggested it to her. In her way, she was trying to call attention to what was going on."

"The bookstore, with objects of art imported from around the world, was the perfect cover." Camilla shifted restlessly in her chair. "Over time what Dudley imported changed."

Nishita picked up one of Lena's books and shuffled the pages. Most new-age teachers, gurus, and spiritual guides speak about wealth and how to attain it. Attainment of money was what hooked followers. In everything that Lena wrote, it wasn't about money. Her topics were truth, honesty, and love. Nishita leaned back in his chair. He glanced at the small stack of Lena's books and the deck of contemplation cards resting on his desk. "Did you ever get the notion that Lena knew any of the details of the bookstore?"

Camilla smoothed her hair. "How much was Lena involved in financial decisions? I don't know, but Sophia had to know. A question for Marta today." Camilla shot up from the chair. "I can't drive to Barstow without good coffee."

Nishita chuckled. He packed his laptop and a manilla file folder in his leather case, stood, and signaled he was ready to leave. It didn't take a moment for Camilla to respond and match his stride out the door.

Once they got out of the building, the day was bright. He'd spent long days at his desk and forgot there was another world out there. He needed to ask for some time off after this case. Maybe get in some hiking or rock climbing.

Camilla marched straight to the coffee shop across the street from the station. Nishita paid for two large coffees. While he added cream to his coffee to achieve just the right caramel color he said, "My grandmother used to say a leopard never changes its spots. My brother and I would laugh. Duh, of course they don't. But once someone gets a taste for bending the rules, padding a resume, or smuggling, there's always a trail."

He got no response. Was she even listening? She was holding her cup to her nose and savoring the aroma. But she glanced at him and nodded while she sipped.

Nishita said, "We should get on the road before traffic gets crazy." They headed back to the garage.

Nishita announced he'd drive. Camilla argued due to his stiches it was her job to drive. He said, "I want you to look over the file. It has pictures from the fire." She appeared to have excess energy to burn, or maybe she was feeling the first jolt of caffeine. They needed to build the case together. She needed to know where he was going in questioning Marta. She opened his leather case and shuffled through several of the photographs, focusing on the ones from the fire at the clinic.

Camilla glanced over the photos. "These are horrible."

He glanced at the top photo and shook his head. "Did you ever get the feeling that Lena's memorial was one big deflection? It pulled officers from the area to work traffic, and ambulance crews were on duty there. If my idea about the timing is correct, as the clinic burned, the bookstore was to be burned as well. I think I stopped their first attempt," Nishita said. "They came back because both buildings were slated to burn, to destroy evidence-worse, to get Sophia as well."

They drove in silence after that.

Making good time, they pulled into the parking lot. The Barstow Community Hospital was small but enough to serve the community. Nishita showed his badge to the man at the front desk and after he scrutinized his identification, he said to wait for the head nurse to call them and pointed to a bank of chairs in the center of the floor. They sat on the dark gray plastic-connected chairs. He took a moment to look around. The walls were painted a mint green and the flooring was thick linoleum with a speckled pattern. Camilla commented she hated the smell of hospitals.

The attending nurse waved to Nishita to come speak with her.

"I'll be back," he said in the terminator's voice to Camilla. Her cell buzzed as he walked to the desk, and he heard her answer in her usual playful tone, "Yeah!"

The nurse was older and had a steely reserve. Nishita figured in the years she'd worked she must have seen just about everything humans would throw at one another. She held a file in her arms and said, "As you requested, this is a record of Ms. Stannis's injuries." Her eyes looked tired, but her voice was strong and clear. "Her left wrist was broken, as was her right ankle. There was a stab wound in her right thigh. It was deep, and she lost a good deal of blood."

Nishita thought of his own recent blood loss and how it impacted him, the instant loss of balance and those bright spots in his eyes as he fainted. Once he came around, he felt tossed like a rag doll. As he gained consciousness, he faced another ordeal: searing pain, confusion about where he was and what had happened.

"Detective?" the nurse said, demanding his attention.

"Yes, please go on."

"As I was saying, she has a concussion, and that's what we're watching." She closed her file folder. "These are odd injuries. None of them are fatal, but."

He considered his words before he spoke. "You got the feeling her wounds were half-hearted?"

"Some people will do anything to get narcotics. Self-harm in ways you and I can't imagine. I didn't get that impression from Marta. But why these injuries, I couldn't begin to guess. Anyway, she is going off pain meds today, so she'll be alert and slightly cranky. I'll send someone to escort you to her room." The nurse gave a curt nod and left him.

Was Marta a distraction that gave Dudley time to get out of the country? This could change his line of questioning. If she willingly endured such a beating, where would it stop?

Camilla approached him, took a deep breath, and said, "I just got off the phone with Las Vegas police." She lowered her voice to a soft whisper, "John Towel, Marta's ex-husband, has been declared missing. It doesn't look good."

Nishita said, "We haven't confirmed he was the limo driver, right?" She shook her head.

He asked, "Wait, why did they call you?"

"I was the officer on the report," Camilla said in her matter-of-fact tone.

A young woman, perhaps in her early thirties introduced herself as the nurse in charge of Marta. She said Marta was doing better although a little uncomfortable. Nishita felt the bandage tight to his right arm and thought of the growing list of victims.

As they entered the room, Marta was sitting up in her bed. Half of her head was bandaged including over one eye. Her right leg was in a cast as was her left hand. She was scowling but Nishita thought that might have been due to the decreased medication.

"I was wondering when you'd show up," Marta said. Her voice sounded husky but strong.

"Do you have time to see us today?" Det. Nishita asked in his most polite tone. Officer Camilla stood behind him.

Marta croaked a laugh. "I think I can fit you in between lunch and my date with the physical therapist." She lifted her unbroken hand but was unable to move it because there was an IV drip attached and a blood pressure monitor clipped to her forefinger. She rolled her visible eye as if to communicate her predicament.

Det. Nishita noted her sense of humor and decided the pain meds hadn't quite worn off. He stole a quick glance to Officer Camilla. She remined stoic and hid any enjoyment of Marta's comments.

Marta squirmed. "I watch a lot of crime shows, you know. I love it when a dark-haired handsome officer reads the perp his rights as he claps on handcuffs. Are you going to do that today?" She chuckled which triggered a small coughing fit.

Det. Nishita spotted a plastic chair in the corner, grabbed it, and moved it to her bedside. He decided to sit on the side with Marta's good eye. "When you were found behind the dumpster, you told the police to contact me?" She gave him a blank stare. "You said my name and told the police to call me."

"Funny, I don't remember that." Marta adjusted her arm in the cast and winced.

Her comment interested him but given that she had been hit in the head, he considered her memory might have gaps. How could he jog it? Her mother. He'd start there. "I'm going to record our conversation." Marta sighed and nodded. He set his recorder to the side out of view of Marta's good eye. "I want you to know your mother is doing well. I realize you have had other concerns." He gestured to her surroundings. "But your mother is progressing very well."

Dripping with bitterness Marta said, "Is she getting chocolate pudding every day?"

"She's getting qualified help. She's been able to walk, and her speech is returning. Her progress is remarkable," Det. Nishita said, hoping that would unsettle Marta.

Marta fell silent. She closed her eye and said, "Oh goodie." Marta tried to adjust her neck and sucked air through her teeth in pain. Nishita avoided the temptation to glance back at Camilla.

"A lot has happened since the memorial. Let's begin with that night." Det. Nishita lifted his leather case. "Is it all right if I set this on your bed? Just here at the foot?" She nodded and gave a small grunt. "I'll keep it clear from your leg. How tall are you, five feet?"

"I'm five-foot-one, I weigh one hundred and four pounds, my eyes are brown and my hair," she paused, "I dye dark brown."

Nishita was impressed. Many women her age wouldn't admit to their weight or coloring their hair. His mother would rather move to Canada than admit she dyed her hair. "You remember Officer Camilla Leila," Nishita gestured to Camilla. "She attended the memorial as well."

He opened his case and lifted a manilla folder. He set the folder atop his case and opened it. He gestured deliberately, wanting Marta to follow his movements. "She took many photographs of the crowd." He checked Marta's one eye to see if she was following. "See? Here we have pictures of you working with the volunteers during the memorial. Here's one of you stranding next to Dudley when he made his dedication to Lena. Oh, speaking of photographs, we dug around and found archived photographs from local papers. These go back thirty years to when Lena and your mother bought the old farmhouse. See?" He held up the copy of the newspaper photo. It showed Marta, Lena, and Sophia standing in front of a delipidated farmhouse. The three of them had big smiles on their faces holding up what looked like a deed. "You photographed each bookstore anniversary. Dudley came into the picture in year three." He spread out several photos of the anniversary celebrations of the bookstore including one from the memorial for Lena last week. He wanted Marta to notice he had a photo from that night. "When I look at these pictures, you haven't aged a bit. I can't say the same for Dudley."

Marta's eye softened and a small smile lifted the corners of her mouth. That smile was either a sign of pride in herself or contempt for Dudley. Either way, he hoped to capitalize on it. "The bookstore was an icon. Too bad it's a burned-out shell now." He handed the old photo to Marta's good hand. He held back a current picture of the bookstore for later in the interview.

She fingered the photo, dropped it, and turned away.

He'd love to press her but had to keep moving before she complained of tiredness.

"In this other photograph from the memorial, you can see the woman who attended your mother that night, in the blue smock."

She waved her hand to push away the photograph.

"I think you should look at this one, Marta," he said in a slightly stronger voice.

She tsked her tongue and pouted then looked down at the photo. "Yes, I remember her. She asked to leave early."

"I saw her inside the bookstore returning the blue smock to you. You checked it over for stains. Do you know why she asked to leave early?" Det. Nishita pressed.

"These people always have family emergencies. They still expect to be paid the full amount." Marta spoke with righteousness.

"We'll get back to her. After you excused her, you went into the kitchen and spoke with Dudley and two men. Soon after, you and Dudley left." Nishita paused to watch Marta's reaction. She gave up nothing. "Camilla didn't get any useable pictures. But we were lucky, several fans recorded the event earlier with their cell phones. They managed to get some pictures of those men."

Det. Nishita lifted out another pile of photographs and set out two. Marta flinched when she glanced at the pictures. The men were standing next to a pick-up truck and a white van. Nishita had always wondered if that truck was the same one that drove past him while he stood in the bookstore's garage. "Do you recognize either of these men?"

Det. Nishita wasn't sure if Marta was shaking her head no or just rolling her head against the pillow. "Marta, you and Dudley got in a van and left with them, don't you know?"

"They are connected to Dudley," she said, "his work."

"To his import/export business?" Det. Nishita asked. He waited for an answer. After a long pause, she nodded, he continued. "At what capacity do they work with Dudley?"

She caressed her broken wrist. It was hard to read her emotions as half her face was covered in bandages. "At the clinic," Marta said.

"Curious." He could feel Camilla holding her breath. He had to wait to let her loose on Marta. In his most compassionate voice he asked, "What happened after you drove away with these men?"

"You want to know about the night Lena died."

"I do want to know. Very much. And I think these men are somehow connected to what happened after Lena died. We have been searching for them, but like Dudley, they have vanished." That was the bit of news he wanted to instill in her. That Dudley had escaped, and she was stuck in this hospital bed. "Did Dudley beat you, Marta?"

"No, no. He stopped them." Her blood pressure monitor began to beep. Det. Nishita had to calm her or the nurse would ask him to leave.

"Dudley protected you?" Marta whimpered and nodded her head. Nishita carefully touched her forearm. He gently petted her as if she were a frightened cat. "Why did they beat you? Did these men blame you for Lena?" Marta held her breath. He pressed gently. "Tell me what happened."

She leaned back against her pillow and closed her eyes, then started slowly, in a weak voice. "Dudley and Lena were arguing. They fought almost daily after she got out of rehab. He accused her of hiding profits. He found evidence that in the last two months she'd self-produced two new books and a new set of contemplation cards."

Det. Nishita leaned forward. "So, she hid profits?"

"Lena never did anything herself. She needed constant guidance, constant supervision. Dudley said she couldn't sign a check without his help. That night, I'd never seen him so angry. He pushed her. Had his hands around her neck. I tried to get in between them. Dudley's elbow hit me on my ear. I fell backwards, hit the wall, and the wind was knocked out of me. I was dizzy. Lena screamed, and then a horrible silence. I knew she was gone."

"How did she die?"

"Dudley tossed her like a doll. She fell, hit her head against the edge of the marble stairs."

"And what happened next?"

"Dudley begged me to help him. He said he'd go to jail; they never believe it was an accident. He frightened me. I told him to call his friends."

"He knew what that meant?" Marta nodded slightly. He softened his voice, talking to her as a trusted friend. "What did these friends say?"

"They told us to go to the conference in Las Vegas and they'd take care of all of it." Marta let out a long sigh.

Det. Nishita checked the blood pressure monitor. It looked a little erratic. He pressed on. "Is this you with Dudley at the hotel?" He showed her a photograph from the hotel's security camera. It was a shot of Dudley speaking to the desk clerk. A woman with a scarf wrapped around her head and wearing a trench coat stood behind him. Marta glanced at the photograph and nodded her head.

Nishita had the photo of the woman getting into the limo but set that aside. He continued, "I have one more for you to look at." He retrieved his laptop from his leather case and set it near Marta's line of sight. He pressed play and the clip of the woman wearing the same scarf and trench coat and Dudley leaving the hotel played. He stopped it before the limo showed up.

Marta groaned as if in pain. "Yes, I was sick that weekend. I told you."

Det. Nishita leaned back in his chair. It was a signal to Camilla to take the lead on this next part.

Officer Camilla began, "Marta, that night, I cleared the bookstore, searching for any people from the memorial that might have gotten lost or perhaps were hiding in a closet. I checked the garage, the storeroom and all the family rooms upstairs, in order to secure the building. Funny, I never spotted that scarf and coat. What happened to them?"

Marta murmured something, then made a face as if in pain.

Officer Camilla moved closer to the side of her bed. "This is an expensive scarf. It's a Hermes scarf and cost almost $900. The trench is a London Fog maxi length and costs $1,100. That's a lot of money to not know where it is."

"Someone stole it. We have all types of people in and out of the bookstore, as you said people hide everywhere," Marta said in a huff. Her monitor beeped with increasing speed. Marta focused on Nishita. "I could tell you of the shoplifting I must do my best to stop." She groaned.

"I can imagine." Det. Nishita did his best to offer her compassion and leaned forward in an attempt to cut off Marta's view of Camilla. "Like the people that care for your mother. They have access to the upstairs."

"Yes, that woman, the one you showed me, I've caught her stealing before," Marta said. "Just hubris."

"Did you know the clinic burned down the night of Lena's memorial?" Det. Nishita said. Marta shook her head no. He leaned back to let Officer Camilla take over this part.

Officer Camilla said, "We discovered you have a security feed from the clinic to your home computer. Why?"

Marta focused on her and paused. "That was Dudley. He didn't trust the center to pay for the referrals we sent them."

"Referrals?" Officer Camilla asked.

"Older people who need care. Some need surgeries, some need in-home care, among other things." She sneered.

"Ah, in-home care. Interesting." Officer Camilla stepped forward and took over the laptop and brought up a different video. "Your security cameras were working the night of the fire; did you know that?" Marta didn't answer.

Officer Camilla went on, "I will warn you this next video is graphic." She pressed play.

The video feed began. It was dark and grainy at first but slowly drew into focus as it played. It showed two men with billed hats shading their faces escorting a woman dressed in the scarf and coat that Marta wore in Las Vegas. Along the outside side walkway, they pulled her into the building. The woman appeared to struggle, but one man punched her, and she slumped forward. The men grabbed her under the arms and dragged her along. They entered the elevator. The doors closed, and the light above illuminated the down arrow. From here there was no footage, only empty hallways and bare offices. Nishita watched Marta and she remained stoic.

Officer Camilla let the video footage run until the men reappeared alone, exited out the back of the building. One man placed something by an outside wall near some pipes. The other dumped something from a can along the wall and bushes. The men quickly moved to their truck.

Again, Officer Camilla let the footage run. Det. Nishita listened carefully. He heard Marta's breath shorten and wondered if occurred to her that that might have been her fate. Somehow, she'd escaped with only a broken wrist and ankle.

There was a flash off to the side of one hallway of the building. Within minutes the building caught fire. Then there was a second explosion.

"We found her body in the storage closet. We haven't been able to identify her, but we will."

"What does this mean to me? It's Dudley's doing. Those are Dudley's thugs."

"You are five feet one inch and weigh 104 pounds. This woman from the Las Vegas footage we estimate at almost five-foot-three and weighs about 115. Here is the shot of the woman in the blue smock standing at the memorial. And here the woman at the hotel in Vegas, and here being escorted into the clinic. We believe these are the same woman." He let that sink in. Marta closed her eyes.

Det. Nishita wanted to snap his fingers and wake her up. Instead, he spoke in a soft voice, "You didn't go to Las Vegas. She did."

Marta opened her eyes wide. The blood pressure beeper escalated.

The sound filled the room with an annoying ting-ting-ting and set his teeth on edge. He knew he'd best get in what he came to say before the nurse told him to leave. "It wasn't Dudley who fought with Lena, it was you. You were in charge of the accounts, all the legal issues that surface running a business, the publishing contracts. You knew when something changed. You knew about changes Lena made in her estate and trust. How did it feel to learn that Dudley knew you had been cut out? Did that set you off against Lena, so you fought? Did that fight begin in your office, and you chased her out to the hallway, pushed her against the elevator shaft, causing deep bruises on her back? Perhaps Dudley heard the argument and tried to break up the fight. In the struggle Lena fell and hit her head."

The room got quiet. Then he said, "Dudley didn't plead with you. You pleaded with him to hide the crime. You told him as the husband, he'd be the prime suspect. But Dudley had a world of crimes to hide as well, and Lena's death would cause too much scrutiny for his associates. He called Dr. Hughes for help. Thus began the cover up. First, hide Lena's body in the garage and turn the air conditioner on high to mask time of death. Next, get one of the healthcare workers to pose as you and stay in the hotel room during the conference. But you didn't know about the scarf and coat the woman wore. Perhaps she kept it. When the limo arrived, you emptied out its trunk and let the driver go. But neither of you expected Grant Montgomery to show up at the bookstore Saturday looking for Lena. A long-delayed meeting between a mother and her biological son. Grant said he saw someone on the third floor who ignored him. That was you."

Marta's beeping got louder. The young nurse entered the room in a rush. She checked Marta's vitals and gave Nishita a look. "I must ask you to leave Detective," she said.

He held up his hand and said, "Just one more thing." He turned to face Marta and looked her straight in the eye. "You are under arrest for the murder of Lena Rezenchov. We will keep an officer at your door until you are released."

The beeping got louder. Marta screamed, "I remember why I called out your name, Detective." Nishita and Camilla caught each other's eyes. Marta's thin lips curved upwards at the corners. "I know all about your homosexual brother and how he searched for acceptance," Marta said. "His accident was faked; did you know that?"

Nishita couldn't feel his feet. All he could see was that smirk on Marta's face. It'd been a long time since someone mentioned his brother's murder. She was using it as some kind of bargaining chip. His entire family knew Allen was gay; it never mattered. Through gritted teeth, he said, "If you have evidence of another crime, I suggest you speak with your attorney, or I will add impeding the course of justice and accessory after the fact in the case of my brother's murder to your charges."

How long he and Marta were locked in a battle of silent wills, he couldn't say. He heard the door open, and Camilla repeat his name, demanding his attention. He picked up his leather case and walked out of the room.

THIRTY-SIX

NISHITA PATTED HIS LEFT ARM, CAREFUL not to irritate the stitches. Nurse and doctor alike told him rubbing or scratching would cause an infection, and if he had any plans to return to weightlifting, he'd let his wounds heal. Leaning back in his chair, he took a deep breath and rode the wave of misery. Once it lessened, he reached for the cup of coffee at the edge of his desk. The cup, cool to the touch, meant the coffee was cold. He hated cold coffee. There was something about it that made him feel lonely. Too perfect a metaphor for his life.

It was a few minutes after five. If he left now, he'd have enough time to swing by the drive-thu and grab a fresh cup before arriving at the cliff by six. He didn't want to be late for the festivities. It was an honor to be included. Anya and Grant had set up an intimate sunset ceremony for Lena at the cliff where she was discovered. This would be the complete opposite memorial from the first. It couldn't be held at the Goddess Garden Bookstore because what was left was a charred skeleton. Anya had told him, the bookstore was the creation of Dudley and Marta, destroyed by criminals they did business with, and she wanted to erase that part from memory. What could he say to ease her pain? In these moments, words sound hollow. Her healing would occur at her pace. He returned his attention to the final report on Lena's murder.

Using the accounts found on Marta's computer, it was clear Marta and Dudley had capitalized on Lena's celebrity. The bookstore was a perfect front for smuggling raw diamonds and laundering the money through remodeling the bookstore. Eventually, they turned to human trafficking, bringing women and children to the country to be sold to the highest bidder. Lena, once sober, couldn't ignore what surrounded her. Her integrity would come into question, her reputation destroyed by association, and she wanted out. She began divorce proceedings, and once the divorce was finalized, Dudley would own the bookstore and all its trappings. Sophia would get the rights to her published books. Due to her illness Lena named Rebecca Lopez from the clinic as executor of Sophia's estate. Anya would get all rights to Lena's self-published works including the contemplation cards, her best seller.

That left Marta completely omitted, dependent on Dudley.

Once Marta realized the details of the trust, she attacked Lena. They fought. Dudley tried to break it up, and, in the struggle Lena fell and hit her head against the marble steps. They could have called 911 and admitted to the accident. But they chose to engage in a cover-up. That was their mistake.

Nishita wasn't sure if it was Marta or Dudley who came up with the idea of hiring someone to pose as Marta in Las Vegas, which gave them a full weekend for Marta to hide Lena's body in the underground garage and clean the bookstore. Smart, the garage kept the temperature cold enough to confuse the time of death, but Marta wasn't as excellent of a cleaner as she thought, missing blood and hair fibers on the elevator grate, and blood stains in the grout of the marble floor. All proved to be Lena's.

Early that Monday morning, Marta drove with Lena in the car to the cliff and met the limo driver and the woman impersonating her, paid them in cash—but not without demanding they move Lena's dead body to the driver's side and push the car over the cliff.

The driver, Nishita suspected, was John Towel, Marta's ex. But both he and his limo have disappeared under strange circumstances. The woman was murdered, and her body was left to burn in the Care Center's building. He wondered about Mr. Towel's fate.

He had to add that Dudley and a male companion flew to London and then caught a connecting flight to Amsterdam. After that, Dudley's trail went cold. Nishita wasn't worried. A man like Dudley would find a way to get a new con to run on unsuspecting marks. One way or another he'd leave a trail. It was only a matter of time. With what Marta alluded to about his brother's hit and run, something told him Dudley knew secrets about many crimes. Nishita would dig. He had the energy and now had a new trail to follow.

Staring at the words of the report, he rubbed his forehead. He couldn't understand how Lena, a famous psychic, didn't realize the illegal smuggling surrounding her. She was a psychic! Perhaps, as with many of us, when it came to loved ones, she saw what she wanted to, a loving husband and faithful best friend. Who doesn't have that weakness?

He had focused on his trajectory to become the youngest detective on the force and pushed aside time for family. How many friends paid that price? Returning to his computer, he reread the report and sent it off to the higher-ups. Once it vanished into the ether he saw the other email he had been composing all morning, an apology to former girlfriend, Emma. He couldn't avoid her smiling face, as her wedding photos were still popular on social media. Must be because of the celebrity-filled attendance. He finally settled on a simple "Congratulations. You look very happy." His hand hovered over the send button. "Be a man, Ted," he muttered. After a deep breath, he pressed it.

There was a commotion at the far end of the hallway. Dr. Boyd was speaking with detectives from another department. Deep in discussion, Dr. Boyd looked like he was on the tail end of a long day. Boyd signaled to Nishita that he wanted to speak with him. Nishita nodded that he'd be right there and wondered if had something to do with Lena. Nishita gathered up his keys, and badge with his left hand.

"You're up and about, I see," Dr. Boyd held out his hand to shake.

"Better every day. Just wish it'd stop itching."

"I've got some salve that will help with that. Come to my office," Dr. Boyd said.

"Rain check? I'm meeting my victim's family for a memorial in Topanga."

"I'll drop it off on your desk," Dr. Boyd said.

Nishita gave him a quizzical look. "What was all the fuss about?" He pointed to the men exiting into the elevator.

"It's an arson from a week ago. They thought the building was searched thoroughly, but when they were demolishing it, they found a woman's body stuffed into a Pelican case. I just got assigned the autopsy."

"Oh, that's terrible," Nishita said. But he couldn't help but be intrigued by how such an expensive case got there and if whoever hid it was responsible for the fire.

"Do me a favor. Stay away from fires for a while." Dr. Boyd smiled.

Nishita nodded.

It was too late to grab coffee, so he made his way to the site. It was mid-March and spring had appeared along the hills turning the dusty brown to a faint green as the coyote bushes sprouted new growth. He saw the cars before he saw people. Pulling over, he struggled to get out of the car, hobble along the gravel shoulder, and keep his arm still. Fisher waved and sprinted up to him.

"You need a hand?" Fisher said.

"I've got the required two, I don't need another one," Nishita said and regretted the words as he said them. "No, I just gotta get my balance, but thanks." Fisher nodded and backed up slightly.

"Hey, Little Ted, 'bout time you showed," Camilla called out.

She placed her hands on her hips with a toothy grin. Wearing simple navy pants and a light blue shirt, Nishita was surprised at how small she looked out of uniform.

"Wearing civilian clothes, I see," Nishita teased. He turned and saw the group that had gathered for the memorial. Anya and Rain stood next to Grant and his tall thin husband. Gus Post and Rebecca Lopez stood off to the side, next to a group of musicians. He'd seen this group twice singing and praying for Lena's spirit at this spot. The guitar player gave Nishita a nod.

"Okay let's get this party started," Rain called out clapping her hands her bracelets tinkling with each movement. Rain held out her arms and signaled for people to gather around the new street lantern.

Fisher surprised Nishita by standing behind him. He whispered, "It's solar powered, it won't impact city resources at all."

Nishita's shoulders instantly rose to his ears from the shock of Fisher's voice. "Cool," he said and made a thumbs-up sign. His cell pinged in his pocket. Normally he wouldn't answer, but he wanted to slow down and also move a step away from Fisher. He held up his phone to signal he needed to take the call. He looked at the screen.

Emma texted: Please call.

BRIE HAS BEEN WRITING EVERY DAY since the economy tanked and her job was downsized. It seemed it was time to do the thing she'd been told to do since Sister Rose told her in the third grade: write. She received an MFA in Theatre Arts long before there were cellphones. Despite this handicap, she enjoyed a delightful career as an actress. Performing plays gave her an ear for dialogue and building tension which she tries to apply to her stories. She strives to write stories that are as complex as we are. Currently, she lives in Canada with her husband and their energetic dogs.

9 781684 922505